daydream girl

bella pollen

ISIS
LARGE PRINT
Oxford

First published in Great Britain under the title
B Movies, Blue Love 1999

This revised edition first published 2005 by Pan Books,
an imprint of Pan Macmillan Ltd.

Published in Large Print 2006 by ISIS Publishing Ltd.,
7 Centremead, Osney Mead, Oxford OX2 0ES
by arrangement with
Pan Macmillan Ltd.

British Library Cataloguing in Publication Data
Pollen, Bella
    Daydream girl. – Large print ed.
    1. Love stories
    2. Large type books
    I. Title
    823.9'14 [F]

C45049865A

ISBN 0–7531–7511–8 (hb)
ISBN 978–0–7531–7512–5 (pb)

Printed and bound in Great Britain by
T. J. International Ltd., Padstow, Cornwall

For Mum and Dad

Acknowledgements

With thanks to:

Paul Goldsworthy and the Coronet Cinema

The British Film Institute

Simon Oakes

Colin Francis, Elaine Towers and Andrew Patterson
at Kensington and Chelsea Council

Amelia Granger, Lara Thompson and Rachel Prior
at Working Title

Felicity Ann Sieghart and the Aldeburgh Cinema

Also, for their support and enthusiasm,
Clare Conville and Arabella Stein

And with particular thanks to my sister Susie
for her consistently scary criticism

Prologue

In a small bedsit in Earls Court, Luke Bradshaw, hands on hips, stares into the mirror. Wholly absorbed, he studies his reflection critically. A long minute comes and goes, then another. Finally a car horn, honking repeatedly, breaks his concentration. Easing up the window, he cranes his neck out and waves. Forcing the window shut again he throws on his leather jacket and sprints down the narrow stairs to the street.

His girlfriend waits in the car outside.

"Kit," he says, wrenching open the door and leaning over to kiss her. "You're a real honey."

"I know." She grins at him.

"I thought you had to work late?"

"Johnny Too-Fat's covering for me. Anyway, I reckoned you could do with the support."

"How's the traffic?" He peers at the queue of black taxis blocking the entrance to the Exhibition Hall.

"Not great."

"Take the next left then." He rests his hand on the back of her neck. "It'll be quicker."

Through the windscreen a tailback of cars forms a ladder of brake lights against the horizon. Luke moves his hand away and starts drumming his fingers against the headrest.

"You OK?"

"Nervous."

"There're some Marlboros in the glove compartment."

He eases out the packet from beneath a mangled A–Z. "I just can't believe the amount of castings I've been to in the last year." He opens the window to let the smoke from his cigarette escape.

"What's this one for?"

"Some alien hospital drama."

"You'll make an adorable alien."

"I've got to get some work, Kit."

"It'll happen soon," she says robustly. "Anyway, who says you won't land a part in this and become an overnight sensation?"

"There's no such thing." He snorts.

"Course there is."

"Give me an example?"

"OK." Kit manoeuvres the car into the right-hand lane and jumps the lights into Regent Street.

"Your father wouldn't take this long to come up with one," Luke teases.

She shakes her head. "You know he called me *three* times today?"

"He's got nothing else to do poor sod."

"Still."

"*42nd Street*," she says after a minute or two of silence.

"Where?" he mumbles, lighting another cigarette.

"Ruby Keeler, *42nd Street*. Overnight sensation. Tomorrow your agent will call with a six-figure contract. My screenplay will be ready to send out soon. Six months down the road we'll be a throbbing power couple."

"Hmm." Luke drops the half-smoked cigarette out the window. "What happens if in six months I'm still out of work but you've turned into Nora Ephron?"

"Then obviously I'll drop you."

"You couldn't be so disloyal."

"Course I could. I'm not going to want you dragging me down."

"But you find me irresistible."

"I'll get over it."

"What if I cunningly married you so you couldn't drop me?"

She shoots him an amused look. "I thought love cynics didn't get married."

"Aha, but under every cynic beats the heart of a romantic."

"*Trembles* the heart of a romantic more like." Kit eases the car on to a yellow line.

"Maybe," he concedes. "Still — promise you won't dump me when you're a Big Golden Person."

"Come on, Luke, stop being so pessimistic." She switches off the engine and turns to face him. "Listen. Trailer of our future: you're going to go through that door, tell them you're *only* prepared to read for the lead, then you're going to get it and become a major TV personality. My script will be hailed as a masterpiece and optioned for record figures. Soon we'll move into a nine-bedroom house in West Hollywood and people all over the world will suck up to us."

"You're right." He leans over to kiss her. "I mean look at us . . . we're brilliant, talented —"

"Funny, intelligent . . ."

"Handsome, sensitive and —"

"— and probably late if you don't get out of the car," Kit finishes, giving him a push.

Luke hovers uncertainly on the pavement as Kit rolls down her window.

"Wish me luck then," he says making a face.

"Good luck." She blows him a kiss, then watches him as he swaggers down the street with a confidence she knows he doesn't feel. "Hey Luke," she suddenly shouts after him, "bet you anything . . . Six months' time and you'll have forgotten you ever needed it."

One Year Later

Travels of a script – I

Offices of the prestigious Film A production company, London, England

A large pile of unsolicited screenplays sit on a desk. Voices in the background indicate a meeting is in progress. From the conversation we learn that British pictures are all the rage, that everyone is looking for a successor to Film A's latest hit: one of the voices asks to use a phone to make a private call.

A youngish man comes into shot and sits down at the desk. He is an Independent Producer, at Film A for a meeting with an ex-girlfriend, Louisa, who happens to be the vice Head of Production. He'd like to be in a meeting with someone more senior, Michael Ryan, president of the company, preferably, but unfortunately his reputation doesn't yet warrant it.

On hold for British Airways he absent-mindedly leafs through the pile of scripts. The title of one catches his eye, it has the word "Kissing" in it.

Hey! What a great title, he thinks attempting to extract it with his free hand. His fumblings knock the pile to the floor. Picking them up hurriedly, he notices that the bindings for several have become loose, including the synopsis and cover note of the script he was taken with . . . On a whim, he takes the synopsis and puts it into his briefcase.

CHAPTER ONE

Monday evening, the Oscars. The evening has a smell to it, the potent smell of success. Some of the most intoxicating perfumes in the world are here tonight, hitching a lift on pampered skins, clinging at first to their host, but once safely within the environs of the room, free to roam and mingle with each other in a playful orgy of Rose, Geranium, Vetiver. Calvin Klein's Obsession stalking and curling around DKNY's Innocence producing a whirling, wicked offspring of exotic fumes.

And the Oscar for Best Original Screenplay goes to . . . Wolf whistles drown out her name. In a daze she stands as the noise reverberates around the room. It has a sound to it, a groaning, roaring sound, so concentrated it is almost tribal! Mystical! Religious! A frisson of electricity runs from her crotch to her brain. Oh the joy, the elation: Lord what a high.

She turns her head as if in slow motion; people are all around, 360 degrees. A woman with a mashed-potato Mrs Simpson hairstyle widens her lips as Kit looks her way. Everywhere she turns mouths smeared in different hues of lipstick contort themselves into smiling shapes. Opening, closing, stretching, flapping, they look like hundreds of red admirals, sucking on the faces of the women.

It's time to begin the long approach to the stage. Through the sudden hush she can sense the awe swelling around her and as she floats towards the podium she is blinded by twin circles of light burning hot in her eyes, branding the message into her brain: you are a Goddess, a Goddess, a Goddess . . . A . . .

"Moron, a FREAKING MORON!" The driver's head jerks itself like a giant tortoise back into the fibreglass shell of his Citroën as he flashes his headlights at me for the third time. I blink into the glare, but blinded see nothing. The light must be green. I press on the accelerator, my car lurches towards the crossing — then a scream. I stamp on the brake. Oh God, now I've nearly mashed the toes of some guy stepping off the edge of the pavement, having obediently awaited his signal to cross.

He's a mean-looking bastard whose neck muscles ripple and bulge under his shirt collar like slabs of oiled beef. For a second he stares at me, testosterone zinging through his body. His hands are clenched angrily and I know what to expect. I can expect death. I can expect his fists to come crashing through the window and connect with the side of my head. Why? Because I've transgressed the law of the metropolis that's why; because this is that time of the evening when the city is indeed at war, when traffic anarchy is loose on the street and when every frustrated city-dweller commit-ting a random act of road rage has the mitigating circumstance of mind-numbing commuting, secretaries dating, families waiting.

And me — God knows, no different from anyone else — getting nowhere on a daily basis. I mollify the pedestrian with a rueful grin. Red has merged to orange. Safely across the junction now, I pull into the side of the road and collapse back against the seat. Johnny Too-Fat's number flashes on my ringing mobile. I press the tiny green ear.

"My Superquim." The line crackles with static.

"Hey there."

"What *is* that awful racket? Sounds like you're pulling the phone through your armpit hair or something."

I give the phone a good shake. "That better?"

"It's better but less exciting. Listen, I've got to talk to you about my wife's latest obsession."

"Please, Too-Fat," I implore, "I nearly just flattened Mike Tyson, and anyway, didn't you get my message?"

"*Your problem is held in a queue and will be answered shortly.*" Johnny adopts an operator's voice.

"I got another rejection letter today."

"Oh bollocks, who from?"

"Channel 4."

"Well . . . don't get too worked up about it."

"How many more am I supposed to get before I'm allowed to get worked up?"

"Plenty more fish, my darling."

"You know what I'm thinking? I'm thinking the title was a mistake."

"Come on, it was inspired."

"It was flip, bordering on silly even. You know how crucial a title is. Maybe it's turning people off."

"Maybe you're being neurotic."

"But maybe not. People could be looking at the title and chucking it straight in the bin. We should have thought longer, had a back-up. How about we think up a better title then send it out again?"

"Kit, firstly 'Kissing''s got a great title, secondly it was mine, and therefore thirdly I must apprise you of the fact that, in accordance with my rights as your most long-suffering friend, I will withdraw your licence to its use, word by word, with each hysterical phone call I receive."

"First impressions are everything, Johnny." I'm not listening to him.

"Come on, Kit, keep your nerve." The line sputs again. "Where are you anyway?"

"On my way to Luke's. He's cooking me dinner."

"Perfect, get him to give you some love and affection, and ideally a massage for your ego."

"My ego doesn't need a massage, it needs a course of anabolic steroids." Johnny chuckles at this and the panic that's been gnawing at my insides dies down a little. "Are we still on for lunch tomorrow?" I ask him.

"My whole body quivers at the thought."

"That's very sweet," I say but the dial tone is already buzzing. I toss the phone into my bag, fire up the ignition and pull back out into the fray.

To the left, beyond the roadworks, the concrete arteries of the M40 flow smoothly away from the heart of the city. My car shunts round the circumference of the Shepherd's Bush Green, past the Bingo Hall and now, finally, the traffic is easing up. Overhead navy darkens towards black. God's hand on the dimmer switch of evening.

As soon as the door to Luke's house jump-starts open I can feel it, the unmistakable electric vibe in the air. The television is on.

"Luke," I shout. As I climb the stairs to the bedroom, the whine and cajole of mistress TV grows louder with every step. Sport, by the sound of it. I can make out the animal roar of the crowd, the hushed expectant silences. On the first floor I poke my head around the bedroom door. Dr Hybrid, aka Luke Bradshaw, aka my boyfriend, lies on his bed, inert, staring at the black box in front of him.

"*Honey, I'm home,*" I sing.

"Mmm," he agrees, failing to drag his eyes from the screen. Instead he gives me an almost imperceptible nod causing the tiny part of his brain, not lulled to sleep by the mesmeric light before it, to activate the nerves down the right side of his body. I fancy I can almost see the static running down his arm, the signal causing a twitch in his hand, which in turn forces his thumb to apply pressure to the miniature red arrow of the remote control. Lawnmower Racing switches to Topless Darts.

"So how was your day, my beloved?" I dump my bag on the bed. "How did the mutant gynaecological scene go?" Still silence, then a small grunt signifying penalty disagreement.

I bite my lip thoughtfully. It's very tricky communicating with Luke these days. Surely it doesn't have to be this hard? You ask him about his day, he asks you about yours. No one's saying you have to listen to the reply, it's just the rules, reciprocal common politeness, straight from the *Handbook of Relationships* — Chapter Two, the third year together. Suddenly, a roar from the crowd. Miss Slovakia, nude and shivering on her ice-skates, has just scored the first bull's-eye.

Luke sighs with happiness. "My Pussykitten," he says twisting his immaculate form into an exaggerated stretch, "God, but I'm shattered. You?" He turns in my general direction. "Tired? Fed up? Thirsty?" He peers at me tenderly and I melt. He's just being a lad I think indulgently, and lads do love their sporting activities.

"All of the above," I say, bending down to kiss him, "and starving."

"Me too." Luke nods vigorously, brushing his lips against my cheek. "Why don't you be a honey and bring up something to eat?" He leaves a tiny pause, kisses me again before adding into my ear, "I didn't quite make it to the shops, I'm afraid."

"Luke, you promised." I straighten up.

"Well, yes I know." He looks guilty. "But I was so shagged out after the session I just crashed." Every Monday Luke has a read-through of the week's shooting with the other members of the cast but following that the rest of the day off.

"But you've been home since two o'clock." I look at my watch. "It's past seven now." The whining tone in my voice worries me. It seems I can pretty much rely

14

on whining on regular days of the week, rather like having a period. Recently I've even begun to wonder whether I'm genetically prone to it.

"I know, I know." Luke's features break into a contrite grin that on screen would have every housewife from Venus to Mars swooning over their ironing boards. "But I really was shattered, honest." He holds his hands out. "C'm here and give me a kiss." He takes hold of my hips, hooks his thumbs through the loops on my combat pants and pulls me close. "Ooh, go on," he nuzzles. "I'll take you out to dinner tomorrow, promise, I'll give you fifty pounds to make a salad, sixty kisses, one hundred hours of foreplay, a full year of high quality frottage, come on, please? As you're up? Angel, angel, angel, darling beautiful lovely pudding?" he sings.

And of course I give in and smile, because no matter what anyone says — kissing is a laxative for the blues. He kisses me again and this time I kiss him back, though primly to signify disapproval. Luke, of course, isn't fooled for a second. He knows full well he could snap his fingers and, like a magician's assistant, I'd divest myself of all outer garments and start pulling rabbits out of my pants for him. I can't help it, he has that effect on me. Luke *per se* I have always found attractive. Luke plus charm is irresistible.

"Doesn't have to be anything major." He grins, sensing weakness. "Something healthy, obviously, but whatever's easiest." He releases me, simultaneously flicking the remote to UK Gold. The theme tune of the *Professionals* blasts forth, and by the time I've reached the doorway he's settled comfortably into peak-viewing position. "Oh, and darling," he adds, looking at the screen and shaking his head fondly at Doyle, or is it perhaps Brodie? "while you're about it, you wouldn't just feed the fish would you?"

There are certain words that attach themselves to a person's character like limpets to a rock. The following, I decide as I measure out a teaspoon of designer foodstuff for the designer fish, apply to Luke on good days; and by good days, I mean those days when I'm madly in love with him. These adjectives are:

Gorgeous
Talented
Self-assured

And then there are the adjectives for the days when I'm less madly in love with him:

Gorgeous
Lucky
Smug

So the obvious constant here is Luke's gorgeousness, which must therefore be addressed first — and it has to be said that both on and off screen Luke is visually intoxicating by any standards. One of those people who could be forgiven for scrawling on the line in his passport, where it says Distinguishing Features, the simple words — thank you. More specific than that?

It's hard to describe. When a person's butt ugly you can at least render them recognizable by saying: You know Stan of course? Nose like a hole puncher; or Remember Gloria? Breasts like spaniels' ears. But good looks can often be too smooth to get an angle on. To give an idea though, Phoebe, Luke's agent used to market him, in pre-Dr Hybrid days, as a man-mix of Peter Gallagher (*Sex, Lies and Videotape*) and Matt Dillon (*To Die For*). Whereas I, with my straggly ponytail and Tibetan monk's eyes might have to he marketed more as a cut-rate Maggie Gyllenhaal who's had a disastrous and possibly suable experience at the hairdresser.

Close-up of fingers picking crumbs off a plate, dabbing them on to a tongue, then timing their stay before they dissolve. This nail-biting competition has turned out to be the highlight of the evening's entertainment so far and although it's not the first time that Luke and I have spent a silent evening in such a way, enjoying our electronic *ménage à trois*, it makes me uneasy that since I plopped the tray on his lap, Luke has not actually spoken beyond the grunted affirmation as to whether he required salt or pepper.

So I sit here cross-legged on the bed, trying to plot a way of extracting a little love and attention from my boyfriend, and as I watch him out of the corner of one eye I wonder whether I should try one of those relationship tests magazines are so fond of i.e. not say another word, not attempt conversation in any form thereby forcing him to take the initiative.

"Baby" — I'd like to think he'd respond within seconds — "you seem a tad down. Tell me everything that's bothering you." Which will be the cue for me to say:

"Luke, I've had it with writing. I'm going to give it all up, end this agony now." Which will be the cue for him to gather me into his arms and hold me close.

"Darling," he will lecture sternly, "you are adorable, funny and talented and if a few short-sighted executives are too up their own arses to see the creative force pulsating from your masterpiece, well that's their loss and it will only be a matter of time before somebody out there has the vision to recognize your genius."

At which point I will sob and bury my face into his armpit which will reek of fresh man-sweat, a heady turn on, and in no time at all we will be making passionate love, falling on the floor and smashing lights and bookshelves all around us like Emma Thompson and Jeff Goldblum in *The Tall Guy*.

"Oh, Luke," I will croon into his chest, "whatever would I do without you?"

"Marry me, Kitten," he'll beg. "We'll do it next spring. What with your exceptional writing talents and my looks and expressiveness on screen we could still be a big, fat Golden Couple. Together we could be a Morticia and Gomez, a Hillary and Bill."

"Laurel and Hardy," I will add, overcome with happiness.

So I could do this *Cosmopolitan* test, but it might not be worth the risk. Instead, I put the now crumbless plate on the floor, squirm out of my clothes, slither down the bed until I'm in an identical position to Luke, then stare robotically at the flashing screen in front of me.

Bed. Midnight. Time studiously occupies itself pushing the hands around the clock on the bedside table. As the last of our neighbours return home, the bedroom is finally dark in sharp relief from the car headlights that have been discoing round the ceiling. Next to me Luke breathes deeply while his body shifts in accordance with his dreams but although my every muscle is relaxed with the drug of sleep, my mind is, as usual, immune. This is my stolen time of the night, the point at which I normally creep downstairs, open up my laptop on the kitchen table and write, but tonight I can't even begin to summon the urge. And I'm wondering why. I've always taken it for granted that life was destined to move forward and improve but in the last couple of months this optimism seems to have been eroded by all kinds of self-doubts. I'm trying not to show this to Luke; lack of confidence does not make for great company. But hard as I try, I cannot escape the feeling that I'm being judged by an inner critic, one who is consistently reporting me as being devoid of wit, cheer, depth of feeling, and awarding me one of those tiny silhouetted women falling asleep in a chair that *Hello!* magazine uses to rate boring movies.

After another hour of tossing in the dark, the need to tell Luke about today's bad news becomes so overwhelming that I ease myself over to his side of the bed, plant a tentative kiss on his shoulder, then heave a loud and not unhopeful sigh — then another and another.

"What *is* wrong, Kit?" Luke mumbles eventually.

"I got another rejection letter today." Luke immediately puts an arm around me and my earlier misgivings evaporate like hot air on a cold window. "Oh Luke." I snuggle self-pityingly into his shoulder. "I feel like such a failure . . . maybe I'd just better give up the whole idea." I tack on this last bit as a wanton double-bluff because getting a screenplay made into a movie whether big, small, block, Indie, good, or bad, is my fate, and already inscribed, I'm convinced, on the CV of my life by the God of Personnel.

There's a beat, then some sheet shifting, as Luke extricates his arm from under my shoulder and turns to fix me with a grave look that is curiously familiar.

"Now look, Kit," he begins, and even in the darkness of the room the expression is recognizable; it's one often used on screen relatives when patients in Dr Hybrid's care croak, "maybe this writing lark . . ." He props himself on his elbow and runs a finger round the small mole to the left of my collar bone.

"Yes?" I whisper hopefully, lamb to the slaughter.

"Well, Kitten, you really mustn't pin all your hopes on it."

Horrified to have the entire spectrum of my fears confirmed, I shoot bolt upright and make a choking noise like a diver with the bends.

"It's just that it is *so* competitive," he says carefully, "and I hate to see you torturing yourself like this." He

20

executes a tremendous yawn. "God, what time is it anyway?" He leans across me, reaches for the clock and makes a face. "Don't think I don't understand how much it means to you," Luke continues indulgently, the kind of indulgence that borders so closely on patronizing that it nearly activates my slapping reflex. "But if it doesn't work out, you could do loads of other things." He settles back against the pillows.

"What things?"

"Well," he says doubtfully, "anything you want."

"Like what?"

"Oh, come on, anything. Learn to cook, sew, even make the garden grow . . . Kit?" He continues more soberly when I don't reply. "I'm just saying that maybe now is a good time to stop messing around with a dead-end job and a pipe dream."

I keep my mouth shut. Only a year ago, Luke was a housepainter, an invisible actor scrabbling on the treadwheel of castings and rebuttals. Now he's Mr Big Television Star with his fat pay cheque and throwaway perks, so of course it's OK for him, but the sad truth is that almost everyone else I know *does* still have a dead-end job and a pipe dream.

Johnny Too-Fat, for instance, works weekends at the Orange Cinema, weekdays selling classic cars whilst pursuing his "career" as an actor. Julie (box office), writes endless tunes which she fervently believes will one day be sampled and turned into number one hits. Callum, the Orange's General Dogsbody, is an unpublished poet. And, in reverse order of dead endedness, my job is Manager of the Orange Cinema and my pipe dream? — To hear the lines and see the scenes I've sweated over right up there on the big screen.

Success has not come easy to me. In fact, let's face it, success has not come at all. I got the job at the cinema because of a misplaced romantic obsession with movies, and the pipe dream thing? Well that originally came about through my insomnia.

An odd sound breaks through the silence that has enveloped the room. "Luke?" I say, shaking his shoulder.

"Darling, sorry," he mumbles. "Cheer up." He rolls on to his back. "So, so sleepy."

I shake him again but he's out cold. A gentle smacking motion pushes the Adam's apple in and out from his throat like a miniature accordion. I slide down the bed, shut my eyes and try to ignore the noise, but underneath my lids, my eyeballs roam their sockets like a couple of teenagers trying to escape a detention room. I sit up, switch on the light and pluck yesterday's *Sunday Times Magazine* from the bedside table. I read it for half an hour before dropping it to the floor, angrily shove a pillow over my head to muffle the now orchestral ripple of Luke's snore, then finally settle down for a night of primary sleep deprivation.

CHAPTER
TWO

At twenty to seven the next morning I finally fall asleep
and endure a hideous dream which features me lying
on a crowded beach fully clothed and pregnant. All of a
sudden a dozen men on horseback ride up along the
dunes. One of the men jumps off his horse next to me.
He's tiny, and wearing turquoise racing colours, a
jockey. He kisses me hard on the lips then sticks a long
needle into my stomach and gives me an amniocentesis
as the alarm clock starts ringing. My eyes open a crack.

Luke yawns, pokes at the clock, rolls over, kisses my
cheek, stretches, swivels his lower half out of the bed,
itches his crotch then pads off to the bathroom.

I squeeze my eyes shut and groan. It's a terrible thing
to wake up one day and discover you cannot sleep. To
find something that was once so easy, so impossibly and
persistently difficult, but the day I turned thirty, sleep,
like a good complexion, regular sex and glistening
white teeth became a luxury rather than a basic right.

It's not as if I haven't tried everything. I've tried
drugs, legal, illegal. I've tried pills, regular, herbular.
I've tried crying, jogging, relaxing. I've tried self-help
books and finally against my better judgement,
quackery. Coerced by Luke, I recently allowed Page, his

yoga teacher, to practise something called REM Manipulation on me. Page claims the reason I don't sleep and have been so *hyper-anxious* of late is because I don't breathe, and because I don't breathe, am therefore harbouring stress, pain and, for all I know, one or two criminals and a family of illegal immigrants.

Oh, I've pointed out the obvious — that if I didn't breathe, I'd be dead by now but this logic has so far escaped Page. Quite a lot of things escape Page, who rides happily through life on the bandwagon of New Ageism. Luke, in his current phase of therapy evangelism, believes that a person who spends his weekends peeing in circles in the Savernak Forest is exactly the right person to put my life in order. He is convinced that my sleep problems are to do with my mother, or lack of one, my father, or absence of a decent one. Moreover Luke insists that shrinkage and plenty of it is the route to a brand new me and he may well be right, but I can't escape the feeling that if you let your neuroses fall into the wrong hands, dangerous things might happen to them. Still, for the sake of compromise I saw Page once or twice. I allowed him to murmur in gently reproving tones about stress control. I pretended to be delighted to lie horizontal while he played odd little music tapes in my ear: noises made by birthing whales, tides ebbing and flowing etc. All of which were apparently designed to calm me down, but which conversely only stressed me further. After the second session, having come to the conclusion that Page was extremely creepy, I resolved never to return.

Before the sleep problem I worked in the music industry, assisting on pop videos. Here was the game plan back in my twenties: pop videos would be a training ground for a career in writing/directing. I'd attach myself to coat-tails. Learn at the elbow of the Greats. For seven years I sidestepped most of the snakes and shimmied up quite a few ladders. The game plan always remained but as time went on deadlines came and went, rules blurred. Then lack of sleep put paid to even those. After a year of faking compos mentis, of falling asleep into coffee, over sandwiches, in edit suites, of garbled excuses for being late, being slow, being stupid, I quit. Resigned. Resigned myself to the inevitability of permanent insomnia, and looked at the career options available:

1) Night watchman
2) Grave robber
3) Vampire

Vampire was the only one with any romance and there were obvious drawbacks to that: firstly, rats, bats and insects don't rank high on my list of favourite foods and secondly it has to be said, those teeth just don't look good on anyone.

It was Johnny Too-Fat who told me to get on with the writing. The cliché used to be that everyone had a book in them. These days it's a screenplay. The things can be found all over the place; scribbled on to the back of envelopes, lurking in the glove compartment of taxi cabs, nestling in the lycra shorts of countless personal trainers. Everyone I knew was pouring their efforts like Baby Bio on to germs of ideas. To join them was an invitation to the land of the self-deluded that, with my hours of night boredom to fill, I was delighted to accept. In many ways, I suppose, I fit well into this world of make-believe and expectant dreamers; where nobody is quite happy with what they are and everybody's greatest ambition is to be something they are not.

I pass out and regain consciousness around ten-thirty when Luke leaves for his regular Tuesday slot with Janet Taylor, supashrink, and my auto-pilot switches on enabling me to shower, get dressed and make my way to the kitchen where I glug down a mug of coffee while Anjelika, Luke's daily, ostentatiously waxes the floor beneath my feet and squawks some unidentifiable language into her mobile. Finally at eleven I manage to get myself off to work.

Somewhere in London, the United Kingdom, or even the world, I would like to believe there exists such a thing as a cinema teeming with punters, all dutifully lined up in a crocodile of fresh-faced movie fans glowing at the prospect of early afternoon entertainment. It is in such a place that Cinema Nirvana is struck: full house, every performance, every day. The Orange Cinema, Shepherd's Bush, London, tragically does not fall into this category.

Traditionally there are very few takers for the midday performance and they invariably consist of the following:

1–3 middle-aged ladies, plus Asda shopping bags
1 creative person, needing a break (desperate authors, struggling painters)
1 heavily pregnant woman
1 hairbrush salesman from Leeds or similar, in London for an evening meeting/illicit affair
1 person with lots of luggage
Several perverts

In fact, as I push my way through the heavy doors of the cinema, coffee and glutinous doughnut in hand, I can see Julie and Callum in the box office doling out tickets and snacks to a couple of obscenely pregnant girls who then, in an admirable display of female ingenuity, manage to balance stomach, breasts, handbags, popcorn and fizzy drinks, all whilst waddling up the paint-chipped steps to the Ladies' toilets without visible mishap.

"Did you hear that?" Julie is saying incredulously as the doors close behind them. "Triplets! Jesus, Callum, imagine what a girl's insides would look like after that? A giant labia on legs. Think of the flotsam and jetsam of life caught on that sticky Venus flytrap of childbirth as it walked down the street: dust, coins, bus tickets" — she draws breath as Callum turns his customary dull red — "apple cores, crisp packets." Julie breaks off to register my arrival with a wave. "Morning, Kit."

"Morning, Medusa." I walk by them through to the office and dump breakfast on the desk, leaving the door open to keep an eye out for the arrival of the mail.

If Waddingtons were to make a contemporary happy families; say one specifically aimed at your average racially stereotyped view of London, with pot-bellied cab driver, Sikh traffic warden, Paki shop owner, Geordie-style football hooligan and so on, then Julie would certainly be used as the model for Ballbuster. With her blackened eyebrows, scary hair and utter disdain for any garment of clothing excepting a stained T-shirt, Julie has such a She-Devil look you could be forgiven for thinking that she ate men for breakfast, spread sparingly on toast. A lot of it's a front though. Underneath all the angry stuff, there is talent. Granted she writes mostly rubbish but occasionally she comes up with a tune so haunting it makes your teeth hurt. This however is a rarity probably because much of her life is spent pursuing some kind of scam or other — an immediate example of which is apparent as she and Callum service the next punters, two women of indeterminate age who are umming and aahing over their choice at the sweet counter. The shorter of the two is wearing a pink anorak, white pop socks and a bluish queen-mother pillbox hat, an ensemble that cunningly disguises her as a Liquorice Allsort, whilst her friend sports a dubious perm and translucent raincoat poignantly decorated with small gold stars.

"Pity you don't have those nice ice-creams in the black tubs any more," complains the Liquorice Allsort lady.

"Ah, well," says Julie then she's off. "Made individually to order you see, small farm in the Isle of Man supplied them, very exclusive, fatality of nineties politics," she grunts. "Now these," she points to the Häagen-Dazs, "are mass market, but they're nice quality, trust me."

"And if you're interested in ice-cream," Callum adds politely, "why don't you get an ice-cream machine. My mum swears by hers." He gazes at the ladies with his pet rabbit eyes. In contrast to Julie, Callum is the housewives' choice. Something to do with the fact that he looks like he needs bundling up in some comely female's arms, popping into the sink to have his dirty spots dabbed off then ironed and folded before being put back on the shelf of life.

The Liquorice Allsort's friend is not convinced. "It's an awful lot of bother though isn't it?" She sniffs peevishly. "You still have to mix the eggs and the cream and the what-not."

"Perhaps sorbet," Callum offers, "would be a good alternative. My mum makes a terrific Fruits of the Forest."

Now firstly Callum's mother is a stumbling Glaswegian drunk and his portrayal of her as Greer Garson in *Mrs Miniver*, wearing a chequered apron while she makes slap-up teas out of paper clips and potato to serve the war effort, is frankly despicable, and, secondly, Julie implying that she is prepared to take an interest in anything that passes her lips other than alcohol or Pot Noodles is also a load of rubbish. You have to laugh though, it will only be a matter of seconds before these two old biddies are charmed then fleeced, and as I carefully set down the coffee on the scratched surface of my desk, I watch them through the open door walking away with a bumper pack of wine gums, one vanilla tub and the daring choice of strawberry daiquiri on a stick, chalking up another eight quid for the Orange's ailing kitty.

The Orange is a former theatre which has operated for the last forty years as a cinema. Inside, the building has been left untouched since the thirties. It's beautiful in a squalid way. When I first took the job it was owned by an old man called Neville Chambers. Even after my role as manager made it no longer necessary, Neville used to turn up for work every morning at nine o'clock on the dot. A scrawny man with such pre-war features it made you sob with nostalgia just to look at him. Neville had been in love with the business of cinema his whole life, working the projection box personally since the seventies but by the time I arrived he was eighty-one and too frail to continue.

As with everything else in my life I soon acquired a secret fantasy for the place. Impressed by my dedication and love of the visual arts, I would become, if only for a brief moment, the daughter Neville never had. When he died, the Orange would be left to me. I would receive news of my inheritance, sitting in his lawyers' offices, veiled and attired in Victorian lace and after a decent period of mourning, I'd get to work.

I'd restore the balconies, the stalls, the green velvet seats. Re-flock the walls, install Dolby Stereo and renovate the loos complete with ball and chain flush. I'd lay a new floor in the box office, paint the outside of the building back to its original colour and re-introduce the Wurlitzer to pep up the start of each performance.

Sensitive to the plight of movie-goers with competing popcorn indigestion and hunger pangs, I'd introduce all kinds of foodological possibilities. In the boxes (extra charge), total privacy and a two-course supper option. In the stalls, fried potatoes on skewers with chilli sauce and in the circles, strips of grilled chicken would come packaged in paper napkins. For movies over two hours, an interval would be created during which I'd serve portions of bread and butter pudding and sell tickets for Future Presentations. Hot chocolate with cinnamon would be on constant offer and for the late-night performances, huge espressos with of course just a *tweest* of lemon.

There would be members' evenings, non-members' evenings, Girls' Nights Out once a month. There would be film parties for bar mitzvahs and anniversaries, Cult Classics every Friday and free Vera Lynn movies in scratchy black and white for the Chelsea Pensioners.

Before long I'd find myself inviting directors from all over the world to present their screenings at the Orange. Martin Scorsese and I would become best friends; he, my mentor, I, his muse. Some of the finer documentary makers in England would clamour to have seasons. Barry Norman would hang. Premières would happen. Royalty would attend.

Sooner or later I would have the luck and eye to recognize a divinely talented young director with intellectual John Hustonian features and barely any money. For a whisper and a promise I would allow him to show his revolutionary short movie for one week exactly during which he would be discovered by Hollywood and internationally revered as the new Orson Welles. Eternally grateful and mesmerized by my haunting personality he would shag me once on the floor of the box office before departing for LA, my latest screenplay under his arm. I would never tell Luke but as my reward for services to society, *Halliwell's Film Guide* would include me in the category of Most Influential People of the Post-Tarantino Era.

It's a good fantasy, but not entirely practical because when Neville Chambers finally died he left the Orange to his only living relative, Ron, and in all the movies I've ever seen, when such a thing exists as "an only living relative" there are two absolute givens:

1) That this person will turn out to be a wanker,

and

2) That someone in the family will leave them something they don't deserve.

When Ron Chambers inherited the Orange everything changed. Loosely described, Ron is a contractor, with a business based in Manchester. From the few snippets periodically reported by his uncle, he'd started out as a builder and made good in the eighties before falling prey to the rollercoaster of the recession. It would appear that some dodgy mortgage scheme carried him through a couple of near bankruptcies which in turn forced him into the teeth of a borrowing spiral which now, I can only imagine, is nipping painfully at his heels. When Ron first inherited the Orange he didn't see much potential in it. Shepherd's Bush had not yet become part of the property boom that was sweeping across West London, but nobody could fail to miss the suburbaning up of the area in the last few years. Cafés transforming into restaurants, newsagents mutating into trendy surf shops and estate agents everywhere dancing in the streets. All this coupled with Ron's increasing need for ready cash has fuelled his own particular fantasy: to flatten the Orange with a customized bulldozer and sell the real estate for an indecent sum of money.

Fortunately, this cannot happen. The Orange is protected by various council and English Heritage listed-building laws, Neville Chambers's legal proviso that the cinema should remain an Independent and, that I should remain as manager as long as I want the job. The downside is that we have one very frustrated and not particularly honest landlord with a burning desire to cash in on his inheritance. But until he manages to do so Callum, Too-Fat, myself will endeavour to run the place as best we can.

Callum brings in the mail. I sift feverishly through bills, a request for a Kids' club and booking forms looking for anything resembling a production logo on the envelope. There are still other companies to hear from but I am not holding my breath. Everyone warned me. Don't send out unsolicited manuscripts, and don't expect any response if you do. Never work without an agent. Well, I had an agent, Anthony Rogers. Unfortunately, he was also a crook. He skipped the country six months ago owing a lot of people a lot of money. Oh, not me obviously because I haven't actually earned any yet, but still, there were plenty of others left scrabbling around for new agents. After I'd unsuccessfully plagued Universal Talent, William Morris, ICM and God only knows how many others for weeks on end, I was suddenly overcome by a terrifying vision of myself fifty, unfulfilled, answering one of those ads at the back of the *Telegraph* Weekend Supplement which read:

NEW WRITERS, PUBLISH YOUR WORK HERE!
We consider everything: plagiarism, verbosity, literary atrocity, pseudism, desperatism.

So I decided, what the hell and sent my screenplay out to the production companies Anthony had originally targeted in one of the rare moments he was acting as an agent rather than tossing off over his burgeoning accounts in the Cayman Islands.

And here's the joke. I was so pleased with it that I didn't just post it, I *biked* the thing round at great expense, like it deserved and was going to get immediate attention. Like someone might actually read it on the spot, option it, cast, direct and distribute it all while the biker was waiting outside, patiently having a quick spliff in the lobby. Ha!

But I'm now at the bottom of the post and there is nothing, nothing in it for me. Good. This means I can simply breathe a sigh of relief, perkily remark "No news is good news" to the desk and find myself genuinely grateful to discover that there can still be comfort in the oldest of clichés.

The Bush Restaurant, lunchtime.

"So the new obsession," says Johnny Too-Fat, "is Fridge Patrol. Linda now insists everything must be compartmentalized. Milk and yogurts to the left, meat and veg to the right, it's like a mini-Sainsbury's in there. Every time I open the door, I'm terrified somebody's going to burst out and offer me cash-back facilities."

"Clean is good, good is tidy, tidy is clean," I chant Linda's favourite maxim and giggle.

"It's not funny, Kit. It's extended to everything. Every time I take off my clothes these days, I can see her itching to tidy up my body, 'Hey, Johnny, what are these?'" he mimics. "'Oh yes, I see they're balls, but they're far too loose and they're swinging around all over the place, they'll have to be pinned down and this mess between your legs, what is it? Pubic hair? Well it's ridiculously long, too curly, too *untidy*.'"

For as long as I can remember, Johnny Too-Fat's marriage has been miserable. Linda is frigid, mind, body and soul, body being the one that irks Johnny the most. "Oh well," he says, "at least a man can always eat." He looks around him. The Bush is virtually deserted, just the usual background scratchings of a Ray Charles compilation on the record player. "Anyone at home?" he shouts. Rufus, the manager, pops up from behind the bar and strolls over to our table.

"So, what'll you have today?" He hovers his pencil over the pad.

"Cappuccino and treble sausage burger for the sexually repressed." Johnny orders without looking at the menu on the blackboard.

"Kit?"

"Apple juice and sweet potato soup for the manic depressive, please."

"Here you go," Rufus says ten minutes later. "Coffee and juice served to you today by one of Life's No Hopers."

We all grin cheerfully.

"How's it going then?" Johnny asks. It should go without saying that Rufus isn't a waiter/manager by trade. He gave up a perfectly decent job as art editor on some architectural magazine to go to film school and has been trying to get his various pipe dreams off the ground ever since.

"Oh," he answers, "not so bad. What about you?"

There is a code for the unemployed creative world, all of us have had this conversation so many times we can put subtitles to it.

How's it going? = *Have you been working on anything?*

Not so bad = *Nothing, how about we change the subject?*

"Oh me? Pretty good," says Johnny, *No work at all for a very long time.* "Any movement on financing for your short?"

"Amazingly enough" — he nods thoughtfully and rubs the top of his buzz-cut — "some really good things are finally happening." He turns to me. Rufus is strange looking, he has a kind of cartoon bone structure, where everything sticks out of his face at impossible and conflicting angles and not one single feature, excluding a pair of rather large grey eyes, appears to be symmetrical. "Johnny told me you've got a script out, have you heard anything?"

"Oh sure," I say, throwing Johnny a filthy look, "actually there are a few people interested." I pick up my knife and clean it with the paper napkin.

There's only one thing more frightening than thinking you might be a failure, and that's everyone else thinking it too. Although it's intensely reassuring to have these conversations. There is camaraderie in the feeling of worthlessness engendered by lack of success in your chosen field. What's more, there are enough of us around here to form a club, and once there's a club, there's a point to us, a focus. We can all feel we belong someplace, even if it isn't the place we would most like to be, but every club has its rules and Rufus at least knows not to dig for further details, instead he smiles his asymmetric smile, tells us our food order won't be long and ambles through to the kitchen on his long skinny legs.

"Hey, any chance of some sugar this side of Christmas?" Johnny shouts after him.

"Sorry," comes the muffled reply, "bit busy as you can see."

"What do you reckon," I eye the empty tables around us, "is he permanently stoned or just goofy?"

"Still in love is my guess, he's only goofy when you're around."

"Oh, come on. That was ages ago." Before Luke appeared on the scene, Rufus asked me out once or twice. I don't think I had a specific reason *not* to go, I just never really fancied it somehow.

"Ah," Johnny looks at me slyly, "but the flame of true love never dies."

"Johnny, first of all he's heavily ensconced with that Björk lookalike he's always bringing to the Orange, and secondly why do you only ever come up with men who fancy me when I'm in a relationship?"

"Because that's when women are at their most attractive."

"You could at least magic up someone with decent prospects."

"You could do worse, sounds like he's getting his film together."

"Terrific, another home video from the Production Company of Bullshit."

"You never know, he might turn out to be your divinely talented young director."

"Too-Fat, he can't even direct the milk, sugar and coffee at the same time, let alone a movie. The very notion of someone as lackadaisical in his approach to life as Rufus coming good is galling on an epic scale."

"Don't be upset about Channel 4, Kit."

"I'm not."

"You are."

"I know."

"I think you're clever and talented."

"You do?"

"Of course I do."

"Say more things like that please, Johnny." (small voice)

"And funny," he adds obligingly.

"And?" (piteously small voice)

"Um . . . Beautiful?"

"Oh right," I laugh, "now you've really convinced me."

"OK, so perhaps you're not beautiful in the *strictest* sense of the word," he takes a swipe at his sausage burger, "but you are definitely cute."

"You're biased."

"Biased is better than nothing my Quimski Korsikoff." He wipes a smear of sweetcorn chutney off his mouth. "How many people do you have left to hear from?"

"A couple. Final Cut's the main one; they were definitely interested when Anthony originally pitched, but hey," I wave my hand airily, "too much time has passed."

"Don't be silly, it's only been out what? Three, four months? That's nothing, Jimmy McGo —"

"Yes, yes I know the story." Jimmy McGovern before he got famous with *Cracker* sent a script to the BBC. After a year of hearing nothing, he apparently sent his script a birthday card. Ha, ha, ha.

"So there you go," Johnny says lamely.

I shred some bread and dangle it into my soup. "When was your last acting job, Too-Fat?"

"Ho-hum, let me see now," Johnny pretends to consider, "it was that ad wasn't it?"

"Which one exactly?"

"Um, I suppose it must have been that one for Smith and Beauchamp," he hedges. "The one my agent got such good feedback on."

"The one last summer, where you were dressed in a brown shiny suit?"

"Yes."

"Johnny, you were a *haemorrhoid* in that ad."

"All right, all right," he sighs. "I know."

"And how old are you next birthday?"

"Kit, do we have to do this?"

"Yes we do, we do." I clatter my spoon into the bowl. "Orson Welles made *Citizen Kane* when he was twenty-four. Fassbinder made forty films before he croaked aged thirty-six. You're *already* thirty-six and I'm thirty-five next birthday, that's not a million miles from forty and forty is ten years over our university deadline."

Johnny and I met at UCL. I read philosophy and Johnny read economics. Johnny Too-Fat was Johnny

40

Less-Fat at that stage. The first time I saw him was in his customary haunt, the library. He wore a puce Cuban shirt and was already in love with every female on his course. Tragically, due to the unprecedented time he spent skulking in the erotica section every female on his course thought he was a pervert. We became instant friends. Both of us were bored with our chosen subjects; for three dreary years I discussed ideology and social control, dwelled briefly on the meaning of existentialism and too late realized I should have signed up for Film School and Johnny likewise for RADA, where no doubt his sardonic fashion style and lascivious humour would have been better camouflaged. The day we left we both made a list of what we would achieve before thirty.

"University shores you up for many things in life," Too-Fat says ruefully. "I guess failure is not one of them. Anyway," he adds, an edge to his voice, "talking about failure. How's Luke? How's it going with you two?"

"Great, great. I mean thank God at least that's all fine."

"You're lucky. What am I going to do about my wife?"

"Leave her."

"How can I leave her? She's a dreamboat — and she chose *me*."

"It doesn't matter how much of a dreamboat she is if you don't have any fun with her."

"She says I'm too fat."

"You are." I watch him mop up the last of the ketchup on his plate with the remainder of his bun. Johnny's eating habits are legendary. "It wouldn't kill you to diet you know."

"Yes it would," he says simply. He wipes his mouth on a napkin. "Anyway I'm a character actor. Nobody has ever said to me, Johnny if you lose weight you could be a romantic lead, you know? It's not like there's a thin good-looking man in me trying to get out. A fat person is who I am, Kit. I was a tubby baby, an overweight teenager and now I'm a fat frigging adult."

Actually, given the appallingly high cholesterol content of Johnny's diet, he's not that large and I often feel his body should be applauded for its heroic attempts to break down the constant intake of foody substances.

"But I'm not repulsive am I?" He looks beseechingly at me. "I'm John Belushi in a bad wig. I'm just Oliver Platt although not all six foot five of him. You'd have a torrid affair with me given half a chance?"

Poor Johnny, I examine him objectively. Five foot seven with straggly hair and a pot-belly. Packaging has really let him down badly. If I was Luke I would probably say, "Actually, Johnny, no, I could no more sleep with you than eat a barbed-wire sandwich for tea," but I don't have the heart, the guts or whatever it takes to hand out those kind of truths. So I reach over, pinch his arm fondly and say, "Of course I would, Johnny. It's hard to keep my hands off you at the best of times."

★ ★ ★

People imagine there's not all that much to running a cinema — you turn off the lights, flick on a projector and spend the rest of the day, feet up watching *From Here to Eternity* with a bucket of popcorn and a litre of Tango: all of which is true but still, in between, there are a few other paltry matters that need attending to: choosing the programming, negotiating with distributors, maintaining repairs on the building, dealing with endless visits from the council and above all, answering the telephone which rings all day. It's ringing when I walk into the office and still ringing by the time I've pulled a chair up to the desk. I pick it up.

"What's on today then?"

"David Cronenberg double bill," I reply in a friendly professional manner. "*Crash* 5.30, *Naked Lunch* 7.30."

A muffled grunt while this information is digested then passed to a third party. The voice comes back on the line.

"And what's the trailer for?"

As soon as I hang up the receiver, the red light flashes again.

"Percy Quill for Mrs Fazackalee," bellows a familiar voice in my ear. I have to think for a second before I get it. Percy Quill is Peter Sellers, the drunk projectionist from *The Smallest Show on Earth*, Mrs Fazackalee was . . .

"Dad," I say briskly, determined not to fall into his trap, "I can't talk to you, we're up to our necks." I tip my chair back and squint through the open door to where the foyer is deserted and Julie and Callum appear to be doing the equivalent of filing their nails.

43

Julie is in fact flicking through *Loaded* magazine, and occasionally torturing Callum by trying to read the scribbled verses of poetry from the private notebook he normally keeps shut with a rubber band and locked in his drawer. But I fib out of habit because Dad's and my relationship has been successfully built on lies for the past two decades and there seems little point in messing around with its precarious balance now. It's ironic of course. When Dad worked as a war correspondent, a father absent without leave, life revolved around these phone calls. That's all I had of him, snatched fragments of long distance love and the annual birthday card — and it was never enough. After Mum died though, when Dad was forced to take up the shared and patched job of parenting with Aunt Pauly, there he was, every day, every night. I'd spent my whole life wanting this, it should have been a dream come true and yet by the time it happened, it was already too late; I'd grown up enough to resent him. Following that I hated him for a while and now, because it's easier, I tolerate him. Despite the fibs and put-offs our relationship teeters on one unequivocal truth: the more he wants of me, the less I have to give.

"I just thought you might be interested to know that Burt Reynolds is renting the houseboat next to me."

"Dad," I say sighing, "Burt Reynolds probably lives in a mock Grecian mansion in Beverly Hills, he does not live on a leaky houseboat in Hammersmith."

"We're all rather excited." He ignores me. "Your Aunt Pauly thinks if I play my cards right he might ask me to join him in a round of golf in which case I'm going to treat myself to one of those nice leather hats. Anyway . . ." he falters into the silence. "Obviously if you're busy, I must let you get on." He hangs up. Last week my father bumped into Julia Roberts in his local pub. Apparently she was playing darts, swearing broadly and drinking Tenants lager. My father is sixty-something. For the sake of clarity he is not senile. He's simply movie obsessed.

For the next hour or so I sit behind my desk, catch up on some forms, reflecting on the happy fact that it is now late afternoon and through the combination of daydreaming and time-wasting I have today, as in every day since I sent out the stupid thing, achieved nothing, which has in turn led me to discover two interesting truths.

1) That waiting for the mail is not dissimilar to waiting for a one-night stand to telephone. You go through the same stages of excitement, hope, frustration, despair, abject humiliation, before finally nervous breakdown.
2) That if you have an engrossing enough fantasy, you can get through most of these stages fairly painlessly.

I've got it all worked out. The ideal daydream runs for twenty-four hours, looping continually after that. The only obvious drawback to twenty-four-hour coverage is that it requires a degree of solitude — and should you seek this kind of solitude on a permanent basis it's only a matter of time before you find yourself in a padded room, dressed like Houdini and surrounded by scary male nurses brandishing electrodes.

The afternoon mail arrives late at four-thirty, but there is nothing, nyet, nilch, zilch, in it for me. I struggle through a little more admin shuffling until, Pam!, before you know it, it's seven o'clock, my hard day's work is officially over, and I am free to mosey on home.

Travels of a script – 2

Offices of Paramount, Los Angeles

The Independent Producer is now in a meeting with Development Executives. He is pitching his projects. The meeting has been in progress for exactly seven and a half minutes. So far the executives are not impressed. This guy is flaky, they've always thought so.

"What else have you got?" they say impatiently.

Sweat trickles down the Independent Producer's back. This is the story of his career so far. He hasn't got anything else. Then he remembers the "Kissing" title. It just jumps into his head.

"Well I do have one more project for you," he says, "but you must understand . . . it's all very secret at the moment."

The executives are shuffling their papers. "One more project huh?" they say, bored. "What's it called?"

He tells them. Their ears prick up. "That sounds like it might be interesting, what's it about?"

Frantically his brain turns over. He hasn't of course read the script, but no matter, he has a vague recollection of the synopsis. He makes a desperate thirty-second pitch.

"But I'm afraid that's all I'm prepared to tell you right now," he finishes. "It's already involved in a bidding war for the rights." He's winging it badly.

There's a short silence.

"We like it," they say finally. "English you say? Great title."

The Independent Producer breathes a sigh of relief. "I'll get back to you," he says.

CHAPTER
THREE

This evening for some reason the traffic's smooth. By the entrance to the park the volume has already thinned and dispersed. Cars scuttle down the side streets off the Uxbridge and Goldhawk roads, a rabbit warren of post-preppy homes for the late nineties. I whizz past the blue water tower on the Shepherd's Bush roundabout, speed up Holland Park Avenue, then turn left down Ladbroke Grove.

I pull into a meter in the Golborne Road. Outside Gordon's, a pretentious delicatessen that's recently opened, a boy stands with his dog. Ironic really that the copy of the *Big Issue* he's selling is almost as trendy and socially desirable on local side tables as *Wallpaper* magazine, but this irony is not lost on we, the inhabitants of North Kensington.

Giraffe decapitated by low-flying plane reads the *Evening Standard* billboard. I buy a new *Time Out* from the newsagents, then in defiance of my haemorrhaging bank balance a very expensive loaf of breakfast bread with figs from Gordon's before heading north-west towards the Harrow Road.

Axbridge Villas sits fashionably, half its shaky foundations in tenement hell, the other half perched hopefully in the cocaine catchment area. Luke has recently rented a house in this street for the sum of £1,000 per week. £1,000 a week! This is extraordinary, representing over a thousand per cent rise in rental obligations for Luke who until this year paid £70 for his bedsit in Earl's Court — and it's not as if we're talking Millionaire's Row here. We are not talking Mayfair, Cheyne Walk, view of the river; lights sparkling in the distance like a choker of diamonds over the throat of the Thames. No, this is for a rental in a small road still not a million miles from the sausage and onion end of White City, within a stone's throw of World of Leather, and closer than you might imagine to the drunks and homeless squatting in their cardboard purgatory under the A40 flyover.

This street is still, let's face it, shit alley. A watering of urine on every blade of grass growing in stunted clumps around the trees and God only knows what kind of suspect goings-on in the flat at the end of the road, but for that one thousand per cent upgrade, there is a certain kudos: a tinge of bohemian, that all important tag of "local" which can now be applied to any number of watering holes and most important of all, its proximity to the burgeoning power base of Notting Hill.

I park the car on a yellow line and lean against the door of no. 27, fumbling for the appropriate key on my ring, trying to remember the last time Luke and I spent an evening at my place. In pre-Axbridge days we used to divide time roughly 50/50 at our respective dwellings. Chapter One of the *Handbook of Relationships*: establish a mutual respect for your partner's space and travel distances. We both kept a set of each other's keys and despite the irritation of never having the right clothes in the right flat, the arrangement worked just fine. Since the move, however, we've probably spent no more than two, three nights at the most at my place, but then, I suppose, it's not altogether surprising. Compared to Luke's new three-storey palace, Praed Street, Paddington, which I bought as a short lease in the trough of the real estate market, is, even by my own suspect standards, a bit of a dump.

Still, however much time I spend in Axbridge Villas, I'm uncomfortably aware that it's not my territory. Luke has policed its furnishing to the point where everything is frighteningly new and cutting edge, a reflection of Dr Hybrid's recent and superior earning power. And despite the fact we swore we'd christen every room in the house by having sex in them, I've discovered yet another interesting truth recently: that it's surprisingly hard to have good sex in very anal surroundings. (No *double entendre* intended.)

As the key finally turns in the lock, there's a great clunk as the door opens from within.

"Kit!" Luke sounds surprised as I trip clumsily into his arms. "You're early tonight." He kisses me, straightens me up, then turns and starts tidying the junk mail on the hall table into rectangular piles of orderly rubbish. "Good day?"

"Are you going somewhere?" I eye the jacket in his hand.

"Kit, actually yes. I'm sorry, I've messed up a bit." He slides his wallet off the table and stows it in his pocket. "I forgot I promised to watch the hour-special with the rest of the cast tonight."

"I thought we were going out to dinner?"

"I know, it's a real drag." Luke looks sheepish. "But if I go now, I'll only have to stay until after the show's over. Then I'll come straight home. Swear."

"Oh, Luke!"

"I know, Kit, but it's a work dinner, so what can I do? Besides we see each other most nights after all, one teeny little evening on our own, a bit of personal space, it's not exactly a disaster."

"I'm the one that's spending the teeny little evening on my own — and your personal space is going to be filled with lots of people."

"I'll be back before eleven, promise, oh, and I bought you some delicious goodies from Gordon's to make up." He kisses me and gives me a cracking smile. "C'm on, don't be a nag." He smoothes the hair to the side of my face and kisses my neck, tickling it a little with his chin. I squirm happily, a fish on the line and he reels me in with ease.

I stare in horror at the goodies from Gordon's. A packet of peat-smoked tofu, some vegetarian kebabs and a jar of cannellini beans occupy the slatted racks of the fridge. I shut the door with a shudder, the force of it accidentally knocking loose the magnetic letters that

Anjelika uses for a shopping list. I pluck them off the floor and push them over the smooth enamelled surface waiting for inspiration, which eventually arrives, courtesy of the Patron Saint of Gobbledegook as SAUSAGE SWEAT IS SAD. It's just cryptic enough to be satisfying so I leave it there and look round the spotless kitchen wondering what else I can possibly find to eat on my hand-plaited bread when the phone rings.

"Film Quiz," a voice barks down the line. "*Pay no attention to that man behind the curtain.*"

"Dad," I say sighing, "I'm really not in the mood."

"You just don't know the answer do you?"

"How could I not know the answer? It's *The Wizard of Oz.* OK?" Then before he gets away with anything else. "Look, I can't talk, Luke's waiting for an important call."

"Just a quickie then," he says taking the hit in his stride, "I phoned to tell you that the *Poseidon Adventure*'s on Sky Movies Gold this evening."

"Oh yeah, Dad, that's great." I try to reach my cigarettes from the kitchen table but the telephone wire is curled into an intricate perm and refuses to stretch the distance.

"You remember it don't you? Gene Hackman, Shelley Winters doing synchronized swimming?"

"Of course I remember, Dad. It's a terrible movie." I feel the customary wave of nostalgia followed by the wave of irritation that generally cancels it out. The *Poseidon Adventure* used to be one of *our* films, mine and Dad's. I should think we've seen it at least five times together. We started going to the cinema after

Mum died. It was a treat that turned into a habit that eventually formed a lifeline for both of us — something safe to talk about. It stopped when I left home. God knows there's an all too familiar pattern to these conversations; any second now there will be an invitation from Dad, followed by a half-hearted excuse from me. Dad will press, I will resist, then feeling bad, offer an alternative, preferably a night when I know I'm going to be busy resulting in us having the whole painful conversation again when I inevitably ring to cancel.

"It's better than that pretentious stuff you show at the Orange. I see you've got *Crash* on. What kind of idiot is going to pay the price of a movie ticket when they can get kicks like that on the M25?"

"More people than those wanting to see Gene Hackman in a toupee."

"You'd be surprised," he says. "Anyway," his voice softens, "how about you both come around to the boat tonight and we watch it together."

"We can't," I kick straight in, "we're going bowling with some friends. Maybe the weekend."

"All right." Dad sounds disappointed. "Give us a call on Friday then, don't forget." I can hear the hopelessness in his voice. "Oh, and send my best to whatsisname."

"Yup." I hold the phone close to my ear, saying nothing.

Dad hesitates, nearly gives in to my meanness, but rallies at the last minute. "He's doing pretty well for himself that boyfriend of yours isn't he?"

54

"Yes, he's good, Dad," I say impatiently.

"He might be good," says Dad chuckling like a troll, "but he's a lousy actor, byeee." He hangs up quickly before I can retaliate.

I light a fag and quick-flick through the reviews in *Time Out* but after a few minutes the guilt starts to bubble up inside me just as I knew it would. I swallow it down with a vodka and ginger ale, sitting at the table with the glass and sparking up another cigarette off the butt of the first. I breathe in the blue smoke trying to regain a sense of perspective. God knows I shouldn't feel so bad. Dad seems perfectly happy out there on his houseboat, cheating at the occasional game of Scrabble with Aunt Pauly and cooking boil in the bag pasta with his radio cronies but still . . . I don't know how long I sit there but the next time I look at the clock it's almost ten and I'm suddenly so hungry that the notion of a cannellini bean fest appears almost gourmet. I rescue them from the fridge, retire upstairs and spoon them cold out of the jar, lying comfortably in bed and gazing in rapture at the *Poseidon Adventure*.

On secondary insomnia nights I fall asleep easily but by dawn I'm awake again, or at least semi-awake, capable only of a fitful doze between the hours of four and seven a.m. And while I doze I dream. It's as if the brain, cunningly registering the dawn of a new day, decides to indulge in some contorted gymnastics, a psychological workout that ensures these dawn performances are, on the whole, pretty energetic. This morning's dream finds a large cylindrical bullet

55

hurtling my way at one hundred and forty miles an hour, pre-programmed to explode up my nose. Unfortunately I'm unable to move and can only watch as it heads straight for my face. "Mother of God," I scream, in my dream ear-splitting, in reality a mere grunt before taking the bullet straight in the face. I shoot up in bed and snatch the alarm clock from the table beside me. It's five twenty a.m.

Luke lies on his back snoring quietly, rhythmically, neatly. The piped edges of his pyjamas waft softly up and down. The buttons attached to the front are open and the contour of his chest rises like a gentle mountain in the distance, the nipple proclaiming the summit at the top. I consider putting my hand over it, but this is a journey no sane girl would embark on without back-up, provisions and probably weapons. Luke the actor is resting at the moment, literally. He needs his sleep and is now well into the closing quarter of his minimum eight hours. These days Luke does not like to be mounted when in the arms of Morpheus. Even so, last night when I felt him climb into bed well after midnight, I thought I might as well give it a try. I rolled over and slung my leg over his. Squirming round his body I kissed his neck and sneaked my hand up the line of his thigh. Luke immediately turned on to his front. I kissed him again and he hunched his shoulders up to his ears.

"Luke?" I whispered huskily.

"Not now, Kitten," he'd groaned and I'd felt a spark of real alarm. This must have been about the tenth time he'd put me off recently. How many movies have you watched where boy continually spurns advances of girl and is *not* sleeping with someone else?

"Luke?" I reckoned I'd better come out with it. Honesty, after all, is always the best policy, otherwise this tiny pimple of distrust would be left to fester under the skin until it became a pustulous boil.

"Mmmm," he mumbled.

I tried to ease the words out, but before I even got to first base, fumbled and blew it. "Has something happened to your penis?" I hissed into his ear. I realized immediately this was a mistake but the problem is, if you're English, middle class and have to use a silly voice to say I love you, then chances are honesty's going to be a hard one to pull off.

"What do you mean?" He'd answered sounding more alert.

"Just wondered whether you still had it about your person or whether perhaps, well you know, it had dropped off or something." Luke immediately turned over and stared at me. Outside, a couple of cats were serenading our window with some tuneless yowling.

"Maybe you mislaid it, left it somewhere and can't remember where? The Dry Cleaner's perhaps?" The joke was going horribly wrong but I ploughed on regardless. "Could you," I squeaked, "have put it in a safety deposit account and forgotten the combination?"

"What on earth are you talking about, Kit?" he'd said, giving me a stony look. And that was that. Full frontal refusal. Maybe for our anniversary I should have one of those road signs made for the bedroom door, a giant pair of lips with a red line through them, non-copulation zone, official.

I scrutinize the clock again in case in some magical way it's suddenly hours later. It's five twenty-two. I close my eyes but it's no good, I'm awake. My body has begun its craving for coffee. The need to clear my head builds up steadily until it's impossible to ignore. I creep out of bed thinking that if I'm stuck with being an insomniac, then early morning is my favourite time to put up with it. It's quiet and there's no Luke's daily-in-waiting to follow me around cleaning up. There's two and a half hours of peace before Anjelika will let herself in, and as it's Wednesday she'll be followed closely by Page for the yoga workout, at which point I will make myself very scarce.

Downstairs the kitchen is dark and quiet. I release the blind with a snap, put on the kettle and make some treacly black coffee. Despite Luke's food-awareness drive, which has lasted six months now without any perceptible change in our health, coffee addiction is something I have been unable to crack. Sometimes the craving for it is so strong I long to skip the night altogether just to get to the pleasure of the first morning sip — not as dumb as it sounds. Luke, when I first met him, was such a heavy smoker that more than once I caught him setting his alarm for the middle of the night in order to have a quick interval fag.

The hot liquid slides down my throat, crashes like a waterfall on to my stomach then spreads out into a dozen streams, black mingling with red, frothing to a dark bilberry colour as it runs the rapids of ligaments and bones, the weight of it pushing the veins up like computer cabling. It's my Popeye's spinach, my betel juice, and when it hits my head, seconds later, I can feel the fog clearing from my brain as if someone has obligingly put a wind machine to a hole in my skull.

On the fridge door the magnetic pieces have already been pre-arranged for Anjelika's shopping list as:

Mud nuts
Sour bread
Kenco
Yeast
Ham

I study them for a minute, then deftly swap them around to MAD BREAST SMEARS HONEY ON DRUNK, cheating with only one letter, but it isn't until I shut the front door quietly behind me that I stop to consider under what sinisterly healthy ruse mud nuts will soon be forcing an unwelcome appearance into our lives.

Outside the sun has broken through the dawn mist for a brief moment of one-upmanship exposing a single streak of blue overhead. A thick white cloud stands by to cover it; a giant Q tip hovering over the ear of the city. I jog to the small park at the end of the street and squat on a bench by the kids' playground striking up a Camel Light. There is just enough darkness left for the match to flare briefly. I feel bad as the thread of smoke coils itself like a ghostly eel into the breeze. Dawn is the only time the air stands a chance, before it's invaded by the millions of humans inhaling, exhaling, arguing, shouting until by evening it's fugged up with other people's sorry germs and frustration. It's cold on the bench. I picture Luke, warm in bed. I should be there too, awake or not, just for the heat, the closeness and in the beginning I think wistfully, I would have been . . .

What makes you pick someone out of a crowd? What makes you shade in the background, colour the foreground, join the dots until you have a solid portrait of your future with some total stranger: a photomontage of him laughing at all your jokes, the first shag, the flowers that follow, arguing over baby's name, cosy evenings spent watching highlights of Prince Harry's wedding while the teenagers mainline upstairs? Well in my case I guess I'm a sucker for anyone who shows interest first, and Luke, from the moment he swung open the bar on the Orange's door three years ago, caught my eye at the ticket office and began staring at me. He stared so conspicuously that I started making mistakes with the change and had to avoid looking in his direction. By the time the popcorn buying and jabbering had petered out he was still there. He hovered then came over, pushing a single ticket under the perspex barrier of the box office.

"I've written my friend's name on the back, Melanie. OK?" He turned it over and pointed at the letters scrawled in biro. "Thanks," he added before walking off towards the inner doors. Halfway through he stopped. Julie dug me in the ribs with a plastic coffee spoon as he came out backwards, turned and marched towards me with a determined look on his face.

60

"It *is* you, isn't it?" he said and grinned. He had a smile of teeth so shiny you could have tap danced on them.

"Yes," I said faintly, "it's me."

"I thought it was — Ha!" Then before I had the time to even so much as flirt, he'd disappeared back into the theatre looking relieved.

"What was that all about then?" asked Julie.

"Beats me." I shrugged staring after him.

"You don't know the bastard?"

"Never seen him before in my whole life."

"Why did you say you did then?"

"I just said it was me, I thought there would be more conversation to follow."

"Not bad for a pick-up line," said Julie grudgingly.

Two weeks later he was back. Usually the Orange is at its busiest on a Saturday night but *Dead Man Walking* had just changed to Wayne Wang's *Smoke*, and the place was deserted except for a few tight groups of intellectuals in-the-know, girlfriends in pairs and the odd single who'd taken the chance that *Smoke* was a Bomb and Blast action flick. Luke arrived in a group of four. I studied them surreptitiously. Two girls, one Thinnifer, the other, with a Baader–Meinhof look to her, hung on to the arm of a guy with an unsuccessful Fu Manchu beard. They bought tickets then came over to where I was taking a turn on popcorn.

"Well, hi again." Luke sounded discomfited. "So, two sweet, one salty, one fat coke, three slim, and, um, this is Scott, Tanya and Lisa." All three of them nodded vaguely and I nodded back. "Everyone," said Luke, "this is . . ." and I waited fascinated.

"Susie," he said eventually, then looked at me. "This is Susie."

I shook my head slowly. He struggled visibly.

"Sally?"

"Nope."

"Oh." He was dumbfounded.

"Kit," I said.

"Kit," he repeated. "Kit." Then looked at me realization dawning. "It isn't you is it?"

"No, I don't think so."

"We haven't slept together have we?"

"No," I said slowly flushing a rich shade of plum, "I'm afraid we haven't."

Sleeping with someone who has already mistaken you for a one-night stand does not bode well for the relationship, but sod that. I was already smiling. Luke the struggling actor had an energy for life that was deeply sexy. Luke the struggling actor ran from tube station, to casting, to reading, to bus station before finally, back to me with bags of hot curry. He sat in front of the television, criticizing performances of others more successful than himself, chain-smoking, slurping beer and indulging in much spontaneous shagging. He was fanatical about acting, talking incessantly about the future. His future, my future. Our future. Luke had the hunger then. Hunger for success, hunger for money, hunger for recognition, and best of all, hunger for me.

Suddenly it happened. One day I drove him to a casting for the new Channel 5 series of *Space Practice*, a mixture between the *X Files* and *ER* if you can imagine that, and from the moment he got the part as the charming Dr Hybrid he never looked back.

Quasi-fame changed him. He made new friends, was flattered by a small but energetic fan club on the internet, strangers smiled. He even discovered a stalker who claimed she could track him on his mobile phone. He found more self-assurance and of course earned more money than he'd ever dreamed of.

With the money came the acquisitions. Apart from the house and the acquisition of Anjelika to clean it, there was Janet, supashrink, through whom he acquired an emotional awareness and then there was the personal trainer, whose body improvements eventually justified the purchase of a new wardrobe — some of it even made out of cashmere. Before anyone really knew what had happened, there was a brand-new Luke.

He still has the hunger. For money — but different league kind of money. For recognition — but from the right people. For success — but only in the right places. Luke has the hunger all right, but these days I'm not sure that I'm still on the menu.

I walk back along the street. Luke and I have a problem. I don't know whether it's just me or both of us that recognize it, but as seems to be the way with two people who have been living together intimately for a number of years, we are clearly not close enough to discuss it.

The key turns smoothly in the lock. It's nearly eight. Not too late to sneak into bed, turn back time, start over — but as I creep tentatively into the bedroom the alarm is already ringing. Luke sits up and presses the knob on the top of the black and white Sega face. "Ah, Kitten," he says closing his jaw on a vicious yawn, "as you're up, be a munchkin would you and make us a cup of tea?"

CHAPTER
FOUR

For 50p regulars can share the Orange's witty and informed view on all cinema and video releases in London. *Twister*, I tap into the keyboard, then stop.

The mail is late again. I'm glancing through to the foyer with increasing regularity but every time I turn my attention back to the screen, my fingers have disobediently removed themselves from the keyboard, retrieved a pen from the drawer and on the back of an envelope are now occupying themselves with how many days to my next period, how much money left in my bank account and most importantly of all how many hours left before *The Simpsons*, at which point I remember that the print deadline is tomorrow.

It's still Kansas, there's still a small girl and her dog, there's still a homely couple dressed in dungarees and it's pretty windy. So far so familiar in this long awaited *Oz* sequel. But wait! There's a nasty nineties twist (geddit?). Before the opening credits are through, Uncle Henry is pulled to his death into the suck zone.

I delete the entire thing and begin again, keeping half an ear on Julie's lazy dialogue sailing through the open door:

JULIE Do anything interesting last night then, Callum?

CALLUM Watched *Spanking the Monkey* on video.

JULIE David O'Russell? About wanking? Doing a bit of research?

CALLUM (*cautiously*) Actually, a friend of my sisters had an accident in that department once.

I shake my head. Callum falls into this trap every time. Julie taunts him with sexual ignorance then Callum in desperation dredges up some rainy-day information thus setting himself up for the very conversation he was trying to avoid in the first place.

CALLUM (*continuing*) Hurt herself with some kind of kitchen utensil.

JULIE (*snorting*) No way. Got it stuck up her did she? Which one?

CALLUM (*back-pedalling*) Didn't ask.

JULIE (*incredulous*) You didn't ask? For the love of Pete, Callum, I mean was it a parsley chopper? A Braun mini handmixer. Was it a corkscrew? I bet she rammed it up with the arms down, then tried to yank it out and the sides shot up and got stuck.

I switch off the computer. Even under the reddish lights of the foyer, Callum looks green. "Do either of you remember that story about the frustrated songwriter?" They both look up. "Casualty had to remove three miniature busts of Beethoven from her arse. Said she'd sat on them for inspiration."

"Are you sure that story's true?" Callum looks horrified.

"Has anyone ever noticed," Julie throws him a withering look, "that Callum's head looks exactly like a cardboard box. In fact I guarantee you that if you could be bothered to check the manufacturing spec for these two British items, i.e. moron's head and a cardboard box, then you would probably discover that they have identical component parts."

"Why do you have to be such a bitch, Julie?" Callum says bitterly.

"Because you're such a bloody wimp."

"Fancy a doughnut anyone?" I break it up. "I'm going to get some air."

"Get me a pasty would you?" Julie says.

"Give me the money then."

"I'd better treat the wimp." She pulls out a brown leather wallet with Big Mothafucka tooled on it. "He could do with some beefing up." She leafs through a thick wad of notes.

"You're flush." Callum peers over her shoulder.

"Oh, yeah well, that signature I was working on got sampled." Julie looks up quickly to gauge our reaction.

"Another one?" I ask incredulously. "What was the money for last month then?"

"That was the option on the stuff for the telly ad remember?" She pulls out a fiver.

"So who have you sold this one to?" asks Callum.

"Phonogram," she says airily. "They're interested in it for Kylie, maybe for Robbie. In fact they're tinkering around with a couple more. We could be talking an album."

"Yeah, well great, Julie, well done." I snatch the money and escape out of the double doors. Julie and Phonogram? Annoyed, I scuff my trainers against the pavement. Along the street the Bush Restaurant is empty except for a burly-looking Mexican guy sweeping the floor.

I've already polished off two blueberry doughnuts by the time I'm back on Queen Street, and the minute I turn the corner my hackles rise. Ron Chambers's black Range Rover is double-parked outside the Orange. I cover the rest of the street at a sprint, and, a stitch nipping at my side, limp through the doors. Callum makes a face and points across the foyer. "Toilets," he mouths. Almost as he says it, the door to the Men's opens and a thickset man appears brushing down the side of his camel coat with his hands.

"Ah, Kit, you're back, good, good, been waiting for you, a word in your ear." He strolls towards me. I look at him trying to conceal my distaste. I think it's Fay

Weldon or Germaine Greer who said something along the lines of "when you're old you get the face and the children you deserve" — an observation I always thought remarkably astute. Well, Ron can't be much more than fifty, and I don't know about any children but his face bears the indelible stamp of questioning bitterness, as if to proclaim to the outer world: here's a man who knows he's been shortchanged in life and simply cannot work out why.

"Lovely to see you, Ron," I say insincerely. "Can I get you anything? Coffee, tea, me?" The reference goes way over his head. I wave the greasy bag in front of him. "Cornish pasty perhaps?"

"Nope." He wags his finger. "Watching the cholesterol darling. Can we go private?" He jabs his thumb towards the office.

"By all means," I make an extravagant sweep to the door then follow behind, giving Callum a huge eyes-rolling-to-heaven take over my shoulder.

As soon as we're in the office though I falter. Sitting on my desk is a newly delivered mound of post. Before I can reach round the corner of the desk and grab it, Ron deposits himself in a chair, leans forward and rests his elbows on the cellophaned copy of *Variety* magazine perching on its top. Thwarted, I pull back and lounge against the shelves.

Ron slaps his pocket and extracts a pack of Embassy Filters. He takes out a cigarette and pokes it in one corner of his mouth. "What are you staring at?" he asks looking up.

"Nothing." I drag my eyes away from the desk. "Nothing. Nice coat." Hoping he might want to take it off actually, then he could hang it up while I snatch the post —

"Hugo Boss." He eases a gold lighter out of its breast pocket. "Warehouse sale." He fingers the lapel lovingly. "Not even the bleeding Pope has cashmere this quality."

"Well, it certainly makes you look very trim."

"As a matter of fact, the girls at the gym say I've lost weight."

"Well," I say politely, "let's hope it's not all lung tissue."

There's a bit of a silence here: Ron belches out a stream of smoke releasing a sibilant cloud of last night's garlic. I look at him curiously. I've always treated him pretty much as a joke. It's hard not to for someone who has such a quixotic view of his own petty thuggery. From the Mafiosi-style restaurants he favours, to the diamond ear stud and the rounded vowels of not entirely genuine *Long Good Friday* slang, Ron cuts something of a pantomime figure, but today there's something different about him, not menacing exactly but a look of suppressed agitation in those narrow ratty eyes.

"Come on, Ron. What do you want? Why are you here?"

"Proposition for you, good deal. Straight up."

"Oh." I resist making a hammy surprised face. Straight is not Ron's favoured means of approach. A visit from Ron, ostensibly to check up on the accounts, almost always precedes a visit from the authorities whom he has alerted (purely as a concerned citizen you understand) to the dreadful state of the Orange. Ron arrives, snoops around for a bit before leaving with some spurious complaint; the drainage is fucked, the noise level is too high, a pubic hair has been found in the popcorn and most recently, a month ago, shock horror! A dead cat — how could it possibly have got there? — decomposing in the Ladies' loos. What he hopes to achieve by all this is a five-year-old's guess; but it won't do him any good. Even if he were to get the Orange closed down, the building is firmly listed and it would take years before it disintegrated badly enough to force a compulsory purchase order. Besides, the council are an affable lot, they're fond of their local cinema and when somebody from Environmental Health does eventually turn up, all they do is give us a mild ticking off, take us through the niceties of the Health and Safety at Work Act, then leave perfectly content with a fistful of complimentary tickets. The long and the short of it is that Ron is powerless. He knows it, I know it, and he knows that I know it, if you see what I mean.

"I've worked out a deal," he says, amiability personified.

"What kind of deal?" I ask curiously.

"You resign from here, help me sort the council, and I'll make it worth your while when I offload the place."

"I see." I pretend to consider. "Offload it as what? You want to sell it as a going concern, right? As an Independent?" I know perfectly well this isn't the case, but I'm genuinely taken aback that he's being so upfront.

"Oh, for Chrissake." His manner takes on a slight edge. "The cinema's worthless, but the site's another matter. I could sell it in a flash to any of the big chains."

"For what? So the inhabitants of Shepherd's Bush can enjoy the unparalleled thrill of buying garden gnomes twenty-four hours a day from some tacky hardware emporium? No way."

"You're all the bloody same." His voice rises, real resentment in it now. "Save this, save that, save cats, save foxes, save cinemas, ban beef, ban the motorways." He reins himself in with obvious difficulty then shifts his weight off the mail and prises a second Embassy Filter from the packet, holding it carefully between thumb and forefinger. "How will you ever pay off that overdraft of yours?" he asks in a more conversational tone. "Nearly a couple of thou isn't it?" He torches the waiting cigarette failing to look me in the eye.

"How do you know that?" I ask uneasily.

"Same way I know you've got a mortgage," he says promptly, "third party car insurance and dad with a houseboat. I know everything." He snorts defensively as if I might be doubting his criminal credentials. "My business employs somebody who's pretty special on information."

The business is just bigtalk and covers the few rundown property pies Ron's got his fingers stuck into — namely a storage business near Shoreditch and a share in a girlie club in Manchester.

"Are you trying to threaten me somehow?"

72

"No, darling," he exclaims exasperated. "I'm trying to chuck you some serious money." He grinds the barely smoked cigarette beneath his tan leather slip-on. "This site's worth a packet. Look, work it out for yourself." He sweeps the *Variety* off the top of the mail, grabs the envelope underneath and starts scribbling figures across the back flap. "You help me, I'll bung you three per cent. Three per cent!" With a controlled flick of the wrist he sends the envelope spinning over the desk towards me.

"What about English Heritage? Are you going to *bung* them too?" I laugh, then stop. The envelope has landed face-up. On the top left-hand side the company name Final Cut is printed in heavy green lettering. It's not the usual Manila parcel of manuscript with a rejection letter inside, just a letter . . . My throat constricts.

"Five per cent." Ron is obviously mistaking my silence for something altogether cooler. "That's my top offer. Jesus woman, five fucking per cent. What's wrong with you?"

All I want is for him to leave. I straighten up abruptly. "I'm sorry, Ron, I can see it must be really frustrating, but your uncle wanted the Orange to stay this way."

"I knew it," he says harshly, "I fucking knew it. Why couldn't the old tosser have just sold up and retired to the Bahamas with a couple of lap dancers."

"He wasn't a tosser," I say bridling. "He was a romantic."

"Romantic? What good is being romantic?" Ron shoves back his chair and stands up. "Ronald bleeding Kray was a romantic, look where it got him. Fucked, poor and dead. What a life, what a waste. Not for me. Not for me." He spins round, yanks open the door and slams it hard behind him.

Past caring I snatch the envelope off the table. The folded letter slides out into my hands. Paralysed, I stare at it, willing the words to burn their way through the white paper.

Dear Miss Butler,

In my capacity as senior script reader for development at Final Cut it has never before been my privilege to encounter a screenplay of such stunning talent as the one I have just finished. With its uniquely witty title and grotesquely funny portrayals of the main protagonist and her emotionally disturbed family it is a masterpiece of understated humour whilst retaining real story integrity and you will not be surprised to hear that I have greenlighted it for immediate optioning.

PS No price is too great to pay for a work of this stature!

PPS Are you seeing anyone right now?

The pressure is unbearable. I take a deep breath, unfold the letter and read.

Dear Miss Butler,
Thank you for sending us your manuscript
which we've now had a chance to read. We
very much enjoyed it, and we think if tackled
in the right way, it really does have potential.
However our commitment to our current
development slate is a priority and we're
afraid we just didn't like the material enough
to want to take it any further.
Good luck with setting it up elsewhere.
Yours
Blah.

I drop the piece of paper as if it was sopped with the poison of the Deadly Australian Cigar toad, then snatch it off the floor and re-read it. And again. And again and again and again. But it doesn't change what's written there, the words just stay the same, smarting on the page.

"What did he want?" Callum's head pokes round. I wipe my eyes in the nick of time. "I've checked the toilets but there's nothing dodgy there." His gaze shifts to the envelope on the desk and he sucks in a breath. "Hey, Kit, any news?"

"No, no, no, no they're just acknowledging receipt of the manuscript," I say cheerfully, but as soon as Callum exits the temptation to head-butt something becomes unavoidable. I bang my head down — not on to the soft cushion of stacked *Premiere* magazines, but straight on to the hard surface of the desk. It hurts like hell but makes me feel curiously better. When the telephone rings a couple of times I watch the coruscating light through a haze of tears refusing to pick up till eventually it stops flashing then disappears altogether. Immediately it rings again. This time Julie sticks her head round without knocking. "Your shag's on the phone, claims it's urgent." She looks closer. "What's wrong with you?"

"Nothing, why?"

"You've got a big red mark on your forehead," she points out.

"Eczema." I stare at her with vague animosity till she backs out. God knows I must learn to beef up my disappointment antibodies, but right now, just for this one phone call I wish I could crack, like an egg, and break open but I suspect Luke would tell me it wasn't constructive to collapse every time there's the slightest setback. I suspect he would think I was weak and a failure and I couldn't bear that so instead I pinch my hand hard and pick up the phone. "Luke!" I say brightly.

A blast of studio chaos bursts forth from the earpiece.

"Kit!" Luke's voice is shouting. "Kit, are you there?"

"I'm here." I wipe my nose on my sleeve. "I'm here."

"Look brilliant news but I'm on set so I can't really talk. Andy Kramer and Leila Smith are coming for dinner tonight."

"What?" Simulated buoyancy wanes. Luke says these two names in a casual way as if implying these people are our oldest friends. They're not. Andy Kramer, the most powerful agent in the country, runs Universal Talent and Leila is an actress and the star of Britain's newest "most successful movie ever", *Evil Man*. I attempt to think of a horror equal to the horror of having to entertain these people but fail.

"We're filming till six, so you'll have to get some food together."

"No, Luke," I plead, "I can't. I really can't. Why are they coming anyway?"

"Someone on the show's arranged it for me," Luke whispers down the line. "Apparently Andy is interested in taking me on."

"Can't you meet them in a restaurant?"

"No, I can't meet them in a restaurant," he repeats irritated. "I've already asked them to come to Axbridge Villas, it's more discreet and anyway what's the big deal? It's just a little dinner and this could be an important evening for me. Get enough food for six at least, I might have to ask someone else so it's not just the four of us. Oh, and you'll never guess what" — Luke sounds irrepressibly cheery as if his dearest wish has been granted by the Social Godmother — "Andy has asked us to Justin and Cameron's party this weekend!"

"Luke, that's great," I stammer.

"You don't sound that thrilled. Honestly, Kit, you've become so negative recently."

I open my mouth to tell him about the letter, then shut it quickly. A cold distilled panic is setting in. "But what am I going to cook?" Cooking implies an ability to transform raw ingredients into something fit for the consumption of a human being. "They'll be used to master chefs," I protest, "silver services, linen tablewa —"

"Just keep it simple." Luke cuts through the babble. "Go to that organic fish shop near you, the really expensive one, I don't mind how much you spend. It's worth it. Oh, hang on," he says, "they're calling me." For a minute or two the hold chimes of *Space Practice* waft down the line. I stare at the desk. "I have to go." Luke's back. "I'll see you later and please, *please*, Kit. Don't let me down." And the line clicks dead.

CHAPTER
FIVE

The queue for the fishmonger's stretches in front of me. Three, five, eight people at least and as soon as I join it, two more people shunt in behind. The shop is hot. It smells metallic; of blood, fish, and the sweet perfume of disposable income. On the wall opposite a slogan of quality is nailed. Beneath my feet the tiled floor is gummy with water and sawdust. Surreptitiously I scrape the sole of my shoe against the sharp edge of the lower counter. The queue shuffles forward claustrophobically. A Sloaney woman at the front is asking freshness questions. The clock ticks away and suddenly for no apparent reason my vision skews.

A trailer of the future: accepting defeat I will be forced to give up writing. Luke, on the other hand, will become a global star. I will resign from the Orange, tend to the house and manage his hectic social affairs, organizing dinner parties for which I will nonchalantly whip up complex sauces and lentils reduced in fresh stock. There's a clip of me now, floating around the kitchen, in some Japaneesy if you Pleasy skirt, being amusing and attractive, unfettered by the chains of past inadequacies, because my real forte, and hence my life's work will be Luke.

"Oh, she's quite lovely," I hear his friends saying respectfully. "A Millennium Bohemian, so untouched by the rat race, she has this, well . . . spiritual fey-like quality, completely misleading of course — she is his *rock*. Could have had a big career they say, but gave it all up for love . . . Aaah."

A woman wearing a headscarf printed with Scottish terriers nudges me impatiently as the gap in front widens. I look around. The determined expression on the faces of the other customers rattles me. Why? I don't know. Then it dawns on me: even these people all know exactly what they want and where they're going.

The queue moves forward quickly and efficiently and I'm unprepared. I crane my head to see the display under the counter ahead. I'm not big on raw fish, raw anything for that matter. Traditionally, fish and butcher shops make me retch. Edging up two places a bewildering array of choice comes into focus.

"Who's next?" A large man threatens service in a white apron and a jaunty green cap.

I look round.

"Yes, madam?" I realize to my dismay that he's addressing me. "What will you have today?" he asks helpfully.

"I'd like to buy some fish." My voice is squeaky. There's a short pause. "For cooking," I add unnecessarily and gaze at him beseechingly.

"Yes?" says the fishmonger. My eyes sweep over the different coloured gloopy sauces.

"Er, do you have any cod?" I hazard. God knows I don't care. I hate cod.

"Cod Hamilton

"Sweet cod kebabs," the man recites monotonously.

"Peppered cod fins

"Princess cod marinade

"Free range cod-liver stew

"Cod's ovaries in aspic."

"Um." I've already forgotten the entire list. Someone in the queue sighs.

"What's that?" I point at a luminous pulpy mass in a container straight ahead of me.

"Spicy Salmon Preparation for Scandinavian stew. How much would you like, madam? One pound? Two pounds?" He makes a stab at the dish with his fat Cumberland fingers.

Behind me the whole queue is shuffling its feet and tittering collectively. The fishmonger takes stock, then throws in his lot with the crowd. His lip wobbles with the enormity of effort required in not laughing.

I'm deep in the grips of an indecision panic. If only it wasn't so hot, if only I could make up my mind, if only I had a better job, if only I could get a break, keep up with Luke. Oh God, everyone is racing ahead of me, leaving me behind. Where have I gone wrong in the cycle of life? All I know is that one day I went to bed in Pre-wash and now I feel like I've woken up in Rinse.

Behind the smirking fishmonger, through a door to the freezer room, I can see the hacked carcass of a giant tuna, its flesh raspberry rippled with streaks of blood. I begin to feel nauseous. The counter swims in front of my face. Suddenly, from a container to my right, the fishmonger grabs the curled coil of a moray eel.

Holding it aloft, he opens his mouth and downloads the entire amphibious snack into his throat.

Horrified I blink, but now something is moving in the tripe. Tiny bubbles are appearing from underneath the mixture. I stare hard at it. Triangular pieces of intestine swim violently from one end of the container to the other like a couple of great whites, frothing and boiling the urine-coloured sauce into a frenzy. To my right, a tray of mackerel sausages squirm uncomfortably against each other, spots of sweat on their upper side. The skin stretched tautly from one cinched in end to another. For a second I truly believe I can hear one of them squeaking.

"God no," I cry thoroughly traumatized. I'm shaking violently, my palms are sweating and I'm suddenly aware of an odd little tic pulsing away in my left eye. This is it. It's finally happened. Mum's weirdness, the beginning of the end. *Irene has episodes you know*, I dimly remember the whispered accusation. Sharply I pull myself together. I could be having a simple nervous breakdown.

"Madam?" the voice finally penetrates. I cast around and mercifully alight on something familiar.

"I'll take some eggs," I cry, voice sepulchral. My cheeks redden with relief.

"What kind of egg?" The fishmonger begins reciting with an air of infinite patience that implies to everyone else I'm an imbecile.

"Bantam

"Moorhen

"Eagle

"Gannet

"Peacock, class one, two, three or four?"

"I'll just take that tray," I say, recklessly pointing at the grey corrugated corner sticking out from behind the jars of tartar and dill sauce.

"The whole tray, madam?" he questions slowly as a smirk gels around his mouth. "There are seventy-two Oyster Catcher's eggs on that tray."

"I'm making a soufflé," I say, suddenly inspired.

Behind me the terrier headscarf suppresses a snigger.

The fishmonger shrugs, taps into the till, then tears off a small white ticket which has £144 printed on the bottom.

"Pay at the desk," he says.

Appalled at the size of the bill but knowing it is far too late, I trip to the desk, face burning. Numbly I hand over the ticket stub with my credit card feeling rather than seeing the fishmonger as he places the fragile tray in my hand. Clutching my purchase, I flee wildly towards the door.

I only see the sticky smack of fish goo as the tip of my shoe touches it. For a split second, balance gone, I am weightless, suspended in time, indestructible. In slow motion I watch the eggs fly off the tray, like very premature birds leaving the nest, and I note with interest how my own arms are scrabbling in the air after them. At that precise moment the door ahead swings open and a man I instantly recognize walks in.

"Mind, for God's sake!" I scream and go down like a wounded quarterback. My shoulder crashes against the floor, my skirt flies up around my waist. Legs fold beneath me like bowling pins. The breath I've just inhaled shoots back out of my lungs. As Rufus caves down on top of me I feel my knee connect with his groin. There is an anguished shriek, and then a soft bubbling noise as the wind comes out of his throat. He lands awkwardly. A groan. His face registers an expression midway between irritation at my fatuity and surprise as his wrist is flexed back to an impossible angle. As the force of his fall propels him off me, I watch in horror as his face fades out to white then chalk and finally through to translucence.

"Oh my God." My hand is in front of my mouth. "Oh my God, oh my God." The smell of fish is sour in my nose. The hem of my skirt begins darkening from the white of the Oyster Catcher's eggs.

Rufus disentangles himself and sits upright. The broken eggs gloop down his head, on to his shirt, and trail to the floor. He wipes an entire yolk off his face with the fingers of his right hand leaving a smear of yellow slime on one cheek and only then does he become aware that his left hand is limp, dangling. Useless.

"Oops," he says.

Travels of a script – 3

The very cheapest bedroom: Chateau Marmont, LA

The Independent Producer is pacing. He must get a copy of this "Kissing" script: acquire the rights pronto. He knows Film A won't give it to him if they think there's interest. He must tread very carefully.

He spends the rest of the evening in a fever of anxiety. He waits. He sweats. He goes to the toilet many times. Finally he can wait no longer, he makes the call. In LA it is midnight. In London it is eight a.m. and his luck, miraculously, is in.

In the offices of Film A, a young runner has just arrived for work. He is parking his bicycle gear in the back of the photocopying room when the telephone rings. He runs to answer it. Lucky he's so fit.

The Independent Producer wings it again. "Look I was in a meeting with Louisa last week and I'm now calling from LA," he says. "There's a script I need to get a copy of."

"Let me see if I can find it for you," says the runner eagerly.

The Independent Producer waits nervously at the other end of the line. His piles itch.

"We have it," the runner says breathlessly. "I think it's the one, although it seems to be missing its cover note and title details."

"Never mind about that," says the Independent Producer impatiently. "Just Fed-Ex it straight to the hotel could you?"

CHAPTER
SIX

Luke lies submerged beneath the therapeutic suds of his seaweed bath, big toe plugged up the spout. The muddy consistency of the water is so thick I can barely make out an inch of flesh underneath. He lies so still it's almost creepy, and if life were a Wes Craven horror movie it would be at this point that I might gently pull his hair in loving embrace expecting an affectionate but rueful grin for my trouble and would instead find myself lifting his disembodied skull clean out of the water, sudsy leer intact. Just as my hand creeps out, Luke turns his head, reaffirms life within, blinks once and says petulantly:

"I still don't understand why you've made *stew* of all things. I loathe stew, it's so pedestrian, why couldn't you have bought some salmon kebabs or sea bass cutlets?"

"I told you already, Luke," I say patiently, "Browse and Wilson was closed." I haven't told him about the fish shop. I haven't told him that instead of buying a simple piece of fish for six people I bought seventy-two rare eggs for the same price as a return flight to Prague then threw them all over the manager of our local restaurant, spraining his wrist into the bargain. Having not told him that, it was then hard to explain why I'd felt obligated to drive Rufus back to the Bush, having first bought two *Evening Standards* to spread over the passenger seat of the car, by which point it was near impossible to justify how I came by the vat of leftover rabbit casserole which the Mexican kindly spooned into a plastic container for me.

"How can it have been closed in the middle of the week? It doesn't make sense."

"There was some kind of toxic spillage. It had affected their catch."

"Someone actually told you this?" he says incredulously.

"There was a notice on the door."

"Why didn't you go to another fish shop? There's one in Westbourne Grove or that new one on the Goldhawk Road."

"I didn't want to risk it," I say unconvincingly. "After all, the fish comes out of the same ocean doesn't it?"

"Sea, Mrs Magnus Magnusson, the fish in this country comes from the North Sea." He looks suspiciously at me. "Are you sure you're not making this up?"

"Why on earth would I do that?" I ask turning my back hastily and stripping off my clothes.

"Because you're insane," he says simply.

As this observation thankfully does not require an answer I step into the shower, let the cold water sluice over my head and emerge a few minutes later feeling much calmer.

"By the way, Kit," Luke's eyes are skimming my body, "I meant to tell you Page is starting a twice a week yoga class at the Alternative Centre."

"Really?" I snatch the towel off the radiator and self-consciously wrap it round myself.

Luke turns the hot tap on with his foot, reaches for the loofah and begins to rub at the hardened skin of his heel. "So do you think you might go?"

"Why?" I glare at him suspiciously. "Do I need to?"

"Kit, Kit," he gives a theatrical groan, "you're so spiky at the moment."

I bite my lip, escape to the bedroom and stand in front of the long mirror. These days when I see my reflection through Luke's eyes it's sometimes hard to escape the sense that I am merely a lump of something sub-human. Now as I stare at myself all I can see is ten stone of stodge. Surely it wasn't always this bad? It's as if my real body went on holiday in my late twenties and now some old hag spurned from Club Med, has returned in its place. At least my face hasn't changed. Or has it? Zoom in to my top lip where there is a faint groove tunnelling into the skin. It definitely wasn't there yesterday. Suddenly I feel the tiniest pinprick of an itch, the sensation of a hair being plucked from the exact place I am looking. I rub the spot with my finger. Did the line just get deeper? I tilt the mirror to see if the light makes any difference. It's worse. I tear myself away, disbelieving. One little remark from Luke and I turn into Gloria Swanson from *Sunset Boulevard*.

Quickly I pull my green suede skirt from my suitcase and rummage for the flowery T-shirt to go with it.

"Is that what you're wearing?" Luke asks as soon as I go into the bathroom to put on make-up.

"Why? What's wrong with it?"

"Nothing, nothing," he says quickly, "actually this grungy look for me is cute." He pauses. "In fact so cute that if we had a bit more time I'd like to . . . well. I'm sure you know exactly."

"Really? You would?"

There is a sloshing of water as he pulls himself up to a sitting position. I sidle over to the bath in a sex kittenish sort of a way.

"Mmm." Luke grabs my hands and pulls me close to the edge. He kisses me. I close my eyes. This month I read an article in *Marie Claire* about how often couples have sex. A new couple said they did "it" nine times a night. I ignored them and flipped over the page to the three-year-old couples. Most of them did it once or twice a week. Luke has now managed to resist me for a month. His chin rubs against my cheek. My head starts to spin. "But right now I must shave." Luke slams his body back down causing a swell of water to slide over the bath's edge.

"Luke," I jump back, "you've soaked me."

"Darling, I'm so sorry, your nice skirt."

"Oh God." I dab at the stain with a towel. "I'll have to change now and I've still got to make the mustard sauce."

"What about something a bit more glam?" Luke calls to my retreating form.

"Like what?" I wail.

90

"Oh, you know, something smart but casual, Leila's got great taste, she always looks chic."

I rummage in the suitcase again. I've never cracked this smart yet casual thing. What does it mean? Does it mean my black trousers from Whistles but with a soiled tracksuit top to tone it down, or maybe my shirt with the shoestring lacing, but worn with pyjama bottoms and Dr Scholls? I see Leila entering her thirty-foot walk-in closet, sliding the castors on her immaculate ash veneer drawers, selecting a bra and panty set from Frederick's of Hollywood, removing a pair of Calvin Klein jeans from the solid bronze rail in front of her. "Aah, perhaps the frivolity of pale will do for this evening," she will murmur, plucking a mogadon-coloured cardigan from an incredible array of multi-hued cashmeres. "Yes, indeed, tonight I shall be an essay of mutually exclusive adjectives, a rainbow of neutrals, common yet classy, smart yet casual."

I pull on my only other decent skirt but every pair of tights I find has a ladder in them. I stuff them back into the hood of the case. Why do I do this? What mad illogical gene has decreed that I must hoard tights with ladders in them? It's as bizarre as the peg Mum used to keep in the kitchen labelled "hot-water bottles that leak". As I inch into a pair that have shrunk in the wash the phone rings.

"Is he there, Kit? It's Phoebe."

"If it's Phoebe," Luke shouts from the bathroom, "I'm not in."

I only just get my hand over the receiver in time. "Phoebe, I'm sorry, he must have popped out to get some fags."

"He's given up."

"They're for me."

"You never used to smoke."

"I started when Luke stopped . . . and we're giving a dinner party." *Whoops* I nearly bite my tongue off.

"Really," she sounds suspicious, "who's coming? Oh, never mind." Luckily Phoebe has the concentration span of a two-year-old. "Look tell me the truth," she pleads, "is he avoiding me because . . . Esme!" she bawls suddenly. "Will you *please* take that plastic bag off the baby's head. No, not after Scooby Doo, *right now*. Sorry," she says wearily into the mouthpiece again. "It's just that he's been so impossible to get hold of and then I heard a rumour . . . well you know . . . *Esme!*" she explodes. "Will you stop eating the garbage. Oh God." Her voice breaks dramatically.

I picture Phoebe, chain-smoking with one hand, managing her hellish children and belligerent husband with the other, popping Lean Cuisine meals in the oven and having to phone all of her egotistical clients in the evening.

"Of course he's not, Phoebe. It's just that he's hopeless, you know." Luke now stands dripping by my elbow, I turn to look at him. "All men are hopeless," I say lamely, "but I'll make sure he calls you back I promise."

"Phoebe the Sobbing Agent." Luke rolls his eyes as I hang up. "That woman is becoming a prize pain."

"Luke, she's stuck by you for ever. You can't just spit her out now."

"Come on, Kit, between Andy Kramer and Phoebe Smith, there's no comparison. Phoebe just doesn't have the contacts."

"Just because Andy Kramer scores himself a celebrity wife, and sticks his mug in front of every camera at every party does not necessarily mean he's a better agent."

"How would you know?" he counters.

I stare at him. "You're a real asshole, you know that."

"I'm sorry, I'm sorry." He darts after me and pulls me round. "Of course I feel guilty about Phoebe, but, Kit, Andy is something different. There's a casting for a part in *Evil Man 2* coming up at Film A in a few weeks' time. Andy has a lot of clout. I want the part of Cool Boy, it's perfect for me. I've read the script, it's raw, and realistic, just what I'm into as an actor right now." He grips my shoulders. "Oh Kit, don't you see, this could be big. You want that for me, don't you?"

"Of course I do, Luke," I confirm into his collar bone. "Why wouldn't I?"

Downstairs in the kitchen Luke has laid out six bottles of red wine. They stand by on the sideboard like a line of tipsy soldiers.

"At ease men," I say mock gaily and stab the first through its skull with the Dachshund opener. After an unsuccessful lobotomizing of the cork, I stick the bottle back on the sideboard and wipe the drop of wine blood from the worktop with my finger. It tastes oakish. The bottom of the cork has crumbled into the wine. I try to pour it out but the severed pieces bob rebelliously in the neck. I strain the wine into a jug, get rid of the cork shrapnel then pour the rest into the bottle, losing about a third in the process. When I hear Luke's footsteps on the stairs, I panic for no discernible reason and fill the bottle up with tap water.

"Kit, we need glasses on the table, napkins, and could you please, please clear all that make-up and guff from the downstairs loo."

"Who are the other couple?"

"Kirsten is one of the main writers on the show, very talented. The boyfriend's new, so an unknown quantity, but from what I can make out, bit of a loser, in fact," he cocks his head to one side, "I can't even remember his name."

"It's Ben," says the unknown quantity walking into the sitting room, "Kirsten's partner."

"Kit." We shake hands. "Luke's girlfriend." In the hall, Kirsten is doing kissing and a spot of lovely deco flattery.

I don't know why but I had imagined that one of television's most successful writers would be heavier, shorter, perhaps with thyroid problems and with any luck a poorly executed face-lift, but as soon as Kirsten walks in it's apparent she's a true Thinnifer; early thirties with natural good looks and wearing a pair of stretch flares with a transparent top depicting a female Buddha praying across her breasts.

"Guess what?" Luke says. "The rights to Kirsten's first screenplay have just been picked up by Disney. Haven't they you clever thing?" He puts an arm round her shoulders and gives her a quick hug. Kirsten beams acknowledgement managing to look simultaneously sexy and intelligent. "We'd certainly better drink to that!" Luke turns to me. "Kit, would you mind?"

I trot dutifully downstairs and return with a vodka tonic for Ben, a red wine for Kirsten and a Spring Water Lemonade for Luke.

"Ah lovely," says Kirsten. "Thanks Kim."

"Kit," I correct.

"Munchkin," says Luke, "didn't we have some vegetable chips?"

In the kitchen I light a cigarette and rip open the chip bag with my teeth. I must, I must, I must sparkle and give good hostess. Taking a double hit of nicotine I head stoically for the stairs.

Back in the sitting room, Kirsten is boasting about the efficiency of her bank.

"The thing is I'd forgotten the code and kept tapping it in wrong. Within hours, they'd sent me a new card by bike saying that somebody was abusing the old pin number and they were cancelling it."

"Counselling your pin number," I say, "that's adorable."

"I'm sorry?" says Kirsten politely.

"I mean, they were worried your pin number had been abused and so they were going to counsel it," I trail off. "Oh, never mind. Ben, I see you've finished your wine." I rush downstairs, take a generous slug of vodka straight from the bottle, rush up and slosh more wine into Ben's glass.

"Thanks," he says peering through the glass of the fish tank. "Groovy fish, Luke. What are they?"

"Neon Tetra," says Luke eagerly, jumping up to join him, "the pair with the feathery fins are Kissing Gouramis and those black and white ones darting about are Zebra Danios."

"You must be a real pro to invest in an Ocean Breeze tank, what turned you on to that little hobby?"

Luke looks faintly embarrassed. "Actually my therapist advised me to buy them, apparently their swimming patterns echo the waves of the brain, if you watch them even for a few minutes, they can dispel negative thoughts."

"That's amazing," says Kirsten. "I knew fish were healthy, but I thought only seared or sushi."

"Hey did anyone else read in the paper about the Dolly scientists mating skate with soya beans?" asks Ben.

"Whatever for?" asks Kirsten, helping herself to another beetroot chip.

"Apparently there's some kind of anti-freeze in the genetic structure of fish which they're trying to introduce to vegetables so they can be grown all year round." He shrugs.

"That's disgusting," says Kirsten.

"I don't know," Luke says, "perhaps they can do something useful with the idea?"

"Like what?" demands Ben.

"Oh, let's see now, mate lobster with Hellmans, or corn on the cob with butter or something."

"But sooner or later they'll try it on humans," says Kirsten with a shudder.

— "You mean like bimbos with brains!"

— "Teenagers with manners!"

— "Accountants with a sense of humour!"

The three of them roar with laughter — and usually I would roar too, become a bit pissed and happy, but tonight the area in my head designated for social interaction has been cleaned out, as if someone has secretly been vacuuming brain matter during my sleep.

There's a different trailer of the future playing now: I won't be Luke's *rock* at all. Instead I will be his *drudge*.

And here's an alternative clip of me opening the front door to a phalanx of tasteful media guests. Oh, they'll greet me politely enough, embarrassed that they're not entirely sure whether I'm their hostess or the caterer brought in for the evening. Luke will show them round his new nine-bedroom villa with underground parking in Holland Park while I finish creaming the home-made horseradish and acquiring risotto elbow. At dinner I'll sit at the table silently obsessing whether the placements are professionally compatible while Luke plays footsie with the wife of the Head of Drama at the other.

Back in the present conversation is halted by an alarming noise which appears to be coming from Ben.

"My stomach's like a Jewish Princess," he says patting it cheerfully, "you don't give it what it wants, it begins to moan horribly."

Luke looks at his watch. "Well it *is* nearly ten o'clock," he says, and wonders where the others are. Everyone starts to look uncomfortable. Leila and Andy are now conspicuous by their absence, and the evening starts to gather a vibe about it — that same one you get ten minutes into a really bad movie, when you're sitting there, thinking: this is a washout isn't it? Hoping it'll get better, knowing it won't and wondering at what point you should walk out. Of course it's not so easy to walk out of a bad dinner party, particularly if you're hosting it and by ten-fifteen waiting any longer becomes uncool.

"I'll put the food on," I say firmly.

In the kitchen I lift the lid off the Le Creuset and stare at the rabbit stew aghast. The lemons have run amok stripping meat from the bones which have revengefully impaled the potatoes on their sharpened ends. The remaining ingredients have committed mass suicide by throwing themselves on to the burning pan bottom. I pour in some boiling water and stir vigorously. I feel sorry for Luke. What is it with Golden People? I'm just thinking they could at least have telephoned to cancel when the telephone does in fact ring. I snatch it up.

"*The Blob* is starting on TNT," my father says.

"Dad," I sigh, vowing at the same time to stop this Pavlovian response to his voice, "I'm right in the middle of a dinner party."

"I just thought you might like to know."

"Why? Why in God's name would I want to know?" I bite my tongue. Sometimes I think I will burn in hell for the way I treat my father, but every time I open my mouth, instead of the gold coin, out hops a toad.

There's a short silence down the end of the line, then, "When did you get to be such a snob, Kit? You used to have such good taste. What's happened to you?"

"It's called growing up, OK? Anyway I don't have time to debate this with you now. I'm trying to cook." There's another silence then a bout of coughing. "Dad? Dad, are you all right?"

"I've felt better," he says lightly and coughs again.

The rabbit legs are now firmly stuck to the bottom of the dish. "Hang on a sec." I stick the phone between shoulder and ear and pick up the pan. The handles are red-hot. I shriek with pain and let go. It tips off the edge of the hob and crashes to the ground. "Oh, for God's sake." I slam down the phone furiously. The rabbit gets scooped off the floor, plopped back in the pan and the evidence wiped away with a J-cloth. I run my burning fingers under the cold tap. Through the pain a tiny sensation of unidentifiable worry pricks away at me, as though a blunt pin tack is loose in my head, not sharp enough to do any real damage but just irritating enough to make me aware of its presence. Then I realize what's causing it. I've never heard Dad complain about his health before. Never.

I'm sitting next to Andy Kramer but he's so big and golden he won't speak to me. He turns away, body language confirming his wish to be at the other end of the table where the others are hotly debating the merits of a new play about paedophilia that had apparently been raided by the vice squad on its first night. "Have you seen it?" I lunge in with a polite conversational stab.

"Yes," he parries deftly before again presenting me with his back. I stare at it impotently.

See, the problem with talking to Big Golden People is that courtesy of *OK* and *Hello!* magazine, you know more about them than they know themselves. You're already intimately acquainted with their greatest hopes, their deepest fears, you're painfully aware of the stylish Elvis bar they've had installed into their new £6.5 million mock Gracelands mansion and of course you're determined not to be a jerk and discuss any of these things but really, you've got to think of something . . .

"Your house is in Richmond isn't it?" I soon find myself indulging in some rank sucking up.

"Yeah," yawns Andy tugging at his negligently chic polo neck.

"The colour of the brickwork looked very . . . um pretty in the photographs."

Kirsten breaks from Ben and leans towards us. "Did you hear that Danny Boyle is starting a soup kitchen, Andy?"

"You don't say, where?" Andy perks up.

"Well, Notting Hill, apparently."

"But there are no poor people left round there," Leila says perplexed.

"I thought it was a bit strange," says Kirsten, "but who cares, he's looking for volunteers."

"Well," confides Leila, "I make a marvellous Ribollita. It's River Café, terribly easy to water down."

Soon everyone is happily talking to everyone else except to me. Why? Because they think I'm the village idiot. Why do they think that? Because clearly I'm behaving like one. Why else would Luke be sitting over there giving me filthy looks every time I open my mouth. Normally I'm an articulate person; thoughts are organized, labelled; ideas in one drawer, witticisms in another, verbs, nouns, adjectives slotted in the correct order filed under sentences. Tonight though, it's like some verbal disaster movie where any comment has to make the treacherous journey from head to mouth led only by a maverick idea. Somewhere along the way, half the word construction keeps getting lost, unable to scramble over my tongue, which is tied into a huge wet knot, blocking the exit to my mouth. Even the point itself, like Gene Hackman in the *Poseidon Adventure*, decides to sacrifice itself to allow the others to escape so that in the end those words that do survive, those that stumble out into the open air, are just too confused to make any kind of sense whatsoever.

I take out the pudding. "Hey, did you know," Andy is saying as I plop his bowl in front of him, "David Bencham has moved to Polygram."

"I thought he was working on that Fox movie with John Waterman," says Kirsten.

"Was," Luke says diffidently, "but apparently it was so bad, they didn't want to release it."

"Exactly, but Peter Ham at Miramax saw it, liked it and, bingo, just bought up the worldwide rights," Andy says. "Spoke to him last week, says he's going to cut thirty minutes and get it a release in the spring. He's very excited."

"Amazing isn't it, although you would have thought from a book as successful as that . . ." Kirsten shrugs and pushes away her bowl.

"Yes, come on, Andy," says Ben, "surely you can explain why it is that great books are always made into bad movies." Andy pauses to consider and for some reason it's at this precise point when the pressure peaks to say something intelligible or spontaneously combust with social inadequacy.

"Like *Angels of Discontent*," I interject quick as a ferret.

Appalled silence.

Everyone stares at me. Luke chokes and does the nose trick with his cranberry juice. Actually I can't think why that particular movie comes to mind, it must be ten years old at least but I stand my ground. "I mean, that has to be the best example of a great book ruined by a deeply dreary movie. Don't you remember, Luke?" I appeal for support. "You were saying so only the other night."

Luke grinds his teeth at me. The silence solidifies.

"Of course it's subjective," I falter.

Then into the abyss —

"My first husband wrote and directed that movie," Leila says softly. "Our marriage never recovered from his clinical depression after the reviews came out. Darling," she turns limply to her husband, "it's late, the babysitter?"

102

That's it then. I'm dead, dead. Dead.

"Hello," Luke says cheerfully, "shall we go for a walk?"

"Why, yes," I reply. "It is indeed a fine day outside." I bend down and fasten the lead to his neck.

"You're looking particularly lovely today, my little Kitten, if I may say so."

"Oh!" I blush. "How kind you are, where shall we go?"

"To the Land where the Grass is Greener of course." He raises a hind leg and scratches vigorously at the scar attaching his head to body.

"But I don't know how to get there!" I say dismayed, "and, anyway, I'm not sure I belong."

"Come, come," he says straining impatiently at his leash, "of course you do, why else would I worship at your feet all day?" With that he lets out an affectionate yip, mounts my leg and energetically begins humping it.

I sit up stiffly on the sofa and rub my eyes. The sitting room is dark and fetid as the soft furnishings struggle to digest the lingering fumes of cigarettes and wine. Judging by the stillness outside it must be three at least. I wince as snippets of dinner come back to me. I cannot cook, I cannot sew, I cannot make the garden grow. After everyone had left he accused me of hijacking the dinner.

"Why? Why would I do that?" I'd asked helplessly.

"Because you're jealous," he'd said. "Jealous of my success."

I pad down to the kitchen where the dirty dishes are spotlighted by the gleam of the street-lamp outside and the empty wine bottles bob on a sea of garbage in the black plastic bag. Perhaps I should push a message into one of them. What is the meaning of all this? I could scrawl, brief yet deep and perhaps if the gods were smiling, sunbathing or whatever it is that instills in them enough feel-good factor to grant the wishes of mortals, then maybe hundreds of miles away a lonely and misunderstood philosopher moonlighting as a garbage man will find the message and appear on the doorstep with the answers.

I prod the magnetic letters round for a bit finally leaving DRINK PUPPY JUICE on the centre of the fridge. Then I do the washing up. All of it. Even drying the plates very painstakingly with a dishcloth, Ruby, the moron from *Upstairs Downstairs*, before carefully putting them away on the shelves. I'm so entrenched in my *Upstairs Downstairs* mode that the ring of the telephone makes me jump and I drop the wine glass I'm polishing straight on to the floor. I watch as it bounces over my bare foot then snaps casually in two neat halves under the washing machine. I stoop to retrieve the pieces holding the receiver to my ear.

"It's Aunt Pauly," says the voice on the other end of the line and I can hardly hear her because she is mumbling, crying and sniffing all at the same time. "It's your father, you'd better come. He's had a heart attack."

CHAPTER
SEVEN

Through the window of the Thomas Ellis Ward the thin needle of an aeroplane trails its thread across the sky. Shadows from the modern council blocks opposite cast slanted skyscrapers on the cotton blankets of the beds. The air-conditioning pumps recycled air around the claustrophobic space keeping the temperature to a well-controlled seventy-two degrees.

Outside in the corridor, doors swing open, trolley wheels scrape against lino, cutlery rattles in the centrifugal dishwasher in the kitchen. The hospital janitor sweeps up the germs from the floor before coughing out some more to replace them. All around are noises of the early morning drill of a hospital waking up. But in a small iron bed on the third floor, up here with the weak hearts, the haemorrhoidal hell, the angina and brittle bones, I watch Dad sleeping his sedated sleep, dreaming his dark dreams over and over until finally they are thin and white and soften into fade.

And another hour passes.

Dad lies on his back against the pillows. Even though Aunt Pauly made the nurse give him three before she left they're about as collectively thick as blotting paper and I can see the metal scaffolding of the bed digging uncomfortably into his shoulder blades. Dad looks awful, his skin a pasty veal colour not helped by the sickly green of his hospital gown. All along the ward shrivelled people are lying against threadbare sheets like science-class frogs waiting for vivisection, or maybe just modelling this year's fashion for the old and infirm. You can almost imagine someone selling it to them in Moss Bros. "Why, it certainly suits you, sir, and if I might say so, it gives you a certain look of, shall we say, vulnerability? Yes indeed, no question anyone will respect you in that, sir, shall I have it wrapped?" At least Dad is far less groggy than last night, and when I came back from the canteen with a cup of coffee, someone had turned on the built-in radio by his bed, which surely would not be allowed for patients in any serious danger.

Towering above him a large-boned woman, her hair in a tortoiseshell grip, appears to be taking his blood pressure and checking the drip. A red and white badge saying Elizabeth, Duty Nurse is pinned to her blouse. "This is the last bag," she tells me humourlessly as she screws the ridged ending into the nozzle protruding from Dad's hand like a bloodied garden hose. "Although he'll need medical therapy for a few weeks or so," she adds.

"Fine," I mumble, looking away. Nestling amongst my many phobias which, for the record, include being murdered in public loos, falling down manholes, blinded by umbrellas, lurks an almost pathological fear of needles. Elizabeth finishes and withdraws, wheeling her pudding trolley of medicines before her.

Something brushes my arm. I start. Dad's eyes are still closed. He drops his hand on top of mine then leaves it there motionless as if the small effort of raising it even this far has completely used up the last of his strength.

"Coma," he whispers.

"What?" I pull the chair closer.

"*Coma*," he croaks into my ear.

"No, Dad, you're fine," I tell him soothingly. "You're awake now."

"No, dummy, *Coma! Don't let them take me to OR7*." He winces as the tube pulls at the skin on his hand. "Year, cast and screenplay writer?" His voice is hoarse and whispery.

"1977." I play along automatically. "Geneviève Bujold, Michael Douglas. Robin Cook wrote the screenplay."

"'88, and Michael Crichton wrote the screenplay. Trick question." He coughs triumphantly — if such a thing is possible.

"Hmm." I smile faintly. Dad's eyes close again. I consider giving him a peck on the cheek, then decide against it. Besides, he's already asleep. I think about the way I received the news of his being in hospital. There were no sharp intakes of breath, no tears, no shaft of pain skewering my heart. I would have liked all of those things to have happened, but instead, I appear to have received the news as a bystander, an onlooker of an accident. Sorry for the victim of course, but not emotionally involved. I watch him as he sleeps. He looks like a very familiar stranger and I wonder when it was he got so old.

"Glad to see you're doing OK, Pops," I tell him later when he opens his eyes.

"Never felt better, Kit," he says weakly. "Pass me my glasses would you?"

Another man materializes through the curtain, this time holding a perspex clipboard. He's wearing a pair of chinos and a button-down cotton shirt. Why does no one wear a uniform in this hospital? Or is it just this floor? Maybe it fazes the old folk. The white uniform of the nurse is, after all, only one step away from the black robes of the grim reaper. On the man's chest another badge introduces him as Stephen, Team Leader. I'm tempted to ask him what the game is.

Stephen, Team Leader stands at the foot of Dad's bed and consults his paperwork. His eyes are so close together he might have been spawned from Cyclops. "Well, good morning," he says, smiling first at Dad, then at me. The two smiles are quite different. The one to me is camaraderie-ish. I recognize the Dad smile as well. It is as humouring and patronizing as only smiles can be when they're directed at someone whose brain is clearly a tragic mess of random thoughts and unruly reflexes. A special smile reserved for old people and babies, the very same one in fact that I have been flashing Dad for the last ten years and it enrages me to see someone else using it.

"So," says Stephen, "we appear to have a Mr Butler here and you are . . . ?" He looks at me politely enquiring, whisking a pencil from the breast pocket of his shirt and poising it above the form. The end of the pencil is chewed. The tiny rubber mutilated and damp. I wonder whether he can also apply it to patients. Rub Dad hard against the white papery sheets, just blow him away, a grey residue to disappear for ever. Dad will be remembered as a smudge mark then eventually bleached out by the hospital laundry. Suddenly I feel tired and resentful. "So," Stephen repeats patiently, "what can we call you?"

"You can call me Elton John if you like," I say acidly, "but my name's Kit."

"Kit Audrey Butler," murmurs Dad reprovingly, "that was very rude."

"Audrey," says Stephen scribbling it down. "That's unusual, you don't hear it much these days."

I hate my name, it's ugly and it conjures up an image of cockney tea ladies with varicose veins serving Battenberg cakes in men's clubs. Everyone else thinks it's hideous too as they invariably compliment me on it.

"Pretty though," he adds quickly. "Don't get me wrong."

"Named her after the Hepburn girls," Dad says smugly, "Katharine and Audrey. All the brains and looks available to women between them."

"Ah yes," says Stephen suddenly going all dewy-eyed, "*Bringing up Baby, The Philadelphia Story, Roman Holiday.*"

"*African Queen, Adam's Rib, Wait Until Dark,*" Dad reels off looking delighted. Two spots of colour have appeared on his cheeks.

"*Wait Until Dark*," Stephen chews the end of his pencil. "Now that was a shocker. There was that scene wasn't there, by the —"

"Fridge," Dad finishes for him nodding.

"When Audrey's hit him with the poker and you think he's dead then he leaps across at her."

Dad chuckles. "I must have seen that movie fifty times and it still gives me a heart attack." They both laugh at the unintended joke then look at each other in pally admiration. "Now," says Dad, "about that heart attack." He winks at Stephen. Stephen winks at me. I scowl at the pair of them. Dad's infallible charm. Works on everyone. Part of me finds it detestable, the other part longs to be charmed as well. Story of our relationship. As soon as Stephen leaves a youngish woman in trainers bobs her head round the door and asks Dad if he wants a pedicure.

"Of course he doesn't want a bloody pedicure," I say exasperated, "he's just had a heart attack."

"It was a minor stroke," says Dad calmly, "and I'd love one. Do look," he whispers as she pulls her case through the curtain. "She's a dead ringer for Monika Kelly in *The Corpse Grinders*."

Aunt Pauly returns around nine o'clock with a bunch of flowers, a small suitcase and a vase. She takes a quick look at Dad gently dozing, then whisks his glasses from his hand, puts them on the tray and pokes the tulips, one by one into the narrow neck of the vase, filling it from the water jug by Dad's bedside.

"I might as well go now you're here."

110

I get to my feet but Aunt Pauly whirls round, gives me a hard very un-Aunt Pauly look and says briskly, "Actually, Kit, I was hoping for a quick chat."

"What about?" Aunt Pauly is Dad's only sister, and although around much of the time after Mum died we have not recently been in the habit of exchanging that many words, let alone settling down for cosy chats. "Anyway," I protest weakly, "I'm desperate for a fag."

"Fine," she says taking a grip on my arm, "we can have it in the smoking room."

The smoking room is about ten feet by eight and flanked by easy-style sofas. At the far end sit a couple of tweedy looking chairs. On closer inspection, they turn out to be pink plastic patterned as tweed. On the table in front of us an ashtray sits brimful. The room stinks. I've forgotten to bring my cigarettes. Aunt Pauly hands me a menthol-tipped Carlton.

A few other geriatrics shuffle in sporting a variety of polyester dressing gowns. They sit down and begin to smoke while an old woman in a wheelchair tries to manoeuvre by the side of an abandoned stretcher in order to gain entry through the door. Nobody including myself makes a move to help her. We all watch until she gives up and wheels away making cross hissing noises through her teeth.

"Katharine, are you listening to me?" Aunt Pauly is lecturing. "You've simply got to be more supportive. Your father needs you now and you must make more of an effort to see him."

"Why?" I ask her, exhaling slowly.

"You're all he's got, Kit."

"He's got you, he's got his friends."

"Kit," she sighs, "for goodness sake, it's been nineteen years."

"Twenty."

"Still," she says sharply, "it's a long time to be angry at someone."

I draw hard on the cigarette. The menthol is confusing. I don't know whether to smoke it, chew it, or stick it under the table with the magazines on.

"Kit," Aunt Pauly tries again.

"It's too late, it was too late a long time ago."

"You never gave him a chance."

"He had his chance," I say bitterly, "and he blew it."

"Your father is *not* responsible for what happened to your mother."

"Well he certainly didn't help did he?" As usual I feel the baby tears coming.

"He should have bloody well talked to you ages ago," Aunt Pauly mutters under her breath. "I told him time and time again."

I blow the smoke into a perfect ring. It hovers like a cartoon bubble next to my mouth. I almost expect to see a piece of giant punctuation appear in it. What was there to talk about? I've heard endless excuses for Dad's philandering, for Mum's problems. None of them change anything. Aunt Pauly trails off, and starts fiddling with the clasp on her handbag. It's one of those upright things that smells of dust and invariably has an ink blot on the lining. When she first started coming around after Mum died, she had a different bag, made

112

of patent leather, a daisy sewn on to the front in large stitching. It was the kind of bag that models spend hours browsing through the charity shops for, which is probably where Aunt Pauly took hers the day she decided she was too old to carry it. There should be a word, a dictionary term for that day, somewhere between menopause and death when a woman wakes up one morning, cuts her hair short for the last time, gives away her bags and junk jewellery then hotfoots it off to the Army and Navy for support tights, blue rinse and of course a stiff leather bag with a gold clasp just like the one Aunt Pauly now snaps open and closed, open and closed with irritating regularity.

"There is no easy way of saying this," she says, "but I'm going to say it anyway. You're a tough girl and it's about time you grew up a little, saw things for the way they are."

I look at her resentfully. People aren't born tough, they just get better at coping with the stuff that gets thrown at them.

"Your mother," Aunt Pauly ploughs on.

"What?" *What about my mother?* I want to shout.

I have a photograph of Mum. She's sitting cross-legged on a patch of grass. I don't know where the patch of grass is, but chances are it's English grass, because I don't think Mum ever left the country after she married Dad. In her arms she's holding a baby. The baby is wrapped in a crocheted shawl. The baby is me. What's odd about the photograph is that the mother is me too. Mum and I, well, we are/were very alike. We have the same reddish-brown hair, same old-fashioned face, same fat freckles splattered like chocolate drops on the bridges of our noses. But now when I look at the picture I am thirty-four. My mother was twenty when the photograph was taken. So it is me, but already come and gone. I'm almost old enough to be the mother of my mother in the photograph. Almost. Strange. Sad.

My mother was unhappy. Everybody knew that. Everyone knew she couldn't cope. Couldn't handle anything. With my father, his going away, his wars, his infidelity. She couldn't cope with shopping, with cooking, with me, with life. Irene was *highly strung* they said. Over the years I have heard a lot of adjectives applied to my mother; nervous, shy, neurotic, unstable, mad even, but call her what you like, in the end they all added up to the same thing, she was doomed. She killed herself when I was fourteen.

"Yes, your father played around," says Aunt Pauly.

"Played around?" I give a short laugh. "My father screwed every female born between 1930 and 1950. That's not playing around, Aunt Pauly, that's some kind of mass fuckicide."

"Yes, but your mother was no angel herself."

"What do you mean?" I say sharply.

"What I say, Kit." She leans forward and puts her hand on my knee. "They were both as bad as each other. In actual fact Irene, I mean your mother, not that it matters now, but she had an affair first."

"That's just not true." I stop attempting to suck nicotine out of the wet tip of the cigarette mint and flatten it into the ashtray with my thumb.

"They should never have got married." She squints at an imaginary blob of something on the floor. "I always said so. They were never very happy together, right from the beginning."

"I would have known, I would have seen. Anyway," I add naively, "I never saw Mum with one single other man besides Dad."

Aunt Pauly takes a deep breath, opens, shuts her handbag for the hundredth time, crosses her legs, fumbles with the button on her cardigan, pats my knee again and says awkwardly:

"That's the whole point, Kit. It wasn't just the one other single man."

CHAPTER
EIGHT

In the lift I give way to tears, squeezing out quite a commendable litreage between floors three and two where it stops for no apparent reason and hangs suspended in space. After a couple of minutes, I pull myself together, give the wall a quick head-bang of frustration, whereupon the lift starts again as if solely from the force of my cranium and judders down to one. I leave my head in the corner as the door opens and give it a second bang for good measure.

"Neurology?" A man's voice enquires politely.

Oh, very funny, I think turning round in a vague effort to appear normal and there, standing by the button controls is Rufus, left arm encased in plaster up to the elbow.

"You," I say stupidly. "What are you doing? Oh, your wrist," I trail off staring at the plaster cast. "It was *broken?*"

He nods.

"I *broke* your wrist?" I repeat incredulously. "I thought it was just a sprain?"

"I thought so too, but it didn't work very well this morning so . . ." He shrugs.

"I can't believe it. I'm so sorry."

"It wasn't your fault."

"Well, you know, actually it was."

"OK it was, but still, don't worry about it."

"Is it sore?"

"Better now the plaster's on." He admires it thoughtfully. "What are you doing here?"

"My dad."

"Is he OK?"

"I suppose so."

"And are you OK?" Rufus peers closer. "Because it looks like you've been crying."

"What is it about our parents' generation? They had more fun, better drugs, went to prison. They lay around in poppy fields with long greasy hair, love beads hanging down to their ankles, listened to great music all day and fucked like rabbits." I take a sip of coffee so weak it looks like the hospital cafeteria staff have dipped a brown magic-marker into a cup of boiling water.

"High on rock'n'roll, low on responsibilities. Mine were just the same, actors — both of them." Rufus rips open a sachet of sugar. "When I was small we toured for two years in a mobile home painted with cosmic moonscapes. All I can remember is them sitting around memorizing great chunks of *The L-Shaped Room* and baking hash cookies." He gives his cup a quick stir. "Course the irony is they've raised us, their poor children, on homilies against disease and drugs, making our entire generation fearful of adventure and commitment at the same time, sentencing us to a lifetime addiction to vitamins and organic food."

"Oh, come on," I say suspiciously, "I've never eaten anything even approaching organic food at the Bush."

He grins sheepishly. "Well, that's only because I've never grown out of my rebellious phase. How old is your dad?"

"Oh, you know, getting on." My foot taps against the table leg. It's a very good question, how old *exactly* is my father? He was thirty-something in the seventies. Once I had a photograph of him with sideburns and leather jerkin holding hands with Mum. I've no idea where it is now.

"It must be pretty depressing up there on the old folk's floor," he says.

"Hmm."

"Still you can't help but wonder what kind of sullen monsters we'll be transformed into."

"As long as I'm not Mrs Norman Bates."

"Or my gran, thank you very much." He gulps down a mouthful of coffee and makes a face. "Amazing. Coffee worse than the Mexican's."

"Why not your gran?"

"Oh, she came to live with us, well die with us," he amends, "when I was about ten. Her life was an endless cycle of eating and sleeping. At the table she would make this noise with her food like water draining from the bath. When she'd finished, it was like there'd been some kind of multiple nutrition pile-up: *Food*" — he puts on a Trevor McDonald voice — "*travelling at a*

118

great and illegal speed has once again crashed against Granny's face."

I laugh.

"Yes, but so disgusting," he says. "After meals she'd totter off leaving a trail of broken plates and potted plants in her wake. Then she'd spend the rest of the day in a chair, mouth open, farting in symphonic simultaneousness with her revolting King Charles, while poor Mum and Dad went about their daily regime of match lighting, sulphur burning, and eyes rolled to heaven."

"I bet she lived for years too."

"Actually as luck would have it, not too bad. Died in her sleep."

"Peacefully, so they say."

"Selfishly I call it, to deprive me of such spectacular family entertainment. Made me dread old age though, everyone's so *mean* to you."

"Oh, I'm not settling for it," I say vehemently. "I don't want Dial-a-Ride, I don't want meals-on-wheels, I don't want some souped-up charity deal delivered by pious boy scouts. When I'm eighty and senile I want drugs, plenty of them. I don't want a copper bracelet, I want a gladiator and a sodding big one too."

"Well it's good . . . although perhaps a little sinister that you've given it so much thought." He rubs his buzz-cut. It reminds me of the Bush. He always rubs his head when he's about to take an order. I wonder whether it's a nervous habit but then Rufus doesn't seem like a nervous person. In fact outside the restaurant environment he seems much more self-contained. Amused rather than fazed by life.

"I'm determined to be one of those cool old hags who wear snappy yellow checked trouser suits, leave their hair long and wear dark glasses and sneakers, sort of a Greta Garbo in Jean-Paul Gaultier."

"With my genes," he says sadly, "I'm doomed to have a shrunken frame made entirely of evil-smelling tweed, deliver sloppy kisses to a variety of cringing relations and own three or four fetid terriers who'll take the buck for the loss of my anal sphincter."

"Never mind, perhaps they'll give it back in the afterlife."

"If there is one." He smiles.

"Hmm." I smile back. "Well if there is, here are my questions? What are the entertainment facilities? Is there popcorn? Can you smoke? Is there a bank of screens plugged into the clouds so you can keep up with the latest releases — or maybe a documentary of life below, tailored to your personal preference of family and friends?"

"What a horrible idea. I'm not sure I'd be at all happy with family or friends tuning into me shoplifting or, say, having sex. Gran for starters."

"Or my mother." I stop abruptly and drain the last of the coffee from my plastic cup.

"You're taking this pretty well you know. It's a tough thing to find out."

"Well sure," I say flippantly, "I'm a tough girl."

★ ★ ★

"Oh, Mees Kit," comes the nasal twang of Anjelika's voice as my legs make an unexpected appearance on the kitchen steps. I swear under my breath. I'd forgotten she'd still be here.

"You sick?" A thin Filipino woman wearing a patterned nylon shirt, pair of towelling slippers and denim skirt ceases momentarily from wiping the kitchen surface with her beloved Trigger Dettox (leaves no smell or taint). She glances up and twitches her upper lip in a good morning then without waiting for an answer fires the plastic nozzle of the bottle in her left hand, blasting the immaculate white surface for the sixth time before lunging forward with the cloth in her right. Anjelika is a wipaholic, addicted to cleaning a clean surface over and over again, wipe, wipe, wipe, sponging away the circular damp marks of the J-cloth with another similar damp mark applied in the opposite direction.

"You no look so good," she remarks. Now Anjelika is moving sideways along the work top, crab cleaning, her arm reaching further and further out in ever enlarging concentric circles.

I mumble a reply of sorts then sit gingerly on the stairs, feeling suddenly very weak. "I hope you no wan coffee," Anjelika says suspiciously. She puts down the Dettox and pulls a plastic bucket from under the sink. "Because I make already for Meester Luke and now I am doing the kitchen floor." She pronounces kitchen, keeshen.

"I'll just re-heat the rest of Luke's then," I say.

121

Despite the fact that I have actually witnessed Luke, in search of a particular shade of T-shirt treating Anjelika more like a prosecution witness whose character he is about to shred, whilst I am unfailingly grovelly; despite the fact that Luke has been known to sing, "Itsy bitsy, teeny weeny, yellow-skinned Filipini," under his breath whenever Anjelika stomps up and down the stairs, whilst I fall about wailing with politically correct horror, it's Luke she adores and as I watch her re-heating the dregs of the morning coffee, mouth rucked petulantly like a macadamia nut, it amazes me once again to realize that I am barely tolerated.

"There ees a note," Anjelika adds grudgingly handing me a cup from the dishwasher, "on the hall table."

Am filming Space crash scene nr Croydon.
Will not be home for the night and maybe not
   tomorrow.
Hope your dad is all right.

I'm in the bathroom, sitting in Luke's pyjamas on the closed seat of the loo.

I drink the warm coffee and stare at the walls as the reality of Aunt Pauly's words sinks in. What am I supposed to think? The memories I have of my mother have become static over the years like carefully maintained colour stills. I can't handle having to change those images now to include the one of "Mum being loose". I certainly don't want to re-cast Dad as

122

any kind of victim here, because if I did, it would mean that I've wasted all those years of thinking of him as the bad guy. So I don't know what to think and I don't know what to do. I'm shackled to this relationship with my father and I think that the key to it was probably lost long ago.

After really quite a long time I get up off the loo seat and walk back into the bedroom. I turn the heating up full, lie down underneath the covers, close my eyes and try to sleep but I can't. I open my eyes and stare at the top eight inches of the radiator until the whiteness of the walls turns to grey shadows and the grey shadows turn to black.

"Therapy," says Luke, telephone waking me from a deep sleep at around two o'clock, "is like peeling an onion. Janet says that each layer you strip away reveals something more about your inner self and your relationship to your parents. It could bring you closer to your father."

"Luke," I mumble groggily, "if I discover anything else about my parents I'm going to have to be committed." I shift the receiver to my other ear and bunch my knees up to my chest.

"Go and see Janet Taylor," he insists. "It will help you get your life into perspective, take your father with you. I mean, why not?"

Why not indeed? Wouldn't that be cosy. Frankly I'd sooner die than sit in a room with my father and talk about why we never talk to each other. Besides imagine how absurd. Here's a clip of us in therapy, me saying,

"Dad, the reason I'm so pissed off with you is that you left me and my mother, slept with every woman in England, then took a ten-year sabbatical in war-torn countries." And here's Dad shaking his head saying, "Well, group, I must admit I probably suffer from James Bond complex, but the thing is, I've always been a tits and farce man."

"Come on," says Luke persuasively, "take down the number, give Janet a call today." And I do. I actually write it down obediently in my address book as if I'm considering it, but I'm not and I know I never will.

After Mum died I went to something called a grief workshop in Hampshire. The workshop consisted of about ten children of various ages. All of us had lost a parent. One little boy had lost his entire family. The counsellor encouraged the children to talk but she ended up doing most of it herself. All I remember were the endless hours spent watching rain splattering on to the skylight above. At the end of the week, the boy who had lost his family set fire to his teddy bear.

"Why are you so frightened of the truth?" Luke says. "Isn't it better to know than to hide? What do you think is going to be inside?"

Travels of a script – 4

Chateau Marmont

The Independent Producer is waiting for his Fed-Ex package to arrive. Hanging out by the pool he meets a Grade A actress. They get to talking. He is, after all, English and quite attractive.

"So, what are you working on right now?" she asks him.

"Oh, this and that," he says. "In fact I've got a project with Paramount at the moment." He badly wants to impress her and besides he's had a couple too many martinis. He leans closer, "And I'll tell you something, they really love it, they're *hot* for it."

The Grade A actress is impressed. More than that, she's interested. After all, the reception of her last two movies has been decidedly lukewarm. She gets straight on the phone to her agent.

"Why don't you know anything about this 'Kissing' deal?" she asks. "Apparently it's a hot project for Paramount. I've heard it's got the best female lead since *Death by Flowers*."

The agent gets on to his contacts at Paramount. What do they know about it? He's heard it's going to be a big deal. Knows some key players who'd like to be involved.

Paramount sits up and takes notice. They put in a call to the Independent Producer. The circle begins.

CHAPTER
NINE

". . . unable to stick to the diet Linda imposes on me. My insides will give out from too much white bread and my colostomy bag will leak. It will be only a matter of time before Linda will find someplace to put me: a nursing institute or even Battersea Dogs' home." We're in the Bush restaurant. Ray Charles has been ousted by Presley.

"Is this like that bullshit thing about pain, Too-Fat?"

"What do you mean?"

"Are you trying in some truly obscure way to make me feel better?"

"Sorry," he admits. The Mexican comes over to take our order. I finger the envelope in my pocket. I figured I should give Rufus something as an apology for the wrist. I settled for making him a free cinema voucher, good for two tickets, then wondered if this was a) mean, and b) looked like I was trying to entice him to the cinema for my own depraved reasons, which got me wondering whether I did indeed want to entice him to the cinema for my own depraved reasons, a theory I promptly and sensibly threw out. A cinema voucher is categorically not a pick-up. The idea was borne out of a humble Christian desire to make amends for grievous bodily harm at which point two tickets began to look mean, so I upped the figure to four then to six then back to four and now after all that he's not even here.

"He's shooting in the woods," says the Mexican.

"What, birds?" I say horrified.

"No, his film," says the Mexican, eyeing me compassionately.

"His *film*?"

"That's right," says Johnny. "I forgot to tell you didn't I? He's got all the financing now."

A pause.

"It's just not fair."

"What's not fair?" He leans across the table for the butter.

"Look, Kit, you can't measure your failure by other people's success." Johnny spreads his bread with a duvet of butter then places the slices of banana on top. "Come on. Let's take your problems in alphabetical order. Let's see now." He ticks off his fingers. "Father ill in hospital. Mother a nymphomaniac. Screenplay rejected."

"Third screenplay, Johnny, my third screenplay has been rejected for the millionth time."

"So what," Johnny says, "*Gone with the Wind* was turned down by at least —"

"Say it at your peril." There is nothing worse than someone quoting a Famous Success Story at you, because you know perfectly well that even though your work is undoubtedly a masterpiece, it is categorically not a *Gone with the Wind*, it will not be starring Clark Gable and Vivien Leigh and definitely will not pick up eight Academy Awards. Whenever anybody quotes me *Gone with the Wind* or *The Day of the Jackal*, I want to strangle them.

"Come on, Kit, don't you think you're being just a little impatient?"

"You're right, Johnny. I suffer from Low Tolerance Threshold, Perseverance Deficiency Syndrome; I'm sure there's an official medical term for it, doctors to see, pills to take, therapy to swallow."

"Oh, for pity's sake, stop wallowing." The Mexican appears for the third time with some more peanut butter, Johnny lathers it on thickly.

"You want that fried?" the Mexican asks.

"Ooh, I don't know?" Johnny's eyes light up at the thought. "Do I?"

"Fried banana and peanut butter was Elvis's favourite, man." He picks up Johnny's plate, lumbers off then turns back. "You do know," he fixes me with a heavy stare, "how nearly *Day of the Jackal* didn't get made?"

"Thank you, just what I was telling her," Johnny says as I splutter into my tea. "Right." He continues keeping his eye trained on the kitchen for the re-appearance of his food. "Next and far more importantly, your dad . . ."

With a finger I move some jam round on my plate. On the way to the Bush this afternoon I found myself doing these little tests. Would I choose:

a) Screenplay optioned + Dad ill

or

    b) Dad healthy + another rejection

I immediately chose a) knowing this was evil, undaughterly and ungodly. Soon these scenarios became a perverse kind of torture, and as I worked them over and over in my head, the stakes became higher.

Would I rather, I mused with the dispassionate interest of the seriously disturbed:

nominated for best original screenplay + Dad croak?

or

Dad live to 103 + efforts never see light of day.

Luckily not even I, in my new role as Linda Blair, Exorcist Daughter, could bring myself to continue this line of questioning and anyway it was completely academic as when I called the hospital the doctor told me Dad was as strong as a combine harvester. Nevertheless the fact that I'm more depressed about my lack of career prospects than what Johnny Too-Fat assumes is the main problem makes me feel doubly guilty, but I have just about enough decency to go along with the idea.

"I got this film out the other day, Too-Fat. Gene Hackman and Elizabeth Mastrantonio. They're both lawyers. She had this big father problem, her father fucked around, her mother has a heart attack and drops dead. I'm watching this movie and I suddenly realize that I'm watching it to get clues, you know, see how I should behave, I mean what kind of a person needs to do that?"

"It's OK, some people go to a psychiatrist, you go to Video City."

"It's not the same thing at all."

"Maybe you should stop trying to push the thing with your father into a pigeon hole. When you go to the hospital this evening, talk to him. I mean really talk to him. Don't just play games about who directed *The Beast From 20,000 Fathoms*, or why Howard Hughes was so obsessed with Jane Russell's tits. Let it be the relationship it's going to be. You can't always write everybody's lines for them. As for your mother, well it's no big deal. I mean, it could have been worse, she could have been a dyke or something."

"Hmm?"

"Are you listening, Kit?"

"Course." I beam at him. "You're saying I've reached a moment in life where thwarted ambition doesn't necessarily lead to despair and self-loathing. You're saying I will emerge from this crisis like a butterfly from a chrysalis, a more resolute person able to imbue future work with a sense of emotional depth and pain that was perhaps previously lacking, then above all with my newfound maturity I shall tonight bond instantly with my father, come to terms with my mother's sex addiction and live happily ever after."

"Good girl," Johnny says. "Now, repeat after me. I am a Quim in a million, a Quim in a million."

"Quim in a million," I intone obediently as I watch the Mexican drop a stack of newly washed plates on to the floor in the kitchen. "A Quim in a million."

On Golden Pond we drift. In a boat. Dad and me. We wear matching crushed cotton hats and khakis. We talk about fish and flies and nylon ties, all three a euphemism for deeper, more painful things. The rollocks squeak, a heron mopes on the passing world while behind us the sun loops downwards in the sky. And finally, finally we are at peace with each oth — "Hold the lift!" Someone shouts. I stab the G button and put my foot against the heavy electronic doors to keep them open. An emaciated man with barren eyes is wheeled in on a stretcher by a couple of attendants. The lift whirrs again and stops at three.

I walk through the double doors into the Thomas Ellis Ward. Along the linoleum corridor the faces are already familiar; at the end of the ward Dad looks perky, his curtains are open and he's sitting up in bed, the tall nurse by his side, fussing around with pillows.

"Good news," Dad says before I can even open my mouth, "Elizabeth here, who is better than Florence Nightingale, who is my nurse, my girlfriend, my guru, and even my philosopher, says I'll be back on the boat by the weekend." Elizabeth the melted ice-queen turns to me and gives a radiant smile. Dad adjusts his glasses on the end of his nose. "I can't tell you how ravishing all the sisters are here," he confides. "Not only that but

132

the Monika Kelly lookalike says she'll even come to the houseboat on her day off to give me a pedicure."

I can't believe this. Here he goes again like an old vaudeville player. *And we have with us today Dad and his Fabulous Chat-up Routine, performing live!* All the old resentment starts. The lines I've been practising since I left Johnny dissipate. Why does he do this? What is he trying to prove here? That he's attractive to women? That his charm is irresistible, even betubed and groggy from his hospital bed? I know this already. Like I don't have memories of endless charmed women. Is he showing off for me? I watch to see if his eyes slide my way, but they don't. I realize, and not for the first time, that it just comes naturally to him and he's just oblivious to the insensitivity.

Elizabeth leaves and Dad and I make polite noises at each other. He probably wants more, I don't give it to him. It's impossible not to fall into the pattern of the last twenty years. Like a couple of pieces of machinery we slot into the clunky rhythm of our roles, he flippant, me sulky, both of us greasing the wheels and cogs of our relationship with the slippery oil of pretence. The visit stops when Elizabeth comes back with a tray of suspicious-looking lasagne and a side salad.

"By the way," Dad says, tucking into it with relish, "if I'm not here tomorrow it will only be because Liz and I have either gone to the movies, or eloped to South America." He gives her a little pat on the hand.

"Don't worry, Dad," I say dryly, "it's not like I'm going to lose any sleep over it."

CHAPTER
TEN

Close eyes, lie still, expel rogue thoughts of Mum with variety of different men . . . pass into sleep for a millisecond. Oh joy! The 3 gm of melatonin's working. Then — horror as vast wattage of adrenaline surges through body at realization. Open eyes, light on, sit up. Think about Mum in bed holding hands with Eamon Andrews while Rolf Harris patiently waits his turn outside the door. Ceiling becomes a vast white screen as fragments of memories play in front of my eyes like a home-video show. Mum as a free spirit, embracing free love? Drifting from one dreamy liaison to another? No, no, no. This is not how I remember her at all. I remember her constant distraction, the dragging suspicion that I was never quite the focus of her attention. I remember her "white meals". Pasta and mashed potato, rice with cream sauce. I remember her in a nightdress in the afternoon. Her laughter a note too high. So many things off-kilter. How does it begin, that kind of depression?

It's a bad night all in all but there comes a point not a million minutes from morning when I decide Johnny is right. I'm wallowing. Badly. I am not my mother and never will be. So no way am I going to let Dad or Luke, and certainly not work, get me down and with that I finally drift off to sleep.

In the Orange, the next morning I read in the paper that a two-headed python has been discovered in Venezuela. It is nineteen foot long and apparently eats with both heads at the same time. It's Julie's morning off and I have only served three takers for the midday performance when a couple of pubescents in high-tops and jackets with Nike printed on to every surface, saunter up to the box office and try to blag a couple of tickets.

"Two," the taller of them growls at me, desperately trying to hide the uncontrollable squeak of his just-broken voice.

Normally, I'm ashamed to admit, we endorse a vague policy of blind-eye to morning performances, but it's a tragedy for this pair of walking product placements that their urge to see an X-rated movie happens to coincide with a visit from a certain Mr Rashid Hassop from the council, who is currently inspecting the premises for the annual renewal of our licence. "So," I say sweetly, "you want to see *Last Tango in Paris*, do you?"

"That's whot's on innit?" says the taller of the two. His hair is shaved at the front, long at the back and bleached at the roots. The result sticks out over his hooded sweat-shirt like a badminton shuttlecock.

"And you'll excuse me for asking of course but how old are you?"

"Er . . . eighteen," they chorus. (Throwing a quick glance at the rating on the movie poster to be sure.)

135

"I see, I see, and that would be both of you added together or each of you individually?"

They look at each other. "Are you gonna give us the tickets or not?" The shuttlecock youth's arms are crossed, his chin defiant (though hairless).

"I'll let you in on condition you sing me any one song from *The Jungle Book*."

Blank look from both boys. "What's that about then?"

"Famous horror musical about man-eating tigers from the hit Kipling mini-series," I say gleefully. "Come back when you've memorized it." They slope off. This witty exchange makes me chuckle so hard that for a minute or two I don't notice Rufus watching me, propped languidly against the wall by the ice-cream sign. He makes a salute with his plaster.

"How did you guess?" He has the envelope of tokens with him. "My ideal evening out."

"Oh, I just figured it was everybody's." I ease myself out of the box office, oddly shy to see him. "I mean you can't go wrong with a good movie can you? Ice-cream in one hand, Sam Shepard in the other."

"Especially not if you're Sam Shepard."

Well I fell into that one. There follows a brief interval while I think up something to say.

"I hear you finally raised the finance for your short?"

"First bit of shooting yesterday afternoon. Didn't have a clue what I was doing."

"What's it about then?"

"Oh, you know," he grins, "a cynical exploitation of the vulnerable side of youth, a thinly veiled autobiography masquerading as original thought, shot in cramped locations for under thirty thousand pounds. But what I actually came to ask you," he smiles at me, "is whether you would c —"

"Look," I interrupt embarrassed, "the tickets aren't — I mean . . . I don't want you to think that I was . . ." I trail off. Oh God, back at the Village Idiots Convention again.

"Come with me?" he finishes.

I then surprise myself by thinking yes, yes please. For a second I want to turn to a studio audience, hold up a giant placard saying PLEASE CHEER! It's a long time since anyone's asked me out and I feel disproportionately chuffed.

"Look I know you've got your boyfriend now and everything, and I know I've asked you once before, well twice to be strictly accurate, and it's probably annoying and possibly masochistic to be asking you again, but I thought maybe we could just go one afternoon." He stops and rubs the top of his buzz-cut. "Actually I'm not sure what I was thinking. Perhaps not."

"But the tickets are only good for the Orange."

"I realize that of course, but I thought we could stretch to another cinema — if that wouldn't be a conflict of interest."

"I don't know." I'm still hedging him, and while I'm doing this, he's looking at me as though trying to guess what I'm thinking and what I'm thinking is: OK to hell with it, yes please, I'd really like to, but before I get a chance to open my mouth, something along the wall on the far side of the foyer catches my eye. Something *scuttling*. Transfixed I stare at it, whereupon it changes direction and suddenly races towards us at high speed practically polishing the toe of Rufus's shoe with its fur. Before I know it I've executed a funny little jump into Rufus's good arm as the thing zigzags down the stairs towards the basement.

"Christ," I yelp, "what was that?"

"It was either a very small bear," Rufus says, staring hard at his shoe, "or a very large rat."

I put my hand over my thumping heart. "I just so much hope it was the bear." His arm is still around me. He smells faintly sweaty. Sexy, I think, then to my horror realize I may have actually sniffed out loud. My face turns the colour of boiled shrimp. Rufus drops his arm.

"Well," he says evenly, "they do say that you're never more than four feet away from a rat in London."

"Kind of creepy idea, that means they have to be, yuk, where?" I look around hoping my blush will subside.

"Down there, I suppose." He gazes at the floorboards. "Scurry, scurry, scurry, scurry, scurry."

"What do you think they live on?" I enquire interestedly.

"Are we about to make polite conversation about rats?"

"No. Yes. I mean, I'm genuinely interested."

"In that case, let me see." He's laughing at me now. "I believe they live on human plankton; that is to say dandruff, scurf, the scratchings of eczema, snot, toenail cuttings. I've heard that some are even partial to belly-button fluff."

"Disgusting," I murmur.

"Seems such a waste too, doesn't it, if they're going to be around all the time they might at least make themselves useful."

"You mean like scrubbing the floorboards?"

"Why not? Learn to be subservient, weave those pink little tails into a lattice and carry things around on them, pop up from behind the loo and give you a hand towel and miniature soap." His eyes narrow with amusement.

"They could be Tony Blair's new kind of underclass, an under underclass. Hey! Soon there will be Rats' rights, votes for rats, Rat for President."

"So do we have a date or not?" Rufus asks catching me off guard because I am already deep into a horrendous vision of rats collecting Oscars for best original screenplays dressed from snout to tail in long Armani strapless gowns but once again I'm prevented/saved from answering by the re-appearance of the council man through the back entrance of the foyer.

"Hello, Miss Butler," he calls and bustles our way.

"Kit?" Rufus is waiting for an answer.

"Look, can you hang on a sec while I'm nice to this man?"

"Oh, all right," he says grudgingly, and I don't miss the smile in his eyes. "But I don't see why he can't hang on while you're nice to me."

The council man reaches us and holds out his hand to Rufus. He has a long patrician face with a high forehead partly obscured by a turban.

"Rashid Hassop," he introduces himself. "Temporary Chief Technical Officer, Hammersmith Council." He smiles pleasantly and clicks the top of his biro. "Are you the owner of these premises?"

"No, no." Rufus waves towards the exit. "I manage the restaurant down the road."

"Ah, yes indeed, The Bush." Mr Hassop checks the file in his hands. "And next to this is the property known as Out Out Damn Spot, which is," he runs his finger down the small print, "premises of two thousand square feet currently operating as a laundromat." He looks up enquiringly. "But everyone under the same ownership if I am correct?"

"We are?" This is big news to me. "Ron is your landlord?"

Rufus looks surprised. "He owns all three thirties buildings in the street. You didn't know that?"

"I had no idea."

"Why do you think he's so frustrated. They're *all* listed, every brick. He can't make money out of *any* of them."

"Excuse me please," Hassop interrupts, "but I will need a chat with Mr Chambers about the licence."

The Orange's Cinematographic licence is renewed annually. It's a pretty straightforward affair; the council usually tips up a month or two before it expires and checks we're in decent repair, not having an E-coli outbreak or showing snuff movies or anything.

140

Occasionally we have to tidy things up, shift a bit of the junk from the "satisfactory means of escape" route, tighten up bolts on railings and other snagging items, but that's usually about the sum of it.

"Ron is strictly an absentee landlord," I tell him. "I deal with the day to day running. It's a beautiful building isn't it?"

"It is as you say very beautiful, but of course very *bigR Gaya*, I'm sorry, excuse me," he corrects himself, "very damaged."

"Part of its charm though, don't you think?" I suggest greasily, smelling trouble for the first time. Hassop has the whiff of Red Tape about him, that odour of someone with too little information and too much power.

"I think there will be a number of points that need attention before the council can be considering renewing the licence."

"Like what?" I ask warily. It only occurs to me now that he might have seen the rat.

"The wiring for example. It is currently very dangerous and does not meet the Regulations for the Electrical Equipment of Buildings."

"Meaning?"

"At the moment you have PVC, very old, very unsafe. To comply with" — he flicks through the heavy photocopied document in his hands — "ah, here we are. The Cinematographic Safety regulation 958 section no. 1530 it would have to change to MICC wiring. That is to say Mineral Insulated Copper Cable."

"You're suggesting we re-wire the whole cinema," I say incredulously.

"Yes indeed, also," he continues to read from the report, "the fruity ribs mounted on ornate cornice brackets and elaborate frieze with floral metopes, these are in bad repair and those doors please," he indicates towards the theatre, "are not fireproofed I think." His intonation is a pronounced sing-song.

"Those are original," says Rufus, "and probably listed."

"This is ridiculous," I protest. "Where's the guy that normally comes round, Alan. Why isn't Alan doing the inspection?"

"Ah, now that you ask, I must tell you." Hassop scratches the side of his forehead where a rash of pimples is creeping like the red army from the border of his turban. "Alan is in hospital. He has sustained a terrible accident." Hassop's expression is less grave than it might be.

"What kind of accident?" asks Rufus curiously.

"He was hit —" He cuts himself off to cover a twitch of a smile. "In truth, a Suspended Parking sign fell on to his poor head."

"Oh." Hassop's struggle nearly gives me the giggles as well.

"Yes indeed, and from a very great height. He will be suing the council naturally." Hassop regains control of himself with a shake. "Forgive me, it is not at all Christian to laugh at the misfortunes of others, but then," he adds, apparently without any irony, "I am of

142

course not a Christian. Now these foam chairs, clause three of part five of additional rules states th—"

"OK, look Mr Hassop. Alan is an ex-fireman. He's been checking the Orange ever since I've been here and he's never had any problems with the things you've mentioned."

"I cannot speak for a colleague, but I am new in this job, and I can't be bungling it by being slapdash. Besiding which I have a background in electrics. I am most skilled in balancing safety against risk."

"So what are you saying? You're not going to renew the licence?" Not having our licence renewed would be a catastrophe. We're short enough of funds as it is without risking even temporary closure.

"That is for the committee to decide." Hassop adjusts his knitted tie closer to his throat. "I'm very sorry," he adds closing his file, "I don't wish to appear *kanjoos*, that is to say in English mean or indeed stingy, but I am just doing my very best professional job." He packs his papers back into the document case under his arm.

I follow him helplessly to the exit. "Do you even like the movies, Mr Hassop?" I ask.

"Oh, very much so. My wife is enjoying only Hindi Romantics but I prefer English style."

"Really. What's your favourite?"

"Ah, what a question this is." He pauses at the door and shuts his eyes as if in deep cinematic meditation. His eyelashes are long and thick. "*The Great Gatsby*," he says finally. "Ah, how I am crying in that ending."

★   ★   ★

I do some hurried calculations on a piece of paper. It's got to be eighty, ninety grand at least. A ridiculously large sum.

"How are we going to raise that kind of money?" Callum asks.

"Oh, for the love of Pete, that *is* why we're having this meeting," says Julie.

"If they don't grant the licence we can apply for a temporary one, three months I think. I'll have to check, and maybe Alan will be back by then."

"Bloody Paki," says Julie vehemently. "What does he know anyway?"

"Yes, but I tell you something, Kit," Callum looks worried, "the wiring *is* dangerous here, you remember what happened to my heater last winter."

I gaze around the room. When you open your eyes to the shabbiness, you see it everywhere; from the paint peeling like dead skin from the foot of the skirting to the mouldy surrounds of the windows. I could kick myself. Running this place has long been a question of maintaining a critical financial balance, but there was always going to come a moment when the creeping decay of the Orange destroyed the building too fast for pennies dropping into the till to fix it. I knew that and I did nothing about it. Where the future of the Orange has been concerned my head has been firmly in the sand. Maybe because I've been using it as a convenient job which allowed me the time to sleep, write and earn money, or maybe because deep down I know there is an inevitability about our closure; that the Independent

Cinema is sooner or later doomed to be an extinct animal.

"What about the Arts Funds, Lottery money?" Rufus asks me. "Did you apply?"

"Turned us down. Insufficient historical interest, not the oldest, not the prettiest, not even the ugliest."

"Do you want me to approach some film companies for you?" he volunteers. "Maybe raise some money from the industry?" And this offer, for some reason really annoys me.

The phone blips, Julie picks it up. "Oh, hi Mr Butler. Yeah, she's right here. I'll pass you over. Kit —" She holds out the receiver.

"Tell him I'm coming in tomorrow."

"She says she's coming in tomorrow . . . No, we're just trying to work out how to raise some money, maybe make the Orange more profitable . . . Oxybloodymoron." Julie fingers the line of a scratch on her neck while she listens, then she snorts, putting her hand over the mouthpiece. "Your father says try radically changing the programming." Julie nods enthusiastically, "You're spot on, Mr Butler, it's a great idea, but as you know, your Kit's a fan of all things pseudo intellectual. Yep, course I'll tell her anyway." She hangs up. "Your old man's got his finger on the pulse, Kit. He says you should show all the old kitsch stuff. B movies. Start a cult following. He says you would know exactly what he's on about."

"B movies." Rufus brightens. "Not such a terrible idea. Plus if you showed stuff not on first release you could negotiate a pretty good deal with the distributors.

145

In fact," he warms to the idea, "if you think about it, there must be two or three generations of movie-goers who've never seen some of those real howlers on the big screen."

"*Bolero* and *Lipstick*," says Julie.

"*The Man with X-Ray Eyes*," says Rufus.

"*The V.I.P.s* and *Butterfield 8*," adds Callum wistfully. They all smile at each other in a laddish way.

The virtues of Dad's personal Cinema Paradiso being extolled by all three of them. I might have bloody known.

"So it's the scheduling that's at fault is it?" I say evenly.

"Well of course," says Traitor 1, "aren't I always saying that?"

"It's just an idea," says Traitor 2.

"It's not a question of fault exactly," says Traitor 3, not quite meeting my eyes. "It's just that maybe you should tailor the scheduling a little bit more to the taste of the community."

"Great! We can all go home now." They start at my nasty tone. "I mean you've solved the crisis. To escape vicious baddies, we'll take refuge in this cinema, get a community spirit going, we'll stand outside and polish people's cars while they watch lousy movies, Callum can sell his bloody awful poems and Julie will compose Gospel-inspired hits."

I realize how childish I'm being but I'm motoring on bile now, full tank. "Before long our efforts will come to the attention of the Pope and we'll put on a gala performance of *Emmanuelle Goes to the Vatican* and

146

no doubt be blessed with the entire amount of cash in a suitcase. In fact, what an inspirational premise for a movie. Why don't I write a treatment? Oh wait," I hit the side of my head, "it's been made already. It's called *Sister Act*." They're all staring at me as if I'm having some kind of schizophrenic episode. "Silly, silly me." I head for the door.

Rufus follows me out. "Kit," he says looking bemused, "we were just fooling around."

"Just back off, Rufus. This is none of your business anyway."

"Why don't I at least give you the names of companies that are worth approaching for money? You'd get a lot of support for the Orange. People are really fond of this place."

"Look, I'm delighted you've got your film up and running, but you know what? It doesn't make you the backbone of the cinematic industry."

"OK, OK," he holds up his hands. "I'm sorry, OK? Don't storm off. Anyway what about our date?"

I look at him furiously. I know my anger is completely misdirected and I also know a good idea when I hear one, even if it is Dad's, but right now I'm feeling small and mean. I'm feeling resentful towards my father and guilty that I've let things slip so badly at the Orange. "You know something, Rufus, I'm in a happy, long-term, sexually fulfilling relationship with a wildly attractive man. I have no intention of going out with you. I didn't three years ago, I don't now."

Travels of a script – 5

Chateau Marmont. Bed of the independent producer

The Fed-Ex package has arrived. The "Kissing" script is everything he hoped for, all the necessary ingredients, darkly comic and as if that wasn't enough a great female lead. He nearly weeps with relief. There is of course a minor problem: no cover note = no author details. He remembers how carelessly he tidied back the loose pages in London and kicks himself.

Paramount is bugging him, he needs to establish Chain of Title. He gets on to Louisa at Film A; he realizes a favour like this is stretching friendship pretty far so he turns on the charm. Don't worry she tells him, all unsolicited scripts should be logged in a book, with entry date, name of author, name of the script and what format it was submitted in.

"Get back to me as soon as you can," he begs her.

Meanwhile the agent of the Grade A actress has a drink with a colleague who just happens to work on *Variety*. The article appears the next day . . . the project is now officially "In Development". Word flies around. The Independent Producer is photographed at an event. People he doesn't know talk to him, and he's getting off on it. For the first time in his life he feels like a player, and it feels good. All over town actresses, directors, vanity production companies are all trying to get a piece of him. Fruit bowls start to arrive. He hasn't heard back from Film A yet, but he's not wasting any opportunity. He begins taking meetings . . .

CHAPTER
ELEVEN

Luke sleeps in his Calvin Klein briefs. He looks eight years old. I whip off my clothes and creep naked into bed. Today is the 25th of October, almost one year exactly since I drove Luke to the *Space Practice* casting. When Phoebe rang to tell him he'd got the lead Luke blew his savings on a room at the Lanesborough Hotel in Knightsbridge. After the ludicrously unctuous butler had showed us around every perk and talked us at length through room service he finally bowed subserviently, "Might there be anything special sir requires before I depart?"

"Yes, as it happens," Luke had said, shoving him out the room, "sir requires a vibrator." Then he'd slammed the door shut, stripped off my clothes, tied my wrists to the posts of the bed with his socks and mimicked, "And is there anything special my wild kitten requires?"

Neither of us heard the butler depositing the vibrator neatly packed in its cardboard box on the polished surface of the hall table. The hotel had cost a fortune. Still, we stayed an extra night, talking, giggling, kissing, fucking. Pressed close together, mouth to mouth, the gap between us filled only with heat, sweat, anticipation.

Today the gap between us cannot measure more than two foot but the two foot might just as well be filled with barbed wire, or landmines. Today I long for that closeness, that heat and I cannot believe there's no possibility of getting it back. "Luke," I whisper, "this weekend, let's go away someplace."

"Mmmm?" he yawns. He passes his hands over his eyes and rubs them gently. They make a wet mashing sound as if one or both of them have popped and jellied into two soft grapes under his knuckles. "Luke," I whisper again, tentatively putting my hand out and touching his back. He hunches and curls up like a clam shell shutting.

There then follows an interesting kind of sex ballet. I shift towards him but Luke, conscious of the impending danger, pulls the cover up to his throat and lies perfectly still, as if like a barracuda I can only gauge his position through sensory movement detection. I stretch my hand across the sheets but he pulls his torso away from me, quickly and quietly shuffling his legs and shoulders to follow. I roll closer and closer. Luke is now on the very edge of the bed with nowhere to go. My outstretched hand searches the sheets for him, a tentacle waving redundantly in the ocean. Luke appears to be assessing the situation. An immediate decision has to be made. He must either fall out of bed or meet my attack head on. Suddenly a third option presents itself. Daringly, he puts his hand back and pinches me on the arm.

"Ouch."

"Sorry darling," he says sweetly, "but you were snoring."

"I was not," I say indignantly. "I was wide awake. I was talking to you."

"Strewth," he yawns, "must have been dreaming. I'm shattered." He rolls on to his back, plopping one hand on to his balls protectively.

"I was saying we should go someplace this weekend, just the two of us."

"Mm . . . lovely idea, but can't."

"Why not?" I lie facing him. "Dad's well enough to go home, we haven't got any plans . . ."

"I don't think so . . ."

"Come on, Luke. Let's ring the Lanesborough right now, see if we could get our old room."

Luke sits up and starts pulling on his jeans. "Actually it's that party this weekend."

The Big Movie party. Of course. I'd completely forgotten. In a flash a whole new plan presents itself. I'll get a radical make-over, borrow a frock, glow on Luke's arm like a rare pearl. Together we'll spend the evening laughing at how much Max Factor the Big Golden People are concealed behind. "Great." I'm enchanted by this vision of new togetherness. "Is it really smart? Should I borrow something?"

Luke starts to pull on a T-shirt.

"I only hope this spot on my cheek goes by then."

He turns to look at me.

"What?" Heh, heh. "Is it that big?"

"Kit," he says carefully, "please don't take this the wrong way but I don't think we've both been invited."

A pause.

"The thing is Andy and Leila asked me to come but I don't think we've been asked as a couple."

"But we are a couple," I say stoutly.

"I know, but I think I was asked singly, if you see what I mean, anyway the point is," he says more bluntly, "this is work for me, it's not a social thing."

"Of course it's a social thing, Luke, it's a party."

"Look it's just a stupid wrap-up party. Please, don't make such an issue about it. They probably just needed a spare man."

"But you're not a spare man. You're with me. Anyway are you sure I'm not asked? Did they say *please don't bring Kit with you?*" My voice rises shrewishly. "Did the invitation actually say *Luke minus one?*"

"Kit, stop-pit," Luke says. "You're way over the top. I assumed when Andy mentioned it, it was for both of us, but apparently numbers are tight and . . ."

A terrible suspicion crosses my mind. "You're sleeping with Leila."

"Of course not."

"Someone else then. You're having an affair with Janet Taylor."

"Give me a little credit, Janet looks like an iguana."

"Cameron then."

"Oh, for pity's sake. If it means so much to you then I won't go either."

Why am I bothering? He doesn't want me to come, any retard can see that.

"Screw you, Luke," I say and storm out of the house.

★ ★ ★

154

Somewhere along the Bayswater Road I cool down and attempt to see reason. Luke and I are two grown-up mature people. We have separate and intelligent thoughts. We are not co-dependent, stuck together like super-glue. So what if someone wants to ask one of us and not the other to a party? I'm OK with that. On Saturday night I will rejoice in staying in, stick photographs into my album and wax my legs. By the time I reach Praed Street I'm able to celebrate the fact that I've managed to turn what could have been a nasty, confidence-draining situation into a positive mental experience.

"What a pair of stoats," Johnny says, "to think they sat in your house, ate the food right out of your fridge and as for Luke — listen, Kit, I hate to say it, but what the hell's come over you? You're letting him walk all over you. Since when have you been so personality-free?"

But of course! That's just it, I realize as I hang up. Too-Fat has put his finger on it. Perhaps my personality *has* gone. Rat-like it's left the sinking ship and gone in search of more fulfilling shores. Now that it's become so noticeable, perhaps the authorities might make an effort to look for it. The Bureau of Missing Characteristics could become involved. Dad and Aunt Pauly might appear on television and make a tearful plea. Luke, the chief suspect in the crime will not be able to pin-point the last time he saw it but will provide a water-tight alibi and no motive. After all, the police will reason, he has plenty of personality of his own. No leads will be established and only a few sad desperate measures taken. Advertisements placed on the back of milk cartons: can you help? Notices nailed along the Uxbridge Road in gaudy yellow signs. But it will all be to no avail. My runaway personality will be left to wander, homeless, body-less, dossing on street corners with some man's pride, or living in sin with a fallen woman's self-respect.

CHAPTER
TWELVE

Small irritating birds are chirping outside the window.

It's five a.m. The graveyard shift of the morning. By eight it's all too obvious I've overreacted, but when I call Luke to admit it, the telephone rings unanswered. I call him again over coffees three and four and by the time I get into the car I realize how lucky I really am. I mean let's face facts: there are girls out there who would *kill* for a single date with Dr Hybrid let alone to sleep with him every night. I call him again and when he still doesn't pick up, I realize that this stroke of self-knowledge has come too late. Paranoia strikes deep. Luke has already dumped me and is currently auditioning for a new girlfriend from hundreds of hopefuls, tossing and shaking manes of glossy Timotei hair as they queue round the block and it's only when I make the tenth frenzied call from the Orange that Anjelika picks up the phone and grudgingly reveals that Luke is not actually couch-casting my replacement but is at the Alternative Centre enjoying a Mind Control class, and won't be home before evening. I hang up in some relief.

"Course, I'm no fashion expert," says Julie, coming in with a roll of posters for our Derek Jarman week, "but why are we dressed as Spiderwoman on such a cold day?"

Puzzled I look down to where her fingers are tweaking the cloth of my black jumper. The wool is indeed peppered with thousands of tiny holes. Ugh. I am a walking moth's nest. My dignity is held together by a single crucial thread through which at any second one of the tiny moths might gnaw, leaving me standing buck naked in front of this morning's selection of perverts.

"You could span a series of natural disaster movies off this premise," Julie snickers. "You know plague of giant moths, fab special effects, strong plot. Will the crop of your boyfriend's new designer jackets be destroyed before . . .?"

My hammered old suitcase at Luke's. Of course. Moth Utopia. Feverishly I leaf through the Yellow Pages; there's no time to lose. On the Pay and Display of Love, I'm fast heading for penalty time.

One hour later. Nick, Pest Consultant for Duramoth arrives at Axbridge Villas driving a BMW. He rifles desultorily through the cupboards while I hover behind him scratching imaginary bites on my neck. Eventually he turns around and presents me with a sympathetic smile.

"Well it's not moths," he says.

"Thank heavens for that." I say, relieved.

"It's worse. It's the dreaded variegated beetle. They eat everything, clothes, furniture, kitchen appliances. Fortunately," he opens his hand, "I happen to have caught one already, look." The thing is indeed terrifying, as large as a hamster and much meaner looking. Even after he's put the magnifying glass away it still sends shivers up my spine.

"Just get rid of them before my boyfriend gets home," I say, writing out a crippling cheque. "Will there be any side effects?"

"A slight smell of ammonia, but trust me, these modern toxins are extremely sophisticated, it won't last more than half an hour."

The neighbours think we have an outbreak of Ebola. Curtains twitch, doors slam. Men in red suits zoom in and out looking desperate and professional. A plastic bubble is placed in the bedroom and into the bubble goes the bed, the contents of the cupboards, and nearly by accident Anjelika who is triple polishing Luke's photograph of Dr Hybrid handshaking the *Star Trek* cast on the mantelpiece.

"Meester Lukee, he know about this?" she screeches at me. "Maybe I bedda call him."

"NO, no," I soothe her. "It's fine. He won't want to be disturbed."

When I creep back in to check progress I find three Duramoth men giggling uncontrollably over a copy of a porn mag featuring Forty Plus readers' wives which I bought for Luke last year when he had flu. They stop giggling when they see me and smoothing back the centrefold hinges, carefully put the magazine in the bubble along with everything else.

By lunchtime the mood has changed from *Outbreak* to *E.T.* More men in gas masks rush in controlled unison to their van and charge back to the house, carrying a long flaccid pipe attached to their vehicle. "Make way, make way, make way!" they shout. I entertain a slight hope that Anjelika might, after all, be more than just an illegal alien.

Johnny Too-Fat draws up in a 1960s Zephyr just as they start to pump the gas. "Guess what?" he says breathlessly. "I couldn't resist telling you in person. Linda has agreed to come on a sex weekend with me. Can you believe it?"

Speechless I stare at him.

"Never mind my Quimski." He gives me a hug as the pipe suddenly springs to life. "A sixty foot penis has just had an erection in your house. Surely this must be a record even for you."

Axbridge Villas. That very same evening.

Clip from the new Disney Channel sitcom provisionally titled: "Not so Mad about You"

LUKE Kit, there's a disgusting smell around. What *is* that you're cooking?

KIT (*attired in chef's apron over crotchless pants*) A special dinner, darling, to make up for being such a nagging cow.

LUKE It's like bad eggs or something.

KIT Probably the snails in double strength garlic, my love. Do try one, they're really quite delicious.

One hour later.

LUKE Kit, that ammonia smell's still here.

KIT Ooh. I expect it's just the drains from next door. Say, why don't you come into the sitting room so I can perform fellatio on you.

LUKE (*suspiciously*) But it's coming from the bedroom.

Scary Jaws-style music builds. Luke races to the cupboard and Kit realizes she is looking disaster in the face. She can only wait for the inevitable to happen. Luke is now frantically sniffing the Ozwald Boateng suit he was planning on wearing to the Big Golden People's party.

LUKE (*reeling back in disgust*) Oh my God. (*Then shouts*) Kit. Get in here. NOW!

Blood drains from Kit's face as picture (and relationship) finally dissolves.

Later that evening in the Orange.

161

"Of course smell can put you right off a person," muses Julie. "It's one of those weird things, even if it's a nice smell, which obviously, vomit or bad eggs aren't."

"Tooth decay, body odour, cheesy feet, cough linctus, they're not nice smells either," says Callum.

"People don't just spontaneously smell of cough linctus, moron."

"I'm not saying they do, Julie," Callum argues patiently. "But if they did, I'm simply saying it would be quite a turn-off, OK? Anyway don't you worry, Kit, nobody dumps their girlfriend of three years for wrecking one little suit."

"Bollocks, of course they do," says Julie. "I've dumped shags for far less, I've dumped them for having arms too short, legs too hairy, eyes too brown, teeth too white. I've dumped blokes because I didn't like their taste in beer, in clubs, in music. I've even dumped them for making me breakfast in the morning. There are a million good reasons for off-loading people, I'd say ruining a nice jacket is one of the better ones. Hey," she stops as a car draws up in front of the cinema, "that prick Ron is back, what's he doing here so late?"

"That's not Ron's car," says Callum. "He hasn't got a limo."

"That's not a limo," I say, misery of the last hour lifting like a storm cloud. "It's Luke's car from the Studio. Don't you see, he's coming to get me? It's like that scene from *An Officer and a Gentleman* with Richard Gere striding into the factory and sweeping up Debra Winger, or better still, the one in *Pretty Woman*: Richard Gere singing *La Traviata* through the sunroof and the fat black chauffeur, grinning and blubbing with the romance of the whole thing."

"Actually, I can't see anyone in the back," says Callum apologetically.

"The glass is *darkened*, Callum," Julie sighs.

"Anyway Luke's probably hiding under bunches and bunches of guilt." I peer out excitedly.

"Look," says Julie, "the door's opening."

A uniformed chauffeur climbs out. He checks a piece of paper in his hand, looks up then stops to stare at the name of the cinema as though he can't quite believe he's been dispatched to such an unprepossessing place. Satisfied he pushes through the double doors.

"I'm looking for a Miss Katharine Butler," he says.

CHAPTER
THIRTEEN

There is a notion, spawned by the structuralist theorist Vladimir Propp, that the plot of every movie, however diverse, can be slotted into one of only seven different storylines in existence, as in *Buddy, Buddy* or *Girl Meets Boy*. As I'm lying here, spurned, spat out, stepped on, passed over, not good enough, try harder, 3/10, I'm wondering if this concept is true for all of life, because if it is, it would certainly explain a lot. Perhaps there are only seven kinds of boyfriend, seven kinds of affairs and, of course, only seven ways of getting dumped because although Paul Simon claims there are fifty ways to leave your lover, I note that when push comes to shove he only manages to name five.

So it's Saturday morning, and I'm lying in bed in Praed Street trying to work out a cute rhyming ditty for Luke.

It's because you smelt the puke, Luke.
Give her the nuke, Luke.
Don't behave like a Duke, Luke.
Just set yourself free.

It seems unfair that moments of triumph are exactly that. Moments. Short periods of time, *specific instances*, as explained in the Collins paperback dictionary, whereas Triumph's natural born enemy, Humiliation, is something that manages to hang around in perpetuity. I try to remember details of all the triumphant things that have happened in my life: first prize in the photography competition at school, my English teacher telling Mum I had exceptional imagination, being kissed by Frank Drurie in front of Vanessa Jones; but these are all moments of which I have only the haziest recollection, whereas humiliating episodes: i.e., walking into Universal Talent's office with my skirt tucked into my knickers, telling my friend how much I fancied Frank Drurie when I thought he was on hold and of course, worst of all, Frank asking himself in for a coffee on our first date and me replying "You can't, I've got my period." These are moments that have the power to humiliate you on continual action replay — and last night, no doubt, will join them.

"There's something for you in the car," the chauffeur said.

I rushed out, thinking that that something was Luke, that he might, at any second, burst through the sunroof dressed in white tails and top hat, champagne aloft. In my mind the leather interiors of the limo were strewn with roses, lilies of the valley and forget-me-nots. The Scent of Love. "Aah. You will come to the ball, Cinders," Luke was supposed to say. "But before that my love," he would press a button and the smoky panel would slide back to reveal a grinning priest, berobed and bescented, waiting to perform the ceremony. "Before that my love," Luke will repeat, "you and I will be one."

So I yanked open the door, eyes all piggy with emotion, but inside the car's stale interior, instead of the brass band, instead of aisles of happy families, sobbing bridesmaids, choirboys yodelling, were just piles and piles of clothes. Dirty clothes, clean clothes, some jumbled, some not, a few in plastic bags, most loose on the floor. All my stuff from Luke's flat. Julie and Callum helped me carry them in. Underneath the mess was my ratty old suitcase full of make-up, creams, potions all spilling out on to the carpeting. The driver leant against the bonnet of the car like a fat black toad and smoked a cigarette.

"Of course we never really liked him anyway," Julie had said.

"That's right, we didn't you know," Callum agreed.

"Well you never said anything," I protested.

"Well obviously we were being loyal," Julie said scornfully. "He's been a prat ever since he got his mug on telly. You're better off without him, even Callum couldn't understand what you saw in him."

"Oh, come on, you must admit how attractive he is."

"Kit, what are you talking about?" Julie's satanic eyebrows met in disgust. "He is small and orange."

"You know what, Julie?" Callum said kindly. "I think we should take our Kit out for a little drink."

★　★　★

166

Thinking about it now, it seems fair to assume there must also be seven types of hangover. In the mirror my eyes are so bloodshot it looks like I've Optrexed them with a Bloody Mary. Judging by the orchestral manoeuvres being conducted in my head, my hangover has to rank a grade five at least — but then a grief hangover is far more potent than any other. Crying makes you look and feel terrible every time. Nevertheless, I devote the rest of the morning to it and by lunch feel oddly better.

Pottering around the kitchenette, it never fails to amaze me how quickly and easily a person can turn squalid when living through truly tragic circumstances. Already and only on the first day of grieving I find myself wearing a vodka- and tear-stained nightdress, a grungy pair of socks which have subconsciously been chosen over other less revolting footwear on offer. I've just made a cup of tea without waiting for the kettle to boil and used a dirty mug that's been on the drainer for God only knows how long.

The rest of the afternoon passes undercover in bed where I wonder how long before I become paralysed with grief. I could be beautiful but doomed. There would be an excuse for my past life and a justification for the emptiness of my future. I will spend my days listening to emotionally wrenching concertos and with time and practice become a great musician. I will play the harp with my eyelashes and win the respect of the world. This idea is so appealing that when the telephone rings I forget for a second that I'm not paralysed and find myself unable to answer. In the nick of time I remember I have the full use of all limbs and lunge for it, convinced it will be Luke.

It's Juan the window cleaner. I toy with the idea of asking him round for a drink, telling him my entire life history while he keeps loneliness at bay with stories of the Spanish Inquisition and his family's courage in days of old. Then I remember that Juan is four foot three and comes originally from Manchester.

I go out and get the papers. Being dumped focuses the mind on only the good things in a relationship. I think about Luke stopping to tie my shoelaces when we were running for a bus. Luke, sobbing, holding me tight for the whole night after he'd lost some role he had desperately coveted. Surely he will have a change of heart? Somewhere in the section of my mind that harbours the unlikely and encourages the optimistic I really do believe this is possible. Yes, as I quicken my step past the stereo shop, past the Athenian grocer and the patisserie, there is no doubt Luke will offer me the position of Girlfriend back. Already due to my absence, his emotional input into the show has waned. Ratings have plummeted. Executives are nervous, the most important of whom are at this very moment roundly insisting on my reinstatement before even considering shooting another episode. I can see them now, waiting by the vast glass doors of Channel 5, smiling beatifically, many wearing extra aftershave. A brass band will be rendering a souped-up version of "California Dreamin" somewhere near the lift.

Luke will be standing in the studio expectantly. His marriage proposal will leave me cold. He will put both hands on my shoulders, weeping noisily with emotion.

"At least come to the party tonight with me, Kit. I need you," he will beg, simultaneously offering me a cash incentive.

A car hoots loudly as it speeds by. I've crossed the road without noticing. In the newsagents I pick the *Guardian* and the *Evening Standard* off the stack and fiddle in my purse for some change. The Greek behind the counter is wearing a back to front baseball cap and reading an Ed McBain paperback. He grunts in exchange for the two coins I thrust at him. The front cover of his book shows a giant stiletto shoe, lacquered the same red as his hat. I walk back along the street. "Weybridge housewife killed by a golf ball," reads the *Evening Standard* headline. I feel a surge of anger against the world. Why hasn't anyone called me? Where's my Support System? Where's Johnny Too-Fat, Julie, Callum? Why don't I seem to have any girlfriends? Where's my mother when I need her? Accidentally I bump into an obnoxiously pretty girl clad in a black puffa walking her dog in the opposite direction. She pulls hard on the lead to regain balance. The dog coughs as I murmur an apology.

"Boy was I mistaken in you," it says.

"I know." I hang my head. "I'm sorry, Luke. Really I am."

"There's no use repenting now, you blew it." He sniffs at the few inches of turdy grass circling the tree. "I'm here to tell you that your passport to the Land where the Grass is Greener has been officially revoked." He raises his leg. "And serves you damn well right too," he adds, giving me a wildly malevolent look before stalking off on its stilt-like legs.

I turn back to the story of the felled housewife. The print of the newspaper smells strange, I snuffle at the pages tentatively, there's a definite aroma — somewhere between newly baked bread and high pheasant. I close the newspaper and sniff the air like a Sioux tracker, realizing it's not coming from the newspaper at all. I look down incredulously and see the dog shit pressed into the porous grooves of my shoe.

Evening. The microwaveable tray of the curry and vegetable thali burns into my lap. Peeling back the plastic sleeve, a dazzling array of colours burst forth. A heady smell of exotic fumes fills the bedroom. Aah. This is lovely. I flick on Sky News. A whole weekend off from the Orange, no clink'n'vomit of the Golden People's party. No creepy celebrities. Just a perfect day, a perfect night. I have for the sake of reassurance listed all the things I do better by myself:

1) Cooking. Guilt-free use of microwave. Apologies unnecessary for seven-day baked potato menu
2) Sex. Partner always on hand, so to speak
3) Half the number of parents
4) Double the size of bed

Even telly is an improvement, no hiss and roar of the sports evening, no monotonous commentary, no compulsory viewing of movies set in violent futuristic prison camps. I sigh with pleasure. *Now, Voyager* is starting on TNT. I prepare to sob copiously throughout.

"Don't let's ask for the moon, we have the stars!" Bette Davis says, the credits roll. It's ten o'clock. I blow my nose. God, I'm lonely. Johnny's on his sex weekend, Luke is brown-nosing Cameron and Justin, Dad is having a three-in-a-bed romp with ice-nurse Elizabeth and the Monika Kelly lookalike. All over London, lights are burning in the homes of couples, settling down to Monopoly, Boggle and other happy family activities. I am a sad, celibate, lonely freak. A newly minted spinster.

This is absurd. Perhaps Luke is right. I am jealous. The fact that he got his six-figure contract but I didn't has split us asunder and turned me into a self-obsessed, self-pitying bore. Oh yes, plus there's my father problem; clearly my parents' lousy marriage and my mother's suicide have rendered me incapable of sustaining a relationship of my own. To sum up, I need professional help, and I need it now. Frantically I leaf through my address book and reach for the phone.

"Hello," I say, "I need to speak to Janet Taylor." There's a click and a buzz.

"You have reached the clinic of Dr Taylor," announces a nurse's crisp tones on voice-mail. **"Normal clinic hours are between 7a.m. and**

7p.m. **Please phone between those times or in an emergency wait for the following message.**" Another click, then a different voice with Dalek-like slowness intones:

"**If you would like to book an appointment please press 1.**

"**If you would like to hear a message from Dr Janet Taylor please press 2.**

"**If you would like to — **"

I press 2. Another higher-pitched Dalek states:

"**If you think you are on a mission from God please press 1.**

"**If you are suffering from chronic low self-worth please press 2.**

"**If you cannot stop flower arranging please press 3.**

"**If you have accidentally taken the wrong dosage of your prescription, please hang up quickly and go to casualty.**"

I press 2.

"**You are inevitably a much better person than you think,**" the message is in full flow. "**Others see you in a positive light, one day you will be able to eradicate the chaos from your life.**" I listen to the whole tape until it finally ends with:

"**If you would like to mail order a copy of this tape please press 1.**"

I tap in my credit-card number as instructed and at the end of this exhausting twenty-minute transaction a voice tells me:

172

"You have ordered one copy of the compilation stress tape as read by Dr J. Taylor for £11.99, to be sent to you today, 29th October, by first-class post. This message will repeat every sixty seconds, have a nice crisis."

Travels of a script – 6

Back of a limousine, LA

The Independent Producer is now on his way to a meeting with Havoc Inc., Tim Robbins's Production Company.

Mobile rings.

From Film A there is bad news. A temp filling in for Michael Ryan's pregnant PA has seriously screwed up the office paperwork. No unsolicited script has been logged for the last four months, let alone read. Moreover the temp has now been sacked.

Chateau Marmont

A message is waiting from Amen RA films. They want to know if there's a part for Wesley Snipes. Shoelace telephones on behalf of Julia Roberts. The Independent Producer panics. He rings London and throws his problem like a hot potato into the lap of Michael Ryan: "How about Film A executive produces?" he suggests.

Film A can now put out some calls to their contacts, agents, other production companies etc. "Somewhere there

174

must be another copy of this thing," the Independent Producer says more confidently than he feels, "and as soon as they track one down, they better get the author in and sign them up."

CHAPTER
FOURTEEN

Monday morning in Dunkin' Donuts. ". . . so as of yesterday, sex has officially become a thing of the past, a slight tingle at the back of my legs whenever I pass necking teenagers. The Foreplay Police will become a body in their own right, of which my wife will be named honorary chairman. Linda will finally win her court case to have my penis kept a minimum of 160 yards from her. A small but tight plastic band will be placed over it, which will, in the unlikely event of an erection, cut off my circulation. I'll be left with the shrivelled blackened remains of my manhood, which will be pickled in formaldehyde and displayed in a museum as a rare exhibit of a modern over-libidinous male." Johnny sinks his teeth into the flesh of a raspberry doughnut.

Sympathy Ping-Pong. Two players only, your turn, my turn. All we need here is an egg-timer. Johnny has run far over his allotted go, warbling on and on about his horrible weekend with his frigid wife. I know I'm being a rotten friend but right now I just don't care. I hate his wife and thank God his sex weekend wasn't a success because the idea that Linda might have let go and embraced the orgasm is, today of all days, a notion too rankly depressing to even contemplate.

"Luke dumped me."

"What!" Johnny shoots a pink spray of jam on to the counter in front of him, "Oh my poor Kit. Why didn't you say?" He wipes his mouth looking stricken. "How are you feeling?"

All my life I've wanted to be one of those selfless women like Debra Winger in *Terms of Endearment* who when dying of a painful and incurable disease and are asked how they're feeling just smile bravely and say marvellous thank you so very much, then leap from their hospital bed and cook a ten course Thanksgiving dinner. But I'm not, so instead I just start weeping like a mad animal.

The Orange.

The camera tracks round to the open door of my office through which Julie's conversation wafts like an infantile voice-over:

JULIE (*ranting*) I don't understand about twin towning; what does this mean? Does it mean that this town in Germany is *identical* to my home town? Does it mean therefore that it has the same rankly depressing 1950s housing, the same illiterate Chinese couple running the fish and chip shop, the same paedophiliac vicar orchestrating the boy scouts movement? Does it exist in a parallel universe or what? They should make this clear, because if this place in Germany is a spot with exactly the same number of wankers, the same amount of shop girls with mouse-dropping tits, the identical HB40 count, some shit hole in fact where the misery thermometer measures the same all-time low as my home town, then why the *fuck* would I ever want to go on holiday there?

CALLUM (*confused*) Plus, it would be such a coincidence.

Bandit Queen. I scribble on my note-pad then lean over and slam the door with my foot. In my hand the pen hovers hopefully. It waits for instructions, for the impetus of coherent and intelligent thought that will propel it across the page. Nothing happens. Next I stare at "Ideas for Raising Money" on the computer screen until my eyes begin to blur from the pulsing rays. After that a bluebottle, making its way across the skating rink of the glass provides another ten minutes of visual entertainment.

Writer's Block. Have I got it? Can anyone get it? How does it work? Can you get it if you're not a writer? Can a writer get it without being published? Does pre-published writer's block just mean that you have nothing to say? That you're crap at writing? And another thing: are there degrees, as in Total Block for instance, where not one single idea comes through, or factor fifteen, which screens ideas, and only filters through stuff that's not too hot or controversial?

This film has too much facial hair to be reviewed, the pen finally writes. I slump back against my chair and ease a Twix bar from the stationery drawer.

The telephone rings. I pick it up.

"Is that the Orange?" A crisp female voice is speaking.

"Mm." I attempt to dislodge the top half of my teeth from the toffee goo wedging them to the bottom.

"I'd like to speak to a Katharine Butler. This is Andrea from Film A."

"Excuse me?" I stammer.

"Andrea from Film A," she repeats. "Michael Ryan's assistant."

My hand trembles on the receiver, the muscle seemingly losing its integrity. It weakens quickly then relinquishes its grip as if someone incredibly dexterous, an Edward Scissorhands or Struwwelpeter, has blown in and in the split second between me asking the question and hearing the answer has snipped adroitly through the nerve endings with such burning speed that it cauterizes the severed blood vessels in the process. There's no pain but the phone drops from my hand straight into the wastebasket and while my brain is performing emergency surgery on my nervous system I can hear the voice of this girl capsized from her telephone on to the choppy litter below.

"Hello, hello," she's saying. "Are you there?"

"I'll just get her," I retrieve the phone, "please hold." I light a fag and draw on it hard as if it were an oxygen tank. "Hello, can I help you?" I say breezily, my voice inexplicably adopting a friendly lilt like I'm selling double glazing or French windows.

"Is this Katharine Butler?"

"Indeed it is."

"Good, this is Andrea, Michael Ryan's assistant. Look," she says warmly, "we were really impressed by your —"

I get as far as the word "impressed" then hear no more, because in my head there's an intense flashing; stars, stripes, flags waving. The national anthem playing on brass instruments, girls with fluffy pompoms and bobby socks cheering and high-stepping.

"You were?" I manage, *what can I possibly say? I'm speechless! This is so unexpected, but I feel I must, although it's corny, thank the people who are most responsible for my success: Johnny, Julie, Callum and of course my boyfriend, Luke, with whom, incidentally, I am back together.*

"So how about you coming in tomorrow to discuss taking this a step further," the voice, still talking at the other end of the line, hesitates. "Assuming you're available tomorrow of course?"

"Why yes," I say dreamily, "as it happens, totally available."

I hang up in a daze.

Jay McInerney wrote a piece once about receiving his first call from Hollywood, that archetypal call, "The one that you dream about, the one you would be foolish to believe will ever come but the one that says, more or less, come hither, we want to make you a star . . ."

CHAPTER
FIFTEEN

"Coffee, tea, water, Coke?" asks the girl behind Film A's reception. Her hair is curled in tiny streaked pigtails and cinched neatly on either side of her head.

"Coke for me please and could I use your loo?"

In the Ladies, a face peers hopefully back at me in the mirror. Is this the face of a loser, Luke? No Siree. You're stepping on to the ladder of players, I tell myself, even if it's only the bottom rung. Well Baby, I congratulate my reflection, you've paid your dues and now there's no place for you to go but up.

By the time I've skimmed through *Screen International* twice and been to the loo three more times I'm feeling marginally less in love with myself. I didn't hear Pigtails actually announce my name. The line had been engaged when I arrived, but maybe it's been continually engaged since and she's forgotten to tell them I'm here. Perhaps at this very moment Michael and a bunch of Development Execs are sitting round a table munching custard creams and waiting for me to arrive.

"Michael knows I'm here, right?" I sidle up to Pigtails. I discover my knees are shaking.

"Yes, yes," she says giving me a reassuring smile. "I'm sure Andrea will be along in just a mo. Nother beverage?"

My stomach gurgles evilly. The four Cokes I'd downed during the previous hour in Pret-A-Manger, attempting to transform hyper-nervousness into cool detachment, have in fact made me incontinent. I hardly dare ask for the washroom keys for the fourth time, trying instead to concentrate on an article about how often chief grips marry continuity girls, and moments later I'm rewarded by the sight of a female, in the late stages of pregnancy, charging towards me. "Katherine Butler? Andrea. We spoke on the phone yesterday. I'm so sorry, but you know how it is," she flaps her hands, "meetings, meetings. So the Orange is what kind of production company?" She pumps back down the corridor on her Adidas plimsoles without waiting for an answer, "Small films, Indies, that kind of thing? New companies are springing up all over the place, hard to keep track really, right?" She finally draws breath as we stop in an open plan area with a couple of desks. "Sit." She snatches a look at her watch. "I've got to meet someone at the airport in a minute, but here," she picks up a sheaf of papers from the desk, "I've just got time to take you through the basics."

I will her to hurry. It's only a matter of time before my bladder, already stretched to the capacity of a swimming pool, explodes sending a titanic wave of urine through the building drowning all the development executives in its wake — and there's still no sign of Michael Ryan. I attempt to excuse myself but Andrea

182

is in full flow and after an excruciating minute or two a couple of words filter through the pain and it occurs to me that something is slightly amiss. It's not just because there are no men in sharp suits plying me with custard creams and lucrative contracts, nor because there's precious little discussion about the optioning of Liv Tyler or Natlie Portman. It occurs to me because of really quite specific phrases that are rolling out of Andrea's mouth, such as my duties encompassing total management of Michael's working life, "The whole Mary Poppins approach to Producer Care," is, I believe, how she puts it, and by the time she winds up with details of health care plans, three month trials, and finally requests my P45, the phrases have all joined together to make a huge joke of which, I finally realize, I am the butt.

Andrea stops abruptly. "You OK? Sorry to spring this on you, this used to be my job before I moved on to Scottish/Irish Projects but my replacement was a disaster, screwed up a whole year's paperwork before we axed her. For some reason your application's only just surfaced now."

"Let me get this right," I say (small, newly humbled voice). "You're offering me a job as Michael Ryan's secretary. That's what this meeting is about. A job offer?"

Andrea looks at me a little doubtfully. "Well, yes," she says, "of course. Although personally I always used to prefer the term PA."

"Is that my application?" I stretch out my hand. Andrea passes over the sheets of paper she's holding.

The top page is all too familiar. It's the cover note for the "Kissing" manuscript. Confused I turn over. Unaccountably the page stapled beneath is typed with a long and impressive CV which bears no resemblance whatsoever to my own life.

Right then. Say this was *Working Girl* for instance . . . Melanie Griffith would turn the job down flat. She'd be after something better, she'd have buckets of that rare commodity *pride*, and the God of Opportunity would ultimately reward her for her strength of character. But this isn't the movies, this is real life on a real day in November sometime in my thirties when it's fast becoming clear that my real job is crumbling, my pipe dream leaking and my bank balance slowly being drained. Pride is a luxury for those who live in the Land where the Grass is Greener.

I take the job.

Twenty-four hours ago any fool could have told me not to try to impress friends and colleagues by flaunting pending fame and fortune but the only fool around was me. So I did flaunt it, in spades. I couldn't help myself. And today? Slinking off, proverbial tail between legs? Well now it comes down to it, I find I can't. I'm sorry, I just can't. So the lie, as lies do, spreads and grows until like Dr Seuss's spot it has expanded to a size where it takes on a life force all of its own.

"So you're quitting," says Julie when I get back, "abandoning the Orange in our time of greatest need."

"Of course not," I say (guilty), "it's just temporary, three months while I bang out the second draft, but I'm going to be right here, every evening, every weekend."

"Rubbish, Kit, once you get into that crowd, we'll never see you again, you'll be swanking all over the place shagging media types, and spending your bloody Saturdays and Sundays in analysis. Oh, Callum's got diarrhoea by the way, he's coming in later."

"Fantastic, Kit," Callum says later. "You stand to make some decent money too."

"Oh, I shouldn't think so," I say. "I mean loads of projects get developed then dropped." I sip the cappuccino Callum brought in with him. Studio red-tape, budgetary constraints, star availability. These will be my get-out clauses, all useful stuff for when the second draft, inevitably comes to nothing.

"Course it will get made," Callum says encouragingly. "Rufus said Film A only tend to develop projects they're feeling strong ab —"

"Rufus knows?" I begin to feel a little sick. "Jesus, Callum."

"I didn't tell him. He told *me* when I stopped in for the coffees."

"I told him," Julie says. "He was getting off the bus when I got here this morning. What's the big deal?"

"Why don't you both just make an announcement in front of every performance."

"Oh, chip down," says Julie, "you'll be the first to know if I sign with Phonogram next month. I certainly won't be working weekends and evenings here, that's for sure."

Uh oh. I look at her blank face. Sign with Phonogram? Is this for real? There are two sinister possibilities.

a) Julie is lying because she knows I am a fraud and therefore realizes she will get away with it.

Or worse:

b) She's telling the truth. She has a deal with Phonogram.

The phone rings. "Why didn't you tell me your news?" says Dad.

"What news?" This is fast becoming a nightmare.

"About your script, Dummy! Callum told me when I phoned earlier. We're very proud, your Aunt Pauly's told everyone at afternoon bingo. You'll have to let me read it now, then who knows?" He says cheerfully, "A little word in the ear of my new friend?"

"What friend is that, Dad?" I say dully, trying to work out the odds on anyone from Film A playing afternoon bingo.

"Didn't I tell you? Burt and I have bonded. Saw me coming down the steps to the boat the day I came back from the hospital. Held the gate open for me! Rather polite I thought."

"And I suppose you exchanged discourse on favourite comedy capers?"

"Don't be sarcastic, Kit, we're not on those kind of terms yet. But if there's a part in there for him, well!" He lowers his voice conspiratorially, ". . . you never know where all this might lead."

"This is all leading to frightening territory, My Hallucinogenic One," says Johnny Too-Fat that evening. And he's right. It is. What appeared to be normal, indeed logical behaviour only a few hours ago, now seems criminal and pathological. I'll be caught out like that guy who wanted to be a doctor so badly, he pretended to be a student in spite of the fact he was nearly forty and was consequently roundly pilloried by society. But how could I have come clean after all that trumpeting?

"Why are you doing this, Kit?"

It's a good question, I don't have the answer, but here are some of the reasons.

Because I can still see the embarrassed look on Luke's face at his dinner party.

Because not only has my career hit an air-pocket, but it's just been sucked right into the Bermuda Triangle.

Because maybe this is meant to be. I've picked up the Chance card on the Monopoly board and it read "Clerical error in your favour, advance to Soho."

"I don't know, Johnny, maybe if I can get in, foot through the door, see what's out there. Anyway, is it so insane that I should want a normal job?"

"Yes it is. You can't do a normal job. You're not a normal person. You're a bat. When on earth do you think you're going to sleep?"

"Weekends?"

187

"You're working at the Orange at weekends, raising money remember? And what happens if Ron Chambers finds out?"

"He won't. He only comes once in a while. Anyway I'm due loads of holiday."

"Well what about the Orange? What about 'Kissing'? What about writing something new?"

"Something new? Like what? I'm sick of writing, sick of the Orange."

"That may be," Too-Fat warns, "but at Film A they'll all be flashy, shark-like, super-smug Sammy Glicks. You'll have absolutely nothing in common with them. You'll hate it, you'll see."

In Budd Schulberg's classic novel *What Makes Sammy Run?* the amoral Sammy Glick ruthlessly exploits any opportunity that comes his way to scramble up the Hollywood ladder in the 1930s. As a comparison it's a little over the top, besides, who says it's the Catch 22 of life that the more you want something, the less likely you are to get it? Surely to succeed is a primitive impulse. So it's no use Johnny asking me why I'm doing this because I don't know. All I do know is that I'm terrified of getting to the end of my time, adding then dividing all the emotions of life and coming up with an average of disappointment. From now on I'm dispensing with all superfluous insecurities. I intend not only to spend my days with people who are sane, but I'm actively looking forward to working with people who are certain that they're good at what they do and, moreover, are cool about it.

CHAPTER
SIXTEEN

So far, so good. I've spent the entire morning being hustled through various offices, introduced to dozens of seemingly keen, shark-like, energetic go-getters. Why, the whole company is literally teeming with people who are confident that they're good at what they do and are cool ab —

"Andrea!" The shout comes through the intercom from Michael Ryan's office.

I look at the closed door, "Should I go and introduce myself? I'm kind of on a handshake roll after all."

"Hm. Wouldn't now," she says.

"Be a sweetie and get me a cup of coffee would you?" The intercom crackles again.

"Get it yourself, you great tub of lard," she shouts back. I blink at her.

There's silence, then a loud groan from behind the door. "NO, NO, NO, NO. For God's sake, not today, not today of all days, I simply can't take it!"

"What's he talking about?" I whisper. "What's today? Why were you so rude?"

"Too right it's today, you useless piece of shit," Andrea shouts, ignoring me. "And you're not changing it again either, dog or no dog."

"What dog?" I ask.

"Have a little pity," he moans.

"What dog?" I repeat, looking under my desk.

"The black dog," she says dismissively.

I look at her blankly.

"The black dog. Depression. Ernest Hemingway, William Styron, James Mason, and our very own Michael Ryan, Top People's Producer, all raging manic depressives. Aren't you, Michael?" she shouts. "The black dog's after you. Woof, woof."

"Andrea, I'm begging you," comes the strangled reply.

"No can do." She flicks off the intercom. "I'm surprised you didn't know," she says conversationally, "it's common knowledge in the industry."

"But still," I hiss, "he'll fire you."

"Can't."

"Of course he can."

"Don't worry," she relents and grins at me. "Today is 'Fuck Off Day'."

I'm totally bewildered.

"Michael picked up the idea in LA last year. In this business you have to lick so many arses it was giving us mouth ulcers. On Fuck Off Day you can be as rude as you like — it's a stress reliever."

The phone on my desk rings. "That's Michael's line," she says, "field it could you?"

I pick up the phone, listen as the voice mentions Universal Talent then glance helplessly round the room to see if the God of Cringe is sitting in the corner because it's Andy Kramer on the other end. "He wants to talk to Michael about somebody for Cool Boy." Realizing even as I pass this information on to Andrea, that the somebody must be Luke, a bitter taste seeps into my mouth.

"Michael won't speak to anyone in this mood, get rid of him."

I make an appropriate excuse praying Andy won't recognize my voice. "But he's insisting," I say feebly, beginning already to feel thoroughly stressed.

"Kit, I can look after you today but I'm pretty busy, so be tough."

I grip the receiver. Footage from the rabbit-stew dinner flickers through my memory and all at once I'm overcome by a powerful urge to be rude. "With respect Mr Kramer," I find myself barking, "from the very sound of you, I can be fairly sure that you're the kind of man who goes to spanking parties and has intercourse with all kinds of weird animals: swans, trolls, gerbils even and you are therefore not the kind of agent we at Film A wish to do business with."

Hand slams down phone with a flourish. Andrea covers her mouth in shock.

I grin at her. This is marvellous, I've surprised even myself, the new corporate confident me. "Fuck off Day," I say feeling better than I have done for weeks. "What a truly inspired invention."

A short middle-aged man sits behind a chrome and leather desk. His bowed head is framed by posters on the wall of *Evil Man, Hyper Active* and some other less recent Film A hits. As I creep in he pushes the contract he was flicking through fretfully to one side.

"You know what my problem is?" He looks up accusingly. He has dark hair, cut boyishly and a thin, virtually two-dimensional face that falls sharply away from a great centrepiece of a nose.

"Me?" I say tentatively.

"No one respects me."

"Of course they do," I say soothingly, not entirely sure of the correct response.

"They think I'm a dork."

"I'm sure that's not true."

"Last weekend I'm in LA, I walk into the lift of the Beverly Wilshire and who do you think is there?"

"Um . . . who?"

"Steven fucking Spielberg, that's who."

"Really?" I try not to sound too impressed. "Did you speak to him?"

"Babbled of course, told him how much I admired his work, the usual stuff."

"What did he say?"

"Absolutely nothing, that's what, he thought I was just another schmuck fan."

"Didn't you introduce yourself, tell him who you were?"

"Didn't make any difference, he just looked at me like I was an amoeba and said 'What floor?' By the way I just had Andy Kramer on the line."

"I know, I am really so sorry. I . . ."

Michael holds up his hands, "I told him you were Winona Ryder, in for the day and larking around on the phones."

"You did? Really? What did he say?"

"He said you have a lousy agent and should move immediately to Universal Talent."

"I should?" I grin.

"Yes but first you should wipe that smile off your face. Aloof detachment will get you a better percentage deal."

"Thanks, that was very good of you."

"I'm a very good man."

"*Just a very bad wizard*," I say spouting a Dad-ism before I can stop myself.

Michael looks at me tiredly. "I hope to God you're not a film buff."

"No, no, not really."

"Half the kids who come to work here, you ask them what they think of Arthouse — they ask who's in it. The other half are all geniuses, they want to be a producer, direct an inspired original, write the definitive screenplay. This is a very disheartening business. Christ it's hot in here," he loosens his shirt, "I must be sickening for something."

"Perhaps you just need a break," I say sympathetically.

"I'm always having breaks. The last thing I need is another break." He reaches into a drawer and pops a Prozac into his mouth. "I wouldn't mind a life though."

★ ★ ★

The Orange, Saturday. "Ah, it's Kit," says Julie in a voice that suggests I am just not one of them any more. "Made any contacts and raised some money yet?"

"Give me a chance, will you?"

"Because we've been working on some ideas of our own while you've been away."

"Oh?" Immediately resentful.

"For a start, we thought we'd get people to adopt seats," announces Callum.

"Who's going to adopt one of the Orange seats," I scoff. "They're bloody uncomfortable and besides they haven't been dry-cleaned in seventy years."

"Well people adopt highways," says Callum defensively.

"Yeah, you shouldn't be so dismissive," says Julie. "Childless American couples do it when they get to their sixties and their dog dies."

"It was on *Cutting Edge* last week," adds Callum. "They adopt park benches and sometimes even fire hydrants."

"Callum, you are so without point sometimes," Julie. says fondly. "Oh, and guess what, Kit? We had the vice squad in yesterday. They'd had a complaint we'd been showing porn."

"Derek Jarman week," Callum reminds me, like I've been away a year and can't possibly be expected to remember the programming schedule, "and it wasn't the usual one pervert —"

"The whole place was stuffed with them." Julie scoops her hand into the chute and removes a handful of popcorn. "It was like they'd all come together on an outing or something wasn't it, Cal? You'd think these

194

guys all hang out together and voted *Sebastian* to be their pervy treat of the week."

"Me and Jules figured they probably watch the movie, go back to the club, have a slice of angel cake and a cup of milky tea then throw darts into each other's naked bodies." He blushes.

"Anyway," finishes Julie, "there was this guy in a porkpie hat and flasher's raincoat. He had this big straw bag on him and in the bag the policeman found a copy of *Bridal Magazine*, a bridal gown size 18 complete with veil and an enormous pair of white satin shoes. Can you believe it?" They both fall about laughing.

I stare at them, Cal? Jules? When did Julie and Callum ever figure *anything* together? What kind of sick role reversal is going on here? Julie is the deranged psychopath, Callum the victim and I'm Helen Mirren from *Prime Suspect* who with the right degree of sexiness and authority keeps everyone safely in their correct place. I'm gone for three days and they're already having a relationship and considering applying to Ealing Council for the adoption of an underprivileged baby.

"Oh and by the way," Julie says almost as an after-thought, "Ron Chambers is waiting for you in the office."

Ron sits, bulky frame squished into the wooden chair behind my desk. He fixes me with a crocodile smile as I carefully shut the door behind me. "Hello darling, halfday?"

"Morning Ron." I smile cheerfully back at him.

Whoever is wardrobe consultant in charge of Ron's character has got his weekend outfit spot on. He's wearing a lime checked shirt under a leather bomber and his freshly pressed Guess jeans are so tight that strain forces the denim to adopt Lycra-esque qualities of stretch which the fabric clearly does not possess, instead dissecting his groin in a painful-looking manner which must surely be stopping the blood flow to his testicles.

"Thought I'd help you out by opening the mail this morning." Ron hoicks his briefcase on to his lap and pings the brass catches. "Couple of interesting things as it happens." He removes a large brown envelope placing it on the desk in front of him. "Know what this is by any chance?"

OK, so I'm mildly curious. What will it be? Some kind of blackmail letter? Luke being blown by the two-headed Venezuelan python? A photograph of my father in bed with the whole of Pan's People at once?

"Let's take a little look shall we?" He slides his pinky into the space under the envelope flap and wiggles out a spiral-bound document. I read the heading upside down. Royal Borough of Hammersmith. It's the council report. I try to keep my face unconcerned.

"So." Ron looks me straight in the eye. It's more of a leer really. "The Orange has lost its licence. How long before you would have told me I wonder."

I digest this while he begins flicking through the pages. His eyes are unusually alert, like a pit bull waiting to pounce.

"Loose plasterwork, gas lamps dangerous, no safe exit: seems you've really let this place go, darling." He shakes his head. "My poor uncle would turn in his grave."

"Your uncle was cremated."

"So he was, dust to dust, ashes to bleeding ashes," he quotes affably, turning to the back page. "Here we have it, council's recommendation. Let's see now, anti-flammatory upholstery, visual panels, installation of fire-alarm system. Expensive things, fire and safety regulations."

"We'll be able to raise the money," I say with what I hope sounds like conviction.

"I don't think so. And without a licence, darling — they'll close you down."

"The Orange is still protected by the Theatre's Law."

"You think?" He stabs at the paper in front of him. "Broken panes, dodgy wiring! These old buildings, they're all about to bloody well collapse. Accidents waiting to happen and all that. You'll have a problem protecting a building that's not there won't you?"

"I suppose you think this is a real piece of luck," I say after a beat.

"Too right, Kit," he agrees. "You should have taken my offer up. This Mr Hassop," he says, and I note he's memorized the name already, "he seems a sensible sort of a bloke. Perhaps I should have a word with him."

"We'll raise the money," I repeat stubbornly.

"Oh, give it up, darling." Ron leans back in his chair contentedly. "Sixty, seventy grand? How?"

"Don't worry," I insist. "I'll find a way."

CHAPTER
SEVENTEEN

Michael's face is as baggy and wrinkled as an old man's scrotum. And coincidentally, his scrotum upon which I am currently chewing is as puckered and slack as an old man's face. I swivel my head upwards to take a good look at him.

His eyes are squeezed shut, beads of sweaty concentration perch globulously on his forehead then slide slowly down the side of his face. On his neck a large blue slug of a vein throbs promisingly and I'm pleased to note that he's making puppy-like whimpering sounds through clenched teeth. Thank God. He can't be too far off.

Emitting a few more grunts of thrilled delight I give his cock one final tug with my lips. Even erect it is still only the size of a small French pickle. Luke at least had been hung, I think sadly. I wrap my mouth round his balls and give them a half-hearted roll around, eventually spitting them out like a couple of olive pips before chomping on his penis distractedly until a mild feeling of whiplash makes itself known around the back of my spinal column. Michael's teeth grind against each other. A few seconds more and it will be too late.

198

Swiftly I remove my mouth. "So you'll help me raise the money then," I demand.

"Jesus," he groans, "what are you doing?"

"The Orange. You'll put the word round?"

"Yes, for Chrissake." Belligerently he pushes my head down towards his shaking member keeping a fistful of hair in each hand to prevent me from moving.

"And another thing" — I whip my mouth away again — "my screenplay, you'll read it by the end of the week?"

"Why, you conniving —" his hands scrabble at my face as he pulls me roughly to him again. His body arches backwards as he comes. My eyes prick with tears. I swill the quarter teaspoon of spunk around my mouth, wonder fleetingly at his sperm count then spit deftly into the Jasper Morrison wastebasket by the side of the chrome desk.

"Aren't you going to wash it for me?" he whines, looking down at his limp member.

Just then the buzzer on the intercom sounds. "**Kit**," a voice says.

"Get real." I grab his cock and shovel it back behind the prison bars of his zip. "I have a job to do." I jump nimbly to my feet.

Michael glares spitefully at me. "One day hookers will be bred with a slit instead of a mouth, that way we can just swipe the Amex through while we screw you."

The intercom buzzes again. "Kit, KIT!" Pigtails's shout finally penetrates my sleep-addled brain. "Michael's three o'clock is here." I wake up with a jolt.

Yikes — what a disgusting dream. Look at me. I'm a jangled mess. I mouthwash down some cold coffee. Somewhere along the line I fooled myself that taking this job meant wriggling out of my insecurities like a snake shedding skins, but of course it's not been that simple. The problem isn't Michael Ryan. On the contrary, he's a hoot. I don't think I've ever met anyone quite so mournful in the face of total achievement, but when you're busy keeping your own hang-ups under control, who needs a job baby-sitting someone else's? No, the problem is that nothing has changed. I've not bumped into Rufus, nor heard a squeak from Luke. I still can't sleep and when I'm awake I still can't write. Then there's Dad. Last night, driving aimlessly around, I found myself on the embankment above his houseboat. The lights were on. Four in the morning and the lights were on. I wondered what he was doing. We've barely spoken since I started here.

Although I've applied to the council for a temporary licence for the Orange, I've effectively abandoned it. Unless I pull my finger out it will probably close — something I know I will regret for the rest of my life. But apart from the one or two money-raising schemes I've instigated, I've done precious little about it, trapped by a kind of lethargy that is curiously easy to go along with.

I head for reception. Turning the corner, a man comes into view lounging on the sofa and I stop dead — Michael Ryan's three o'clock is Rufus. Of all the karmic bad luck. But there's no place to hide because Pigtails is already saying, "Here's Michael's assistant now," whereupon Rufus looks up and promptly jumps to his feet in surprise.

"Michael's assistant," he repeats slowly. "Hello." He shakes my hand. "Kit, what are you doing here?" he hisses.

"What are *you* doing here?" I stall. Pigtails watches us from behind the desk.

"Well," he itches his plaster cast against his scalp, "I have an appointment."

"And I have a job."

"I can see that, but I had thought . . . a different sort of a . . ." He looks perplexed, then as realization dawns on him, colours slightly. My own face starts to heat up but I force a clamp on my plummeting ego.

"I'm working as PA to Michael Ryan." I turn on my heel.

"But your script, I thought you were working on it . . ." He follows me up the corridor.

"Is that a fact?" I say over my shoulder.

"I don't know." He catches my arm. "Is it?"

"Well you know what they say. Truth is the biggest bluff of all and facts are all the more interesting when they're made up."

"You're smart but peculiar, Kit. You know that?"

"It's my speciality double act." I can't meet his eyes. "What are you seeing Michael about?"

"I'm trying to get some distribution sorted."

"He's in there." I nod towards Michael's office.

"Kit," he says, "why haven't you been to the Bush for so long — are you avoiding me?"

"No, I'm not avoiding you," I say crossly. "You're stalking me. Look, Michael's waiting, you'd better go in."

"Are you still angry with me?"

"No."

"You're sure."

"I'm sure."

"Great! Does that mean our date's back on?"

I look at him incredulously. "You're right, you are a masochist. Why on earth do you keep asking me out?"

"I don't know, I find it really addictive." He looks serious. "It's beginning to be a real worry."

I frown to prevent myself from laughing.

"Come on, Kit, what are you expecting me to say? That I'm hopelessly in love with you? That I'm asking you out because I'm in a dead-end relationship and you're no longer in a blissful one . . ."

"Who told you that?"

"Johnny happened to mention it."

"Of course," I sigh.

"And because you're no longer in a blissful relationship, you're probably vulnerable now and I figure you will be an easy lay? Or are you prepared to accept the fact that I might possibly be asking you on a no-ulterior-motive, purely platonic, casual, no strings, no expectations, just a tentative two people who like going to the cinema sort of a date?"

CHAPTER
EIGHTEEN

The third floor of Whiteley's Shopping Centre is throbbing with its usual pick'n'mix of ethnic visitors. As I scale the escalator, what looks like a dead Middle Easterner, exhausted by the twin toils of shopping and eating, sits slumped at an outdoor table in Poons. In McDonald's at the far end of the hall, a twelve year old is enjoying his birthday party romping with mates in the play area and stabbing nearby parents with chips, their ends bloodied with congealed ketchup.

The place is buzzing with cruising mobile-phone gangs. Alongside the escalators ranks of post-coital Arabic boys, the toothbrush of new moustache grazing their upper lips, swagger northwards in pressed mohair suits and sharp shoes. Their would-be girlfriends advance south-side from the eatery sections adorned in a variety of mock Versace creations. A few tired tourists, on the run from Queensway sit cramped in Mamma Amalfi, prevented from speaking to each other by the paper flag stuck into a vase proclaiming the all-year-round Italian speciality month.

Dad loves this place. He once told me that the truly inspiring thing about Whiteley's is that it doesn't make any difference what restaurant you choose: Poons, the

Mexican Tortilla, Spudulike, they're all the same! All fare is simply a mix, shipped in one giant vat of grey matter, distributed to the various nationalistic restaurants then squeezed into whatever foodie mould is appropriate to the country serving. Hundreds of little spring roll moulds here, a dozen falafel moulds there, all of which are then quick-conveyed into the massive central microwave. Sauce and flavouring in bottles labelled Italian, French, Spanish are then poured on locally, so to speak. For Dad I guess it's all part of the great Cinema Mall experience he gets off on. Personally I'll take the impoverished charm of the Orange any day.

Rufus is not outside the cinema. It's nine-ten. The movie starts in less than five minutes. I buy two tickets from the girl at the booth. Her blonde hair is permed and black at the roots. She could almost be pretty but her skin is dry and she looks flat-chested in her Happy to Be of Service! UCI outfit. The teenage pinhead behind her at the box office wears Jarvis Cocker glasses and has a lovebite on the side of his neck. From the way they are studiously ignoring each other, it's clear they've had a lovers' tiff. I wonder what their lives are like, certain of one thing only, that when the definitive movie is made about usherettes in love, these two ordinary people will be portrayed with heart-rending glamour by Sandra Bullock and Ewan McGregor.

When Rufus has still not appeared by nine-fifteen I scribble his name on the second ticket, leave it with Ewan and ease myself into G10 just as the ads begin to flash up. For me it's not worth going to the movies unless you get the ads, the current presentations, and of course the trailers. Feature presentation without its accessories is as unsatisfactory and incomplete an experience as say, raisin bran without the raisins, or sex without foreplay, so when Rufus still hasn't shown up by the end of the previews it dawns on me that he's going to stand me up. I peer over my shoulder. The double doors are closed. The theatre is packed full of entwined lovers and scoffing groups of youths. The buttery smell of popcorn begins to play havoc with my taste buds.

A short film for Comic Relief is playing. I make a dash for the food kiosk. In front of me a slow-witted family, thick-lipped twins and their mother, are squinting at a Mars bar wrapper, trying to decipher the Lloyd's Bank sponsored free grub'n'drink offer. The kiosk girl hands the twins two cardboard-dished tacos covered in a volcanic lava of molten plastic.

"I said hot dog, Mam," whines one of them.

"You can't have a hot dog, girl," the mother says swiping her progeny on the side of the head, "it's not part of the deal."

A few minutes later I waddle back down the aisle with a carton of sweet popcorn, a litre of Sprite and the thrilling bulge of a packet of Maltesers in my pocket. Now I'm single there's no shame in allowing myself to become a Fattipuff. I'll eat forty doughnuts a day like Leonardo DiCaprio's mother in *What's Eating Gilbert Grape* and when I finally explode Dad will have me buried in a piano case.

"Shall I get you a trolley?" says a voice at my elbow. I jump. Rufus grins in the dark as he eases the vast container of fizzy stuff out of my hands.

"You're so late." I'm ridiculously pleased to see him. "I thought you weren't coming."

"I'm sorry, I couldn't find a babysitter for the dog."

"Your dog needs a babysitter?"

"He needs a psychiatrist but a babysitter is a lot cheaper." We park ourselves back into the seats. "Want some?" I hold the popcorn out to him. "It's fat free," I add to make myself seem less greedy.

He grabs a fistful. "Which means what by the way?"

"What?"

"I mean how do they get the fat out?"

"Oh, I don't know," I say struck. "I never thought about it."

"New Age men like myself, we worry about mystery claims. Foodological liposuction — how do they get it out, and more importantly, where do they put it afterwards? Is it dangerous, like nuclear waste? Do they burn it, what?"

"Shhh," say the au pairs next door to us.

"Buried is my guess," I lower my voice, "like BSE."

"Imagine the disaster movie," he says taking another handful. "Hot pulsating cholesterol erupts from beneath the earth and is loosed across Route 66 causing fear and panic as it touches the shoe of every thin American. *The coast is toast*. Literally."

"Sort of a cross between *The Nutty Professor* and *Dante's Peak*," I chortle.

"Will it do for secret snackers what *Fatal Attraction* did for adulterers? I think you should pitch it to your boss tomorrow and give me a cut."

"SHHHHH," says everyone as the slickness of Carlton Advertising replaces Pearl and Dean ba, ba, baaing across the screen.

"Hey, another mystery claim," I whisper. "Decaffeinated coffee?"

"Do you always have the last word, Kit?" His lips are close to my ear.

"Always," I reply.

About ten minutes into the film I become aware that the fidgeting and rustling of the audience has risen way beyond its normal volume. A man is standing at the bottom of the theatre, near the screen. He wanders up and down then stops in the middle of the aisle. On film Samuel Jackson is blown backwards by a car bomb. Into the awed silence that follows the man shouts, "Damn." It rings out, far more arresting than the 18-rated movie dialogue. More and more eyes turn. The man's frustration appears to be building. He stalks back down to the front, then across, shadow projecting in front of him. He reaches the far end then begins to prowl up the left-hand side. The people occupying the aisles become wary, shrinking away from him. He stops once more and lets out a furious groan.

The film continues, but without exception the audience watches the man. There's a light tittering, a nervous interest in what's going to happen, the anticipation of a crowd sensing somebody's about to make a fool of himself. I look at Rufus, he shrugs, puzzled. I look back at the man. Hey, this guy is mental, the audience is saying, what a loser. Ha, ha, ha, let's all look at him, stare at him, *laugh* at him.

Then, without warning, the atmosphere changes. The man thrusts his hand inside his jacket pocket and pulls out something small and dark. A metallic flash. Instantly, with one mind the entire audience thinks gun. You can literally feel the panic rising from them. Gun, gun, GUN. This is no longer entertainment; this is Hungerford, Dunblane. This is Whiteley's. There is a Mexican wave of fear as everybody ducks. My head must be down for a clear thirty seconds and I only raise it when the whispering starts again and it's only then that I realize Rufus has gone.

I see him immediately, at the front, his good hand on the man's elbow speaking gently to him. The audience holds its breath. Fear begins to evaporate. Rufus leads the man quietly up the aisle towards the exit, but it suddenly occurs to me with a coldness I find paralysing that the now shuffling gait is as familiar as the old tweed jacket and, as they reach aisle G and continue past, I realize with a terrible jolting shock that the man is my father.

There's a defining moment back on the houseboat. I ask Dad how he's feeling and offer to make a cup of tea. I use a tone of voice that's alien to me, a social services kind of a voice and I realize I'm using it because Rufus is here, and I want to look like a nice person in front of him. Dad must be aware of it too because he fixes me with a look that so clearly says, stop showing off in front of your friends that I instantly blush, scowl to hide it, then take refuge in the kitchen area where I suck in a deep breath and push the switch on the kettle with unnecessary force.

"I got the time of the film wrong," I can hear Dad explaining to Rufus. "I can't bear to miss the beginning and then I couldn't find my seat. The case for my glasses was in my jacket pocket all right, but it was empty. I got myself a bit disorientated that's all."

"You had everyone pretty worked up for a bit." Rufus hands him back the hard metal case.

"Actually I hate watching movies with glasses." Dad chuckles, putting it carefully on the table in front of him. "It's like having a magnifying glass on my face."

"Can you see much without them?"

"I see everything just fine. Detail is tricky of course, but who needs detail? People look like melons with my glasses on, without them, they're skinny shadows, I like them better as skinny shadows, it leaves more for the imagination to build with."

"There's no milk." I dump the tray on the table.

"Oh dear," he says absently, "I forgot."

"I'll go and get some." I'm relieved frankly to have an excuse to get off the boat.

"No, I'll go," Rufus says pointedly. "You stay with your father."

Of course the minute Rufus leaves we fall into awkward silence. Ever since Aunt Pauly in the hospital, I feel like I'm under some kind of insane pressure to forgive him, absolve him, but it's like I'm missing the motive. In *The Rock* and *Absolute Power*, two other father/daughter angst movies I've mysteriously found myself watching recently, Sean Connery and Clint Eastwood spend the entire ninety minutes trying to prove they're just regular family guys. Sean crashes fifty cars in San Francisco and grows his hair unattractively long. Clint keeps breaking into his daughter's flat and stocking up her fridge with healthy salad items. So far though, there's no proof that Dad would even run a red light for me. The crux is that there are really good reasons why these dysfunctional pairs all end up as re-united happy families. But for us, I don't know. There's no CIA conspiracy to foil together, no president to overthrow, there's nothing, just me and Dad and the past blocking the way to the future. God knows, one day I will have to learn to forgive him for feeling his pain in a different way to me.

"You were embarrassed by me in Whiteley's." Dad finally breaks the silence.

"No, no, of course not."

"Yes you were. I saw it in your face," and he says it so matter of factly it nearly splits my heart in two.

"I take it you two don't get on very well?" Rufus asks after we leave.

"Bit of an understatement."

"Do you mind?"

Of course I mind. It's just that I . . . I don't know . . . it's complicated.

"He's a walking, talking *Halliwell's Film Guide*," Rufus says admiringly.

"Obsessed, more like it."

"Did he used to be in the business?"

"He was a war correspondent for the BBC."

"And your mum?" He leaves the question hanging.

"She's dead."

"Oh." He turns to look at me. "I know it sounds an odd thing to say, but I thought maybe she was." There's a beat then, "How did she die?"

It takes me a moment to answer. "One pill too many, I guess." But I've always wondered. A bad night? A worse day? Two anti-depressants. Three sleeping pills. An interminable twenty-four hours. A fifth pill, a sixth, another half? How did she die? Suicide by fractions.

"I'm sorry."

"It was a long time ago."

"My dad died last year. Cancer. I still wish I'd spent more time with him."

"You don't have to sell my father to me you know," I say quietly.

He stops then. He tells me it's OK to drop him somewhere north of the Harrow Road and I don't argue about it. When he gets out he gives me a wave, but he doesn't say anything, there's probably not much he wants to say. Later at the traffic lights, just before the turning to Praed Street, I catch sight of my mouth in the driving mirror. It stretches across my face, an unfamiliar hard line. Is that what I'm becoming? Hard, bitter, ugly? I hate my father, I hate my life, but right now, more than anything, I hate myself.

CHAPTER
NINETEEN

"Michael Ryan's office, can I help you?"

"This is Carla Matterson speaking. I saw the programme about Film A on television last night."

"Yes." Instantly losing attention. This has to be the twentieth call since Michael was featured on the *South Bank Show* last night. Moodily I doodle Rufus's name on my pad of paper, then Luke's.

"The thing is," the woman is droning on, "I've written a treatment about a lesbian with spina bifida, and I'm absolutely sure it will be right up Mr Ryan's street. So I'd like to speak to him, do you understand what I'm saying? In person that is."

This wakes me up. I've never had the guts to be as direct as this. Is this how people get their breaks? It must be. They just need the courage and confidence to really believe in themselves. "Tell me something, Carla, I mean do you believe in it one hundred per cent? What makes you have such absolute faith in your work?"

There's a silence down the other end of the line. "Well," she says finally, "you know how Jesus is the Son of God, right?"

"Um, yes."

"Well see, I'm the daughter of God so it's got to be pretty good hasn't it?"

I hang up, check my diary. Still fourteen more shopping days till Christmas. Time has crawled through the last three weeks despite all the things I've stuffed into it. Even before the *South Bank Show* I've talked to hundreds of people like Carla Matterson. I've wet-nursed Michael through several crises. Pre-production on *Evil Man 2* is nearly finished, except they still haven't cast the part of Cool Boy. (I heard on the office grapevine that Luke fluffed his reading and subsequently enjoyed a bitchy thrill at the thought.) I've even organized tomorrow night's Christmas party.

Then there's the Orange. I've heard back from the council and despite Ron Chambers we've been granted a temporary licence until our appeal case comes up in May next year. Having said that, none of the schemes I've instigated have raised any meaningful cash. This is largely due to my own apathy, but every time I think about doing the correct and heroic thing of going back full-time to the Orange, I'm stymied by the following circular thoughts:

We need to find £90,000. (I've now had it costed.)
I could put heart and soul into money raising, and it might not make any difference.
If I leave Film A, then the Orange closes anyway, I will be out of a job completely.
And it's not like I can fall back on my writing.

Plus I have an overdraft.

But we need to find £90,000.

On a social note, I've seen Johnny (a lot). I've seen Callum and Julie who now claims she's "that far" away from a recording contract, but I've not caught even a glimpse of Rufus, and needless to say I've heard nothing from Luke, until one morning, out of the blue, he rings me.

"Kitten, it's me."

When someone dumps you, returns you (and your belongings) to sender; no explanation, no note, no motive really, then there's only one thing to do, and that's work one out for yourself by means of fair trial — and this I've done over the last six weeks in the objective courtroom of my head. And the verdict? Luke has been pronounced guilty of being a wanker. I on the other hand have been exonerated, awarded costs and given victim's rights to imprison the accused in my psychological jail. The morning Luke calls however, I guess my guard is down.

"What do you want, Luke?"

"Can we talk?"

"No."

"Can we have a coffee or something? Can I come round to Praed Street?"

"No."

"I just wanted to say that I'm sorry if I was a bit brutal."

"Huh," I snort. No way am I going to allow him an appeal.

"I know it's no excuse," he goes on, "you have every right to be angry."

Oh, God help me. Luke is using his underdog voice. A voice he used, I now remember, on the BAFTA-winning episode of *Space Practice*, the one where he accidentally kills the son of the Neutron Minister through liver misdiagnosis and has to come clean with the parents. It's an English thing, this routing for the underdog, and as I feel it sucking the resentment out of me, I excuse my weakness on the grounds that I have been characteristically engineered through the united strength of the British gene pool to support him now he's so obviously feeling low.

"It was me as well, Luke," I sigh.

"When can I see you, Kitten?" His voice softens. "Tonight?"

"Not tonight." Thinking of the mass preparation.

"It has to be tonight," he says mournfully. "I don't think I can wait any longer."

"Oh, all right then," I say it grudgingly but flashing across the screen now dozens of extras dressed as morris dancers have jumped up and are bopping round the maypole swinging bells.

"I'll be over round eight . . . and I'll bring something special for dinner."

OK, so fine. I'm thoroughly weak-willed. This is a foolish and downright idiotic thing to do, asking for trouble, out of the frying pan and into the — oh, whatever.

★   ★   ★

Praed Street, eight-thirty. Luke's running late. I put a bottle of sake into the microwave and lean against the worktop. Dreamily I wonder when exactly the defining moment was for Luke, the moment he realized his life was not worthwhile without me. I pour the warm sake into an egg cup and take a sip ruminatively. Perhaps even now he's in the throes of inner turmoil . . .

The sting of the doorbell snaps reality back into focus. The sake bottle is empty. In the hall mirror my eyes glitter. Luke stands on the steps outside but I don't see the sheepish expression on his face, I don't see that he is empty-handed of that special something for dinner, I just remember how much I've missed him. I have a flash of myself at Aunt Pauly's age, cheeks covered by a criss-crossing of spider veins, boring some well-meaning stranger at the Bingo Hall about how I once found true love but blew it, and a second chance never came my way. And suddenly, despite all other uncertainties, I'm sure about one thing and one thing alone: that if this is my second chance — I'd definitely better not squander it.

Luke's kissing me on the cheek, but my face is already turning one way while his turns the other. Before I can make out whether he's leading me, or I'm pushing him we're kissing hard. I feel flushed, a bit drunk, very sexy and Luke feels good in my arms. After a second he seems to pull up, as though surprised at what's going on but by then I'm already sliding the belt out of his jeans and there's no going back for either of us.

216

Later however, it occurs to me that the warm golden light, the euphoria, the post-coital glow if you like has faded unnaturally fast. I have the vaguest sense that I'm in the middle of a *When Harry Met Sally* moment because whilst I'm smiling idiotically, running my hand over Luke's chest, anticipating the long night in front of us, Luke is withdrawing, standing up, then worse, beginning to get dressed. As he pulls on his jeans and smoothes the creases of his shirt I watch his back dumbly, clasping the sofa cushion to my chin. Finally he turns and my fear dissolves. He gives me a dazzling smile, asks if I'll go to the Film A Christmas party with him, then when I agree begs me, almost shyly really, whether I could do him the favour of a lifetime and use my *influence* to swing a second reading for the part of Cool Boy with Michael Ryan tomorrow.

I don't think to ask him why he's leaving when it's only ten o'clock. I don't wonder where he's going or why we haven't talked because I'm still getting off on the word *influence*, I'm far too busy watching the rushes of myself taking over the reins at Film A when Michael is finally committed for Prozac Dependency. And see, here's a clip of me and Dr Hybrid moving to West Hollywood following his gritty portrayal as Cool Boy, the two of us pursuing our divergent yet compatible careers, wallowing in an orgy of each other's love and support and then, surely, I think as the door shuts quietly behind Luke, surely will life not finally be golden indeed?

Travels of a script – 7

A larger, upgraded bedroom at Chateau Marmont

Close-up on phone: which never stops ringing.

The Independent Producer starts to seriously stall Paramount. They are making a lot of calls, he fails to return them. Paramount are desperate to sign. So's the Independent Producer.

Paramount cannot understand why they're being hedged. This guy's a cool customer, they think, at least a lot cooler than they first reckoned, that's for sure. They up the ante considerably. Four major studios are now in the running. More and more exotic fruit bowls appear. *Variety* announce that Moving Pictures, Demi Moore's production company, is close to signing up for the project.

The Independent Producer hasn't got the time to chase up the Chain of Title any more, he is far too busy taking meetings, squiring his Grade A actress and feeding titbits about his flourishing career to *Variety*. He's counting on Film A to sort it out, and just to make sure, he even gets a rights lawyer to spend a few hours working on it. Obscurity is a smell he can barely remember.

CHAPTER
TWENTY

Ever since I can remember, I've had a shopping neurosis. It works like this: I see something I know will look great on me, I find I can afford it, yet the more I want it, the less likely I am to try it on, usually opting for something completely different that I don't fancy half as much. It's the same family of diseases as Menu Envy; that thing of knowing exactly what you want to eat in a restaurant, but deliberately ordering something different out of perversity/guilt/stupidity and thus spending the rest of the evening in silent misery watching someone else consume your ideal meal.

Tonight however is the Film A Christmas party, and I am going with Luke. Since last night I am a sexual goddess. I have a fabulous job and a great deal of something called *influence*. I am no longer a useless discarded fraction of a person, *a whiff of Spin*. On the contrary, I am somebody's better half who will spend Christmas in bed with my beloved dressed in scanty Agent Provocateur and opening his and hers stockings. Life is, apart from my streaming cold, bliss and I have therefore called in to Film A not only to arrange Luke's meeting with Michael but also to announce some spurious domestic crisis in order to swell my overdraft with the purchase of the most enchanting outfit I can lay my hands on. Thus when I spy this ostrich-feather-trimmed dress in the window of Joseph, I change the habit of a lifetime and push through the glass doors, determined to try it on.

Up close, it's pale lilac and made of a strange crocheted material. Surreptitiously I slide the hanger off the rail. Sensing an enormous purchase, a sales assistant attaches herself to my elbow.

"Oh, my God," she whispers reverently, "that is absolutely my favourite frock." Her accent is pure Sussex Pony Club.

"Is this the only size?"

"Yah, fraid so, Yoki doesn't believe in large. Stupid pouf." She closes one eye then the other as if to measure me. "Bet you anything it'll fit though." She hangs it on the peg in the changing room. "It's got buckets of stretch."

She's right too. On, the dress is sensational. The ostrich feathers settle into a halo around my neck, then plunge down to show just the right amount of cleavage. The rest of the dress is cut small, but the jersey content allows it to magically bypass the hips without the usual roadblocks of fat.

I mince out of the cubicle and gaze at my reflection in the communal mirror.

"You don't think it's a bit tight?"

"I'll say." My pony club friend giggles. "Looks v. sexy though."

"Well, it's really nice. How much is it?"

"One thousand two hundred." She looks stricken as my face falls. "I know, it's such a rip-off, but honestly, you look fab."

I'm just slinking back into the cubicle when over the top of the mirrored door I see a curiously familiar figure whisking through the racks at the far end of the shop. I double take.

"Julie, Julie!" She looks straight through me, then disappears round the back of a Miu Miu display unit. Still in the ostrich outfit with the ticket hanging down the back, I rush round. She's not there. Perplexed I spy her skulking near the Prada section prowling through jumpers on the veneered shelves. "Julie," I say in amazement, "what are you doing here? Are you *shopping*?" To see Julie in a clothes shop is the equivalent of . . . I don't know actually, Bill Gates in a dole queue I suppose.

"Shuttup," she says, "go away."

"What are you doing?"

"I mean it. Piss off."

"But Julie . . ."

She gives me a cold scary look. "Bugger off, Kit, I'm working." I stare at her, astonished then notice the bulge down the side of her hooded sweat top; I catch a glimpse of brown suede and it suddenly dawns on me. She's shoplifting, and as Prada and Miu Miu certainly don't believe in size 16s for women of five foot eleven, she must be shoplifting to order, professionally. All that money, all that cash, all those songs she kept having optioned which we never heard anything more about. For a minute I feel a stab of something really quite close to sisterly love, then I feel sorry for her. But quite soon after that it occurs to me how very fortuitous this meeting is going to be.

CHAPTER
TWENTY-ONE

The Film A Christmas party is in full swing. Throngs of resplendent guests swarm over the floor area of the club. The low burble of ego-stroking and deal-broking is regularly punctuated by a sonata of tinkling pings as private toasts are raised. My eye works the room like a camera, panning back then tracking up to the splendid domed ceiling with its faux Wren proportions, sweeping along the elaborate cornicing until it reaches the circular structure of the staircase down whose cerulean-carpeted steps a waiter glides. As his shoe hits the floor the camera widens to full angle and it is plain to see that in every corner, around every pillar, within every tight circle of the élite gathered here, the international language of networking is taking place.

Hot social stress rises in my head like bread in an oven. I fire up a cigarette and suck the nicotine into my throat. There must be five hundred people here at least and I still can't find Luke. After his reading this afternoon, he'd left a message on the machine saying he'd pick me up at nine. At ten he'd rung to say he'd meet me here. Now it's eleven o'clock and I'm beginning to feel sticky and self-conscious. The filaments of the ostrich feathers keep finding their way up my nose like alien antennae. I smooth them down and gaze over the sea of heads for a friendly face.

A shout in my ear. "Kit!" I flash round to discover a mystery female stage left. The girl is very young, with a Courtney Love hairstyle and blasé look. She slouches confidently on her nine-inch heels.

"Got a fag?" she drawls.

"Wait a minute." I peer at her. "Nina?"

"Yeah. How ya doing, Kit?"

Nina is the daughter of one of Dad's BBC cronies. I reel back remembering halcyon babysitting days of nappies and pink dollies. "Ooh, Nina, poor you," I say, "you probably don't know a soul here do you?" At that moment I spy Luke leaning against a pillar, talking to a man in a Polartec dinner jacket. I give him a merry wave as he catches my eye. "Look, that's Luke Bradshaw, the actor . . . actually," I say confidingly, "I know him pretty well. I could introduce you if you like."

"Naa, s'all right," Nina says, hauling a tab of acid from her bag and letting it dissolve like a lemon sherbet on her tongue, "only shagged him last night didn't I?"

"What?" I stare at her. "Are you sure?"

"Wait a sec." She squints drunkenly in his direction. "Yeah, think so." She grabs the cigarette from my hand and takes herself off.

I stand rooted to the spot. The Christmas fantasy of Luke and I intertwined amongst the remnants of Baby Jesus wrapping paper is replaced by me, old, bent double like a pipe cleaner, eating Tesco's turkey for one.

226

When I open my eyes again Luke is standing in front of me. There's a long painful silence then finally:

"You didn't come round last night to get back together did you, Luke?"

"Not exactly," he admits.

"What was it all about then?"

"Kit," he holds his hands up defensively, "you jumped me."

"You didn't exactly try to stop me."

"You had superhuman strength, like a mad person. Ha, ha." It's a weak laugh for a weak joke and we both know it. "Look, I wanted to square things with you that's all, talk about what went wrong. I didn't want you thinking I was a complete bastard for the rest of your life."

I should have known. Luke wanted to stow the relationship somewhere in a nice guilt-free place with padded walls, as far as possible from his conscience. "Why," I say nastily, "can't bear to lose a fan?"

"I wanted us to be friends."

"Friends? Oh come on, Luke." Going from long-term boyfriend to friend in a month is like expecting the ape to mutate into an astrophysicist within the space of one generation.

Luke just stands there.

"So what did go wrong then?"

Pigtail girl passes by, she throws us a look. Luke pulls me round the corner.

"You really want to know?"

"Yes, of course I do. We had plans you know, Luke. We were going somewhere and we were going to get there together, remember? So maybe it is unnatural and freakish but if it's not too much trouble, yes, I'd like to know." The words taste sour in my mouth, as if carved out of lemon pith.

"Listen to yourself, Kit. Things aren't going your way and you're relying on me to make you feel better about it. You want to say nothing's working out for me right now and for me to keep saying, it doesn't matter, I love you anyway."

I look at him sadly. Of course that's what I want.

"I have always been there for you, Luke, no matter how grim things were, no matter how bad you felt about yourself. I *always* believed in you."

"I'm sorry, Kit, but if you project a negative image of yourself for long enough, then sooner or later you manage to convince everyone around you it's true."

Tears prick at my eyes. Why in God's name are we so insistent on the truth? For the last few weeks I have been the heroine, nursing pain behind a brave face. Suddenly, a role-reversal has taken place; Luke is the long-suffering boyfriend trying to deal with an irretrievably graceless girlfriend. On and on he goes, and although I put up a cursory defence, dredge a mixed bag of excuses from my pocket, take him down a few blind alleys here and there, he manages to complete his character assassination without too much trouble. When it's all over, there's nothing left for me to say because although I know that Luke has changed beyond recognition, that he's become vain, selfish and pleased with himself, the awful truth

228

is that it doesn't make my own failings any more palatable.

"Did you sleep with me to get the reading with Michael this afternoon?"

He looks at me and there's no mistaking the scorn in his face now. "There's one thing I really don't need to screw you for, Kit, and that's your contacts."

For the next ten minutes I splash cold water on my face where it instantly converts to hot salty tears before the loo door swings open and Pigtails comes in with her bag of make-up.

"That was Dr Hybrid wasn't it?" she remarks applying foundation with professional severity to the twenty-something grooves of her face. "He was in the office this afternoon."

"I heard." I yank another piece of towelling paper from the machine and blot my eyes.

"I must say he's always been my dish of the day."

"Yeah well, he's pretty attractive I suppose."

"Oh, do you think so?" She screws the lid down on her Nars foundation. "I thought disappointingly small and orange in the flesh." She expertly chops out a line of coke on the basin ledge.

I smile at her gratefully.

"If you want my advice, Kit," she hands me her fiver, "take some drugs, put on some lipstick, then get out there and work this party."

It's around one a.m. I'm hovering in the middle of a staircase when the crush becomes so intense I'm forced to stop. Glancing down I see Rufus, hand on banister, talking to a group of executives from Granada. I consider back-tracking but at the top of the stairs, Luke is taking his protracted leave of a man in a neck brace. Behind me people have closed off the steps, huddling in little clusters; dealing, wheeling, flirting, conversing. I'm trapped. Escape presents itself in the form of an oversized tropical flora and fauna arrangement. I slip behind it and lean against the wall shutting my eyes. This is marvellous. No one will notice me here. The leaves sway gentle shadows in front of my lids. My face is hot and sweating and except for the lamentable absence of a conch shell held to my ear by a Brazilian in a pair of Speedos I could almost kid myself I'm on a Rio holiday.

Time passes. "So what did you think?" a voice asks close to me. Is it possible? Is somebody speaking to me? My eyes flutter open. Two men to the side of my jungle are lounging against the wall. One is unmistakably Michael Ryan but the foliage is too thick to see the other.

"There's no question he's talented." Michael nods his head. "You were right. I was impressed."

"The part of Cool Boy might have been written for him," says the other man. His mid-Atlantic accent seems horribly familiar. "I've represented him for enough time to recognize his talent has longevity and I would definitely say his appeal is cross-medial. Everyone at Universal Talent thinks he's going to be a huge star."

MICHAEL *(casually)* Gay? I couldn't tell.

ANDY KRAMER Straight — at the moment. Actually we've just extracted him from a real dead-end relationship with some girl.

I press myself flat as possible against the wall and put in a request for special FX of passing Boeing 747 to crash through the ceiling and land on the man's head.

MICHAEL *(sympathetically)* Arm candy?

ANDY Oh, not even, some funny chippy little thing. Here you want a hit? Good strong stuff.

A hand covered in thick black hairs extends into the foliage and flicks ash on to my dress.

MICHAEL Not for me, trying to keep off it. Anyway if he gets Cool Boy, I expect you'll soon find him a Joss or a Reese.

ANDY Oh, you can count on it. Hey *(as Michael moves off)*, we'll keep in touch.

Andy's hand parts the leaves for the second time and feels around for the base of the plant. The fingers deposit the joint into the topsoil where it lies like a turd emitting curls of smoke. Gingerly I take a hit off the butt, then another and another, inhaling it as deep into my lungs as possible. I choke, then swallow the smoke abruptly. My face turns puce. Unable to hold out any longer, I let loose a rasping wheeze and burst through the foliage, flashing Andy a dazzling smile before elbowing my way down the stairs.

Luke is now at the bottom. His presumably ex-agent Phoebe, drunk and in tears, talks at him. To my right a man in brown hipsters is pedantically explaining the difficulty of shooting his new underwater documentary.

"So," he says to the assembled company, "you see my point I assume?"

Seizing the opportunity I throw myself into their midst. "Personally it sounds most frustrating, like a hundred octopuses making love and none of them coming."

Whereupon a man passing, comments, "What a very witty analogy, I may have to borrow it sometime."

I glance in the direction of the voice. Good grief surely it's none other than the movie critic from the *Sunday Times*.

"I'm afraid I don't tend to lend witticisms, although I might consider franchising it for a price." Then I'm away, unleashed like champagne out of a bottle of Bollinger, intoxicating all with my humour, drive and sparkle.

"That dress is a triumph," says someone admiringly.

"And I love the way you've applied that violet blusher," says another. My confidence soars to a new high. I am intensely bright and attractive. I can sense it.

"Perhaps you would like to dance?" asks the Documentary Maker.

232

"Why," I say flirtatiously, "I'd adore to." I take his arm and sweep past Luke.

By the time we work our way into the throng, I have to concentrate really hard on not falling over. Hazily I look at the man opposite me. He seems to have shrunk at least a foot and be conversing rather obscurely about traffic congestion on the M1. I execute a couple of jerky twists until I realize I've reeled to the edge of the dance floor. A hand closes on my shoulder.

"Are you OK?" Rufus is standing behind me. "You look a bit strung out."

"No, no, on the contrary," I manage, "having a smashing time."

"Virtually impossible not to in your state. Who's that little creep you're dancing with?"

"That little creep, I'll have you know, happens to be Seth Walters, famous cutting-edge documentary person."

"Hm, I don't think so, that's Seth up there." I look up to where he's pointing then back to the dance floor. Quite incomprehensibly Seth has been replaced by a complete stranger who is now jigging up and down like a demented troll and looking around hopefully for my whereabouts.

"And why is your face purple?"

"Is this a knock-knock joke?" I ask giggling.

"Look." He pulls me round to the mirror. I stare at my reflection. Two great smears of violet cover each cheek, I turn the palms of my hands upwards, they're purple as well. The dye of the dress must have come off in the heat. Unless of course it was sprayed with anti-theft device, like stolen money. I giggle again,

"Film quiz, Rufus, who am I? I'm *The Purple Rose of Camden*. Oops." I stumble. "Want to dance?"

"Kit," says Rufus, "you're wired." He puts a hand over mine to stop it twitching further.

"You're right." I allow him to manoeuvre me out of the crush. "I should probably go home."

"I'll give you a lift."

"I'll take a cab."

"I think I'd better take you."

My hackles rise at the patronizing edge. "It's fine. I'll get a cab."

"You won't find one at this time of night."

"Look, I don't want a lift, OK?" I snarl.

"Fine." He holds up his hands. "Suit yourself."

Head spinning, girl totters down deserted road.

I stop at the end of the street. Instead of the main road, I appear to be on the edge of a factory estate. I slump against a convenient lamp post and fumble in my coat pocket for cigarettes. Infuriatingly the packet is gone but my hand closes over something hard and square, I pull it out. An old KitKat bar. What a stroke of luck, my stomach rumbles appreciatively. I puncture the edge of the wrapper with my nail experiencing a fleeting sensation that I'm no longer alone. A man is blocking my path. I look up to find a pair of eyes burning.

"You," he says, "give it to me."

"What?" My heart tries to thud, but I'm far too pissed for it to react with anything other than a mild tap.

234

"I said give it to me."

"But I don't have anything, not even a bag look," I turn helpfully to show lack of back pack.

He puts his arm on my shoulder and whisks me round to face him.

"Oi, stop it," I say crossly.

He sticks his hand out.

"Give me the KitKat." For a second I think he says, "give me the cat, Kit." I look at the sweet in my hand, thoroughly mystified. He loses patience, snatches it, rips away the red wrapper, then turning over the slab of chocolate, peels off the silver paper as carefully as wiping the sleep from a baby's eyes.

"Ta," he says, handing back the naked cocoa. "Thanks very much."

"You're welcome," I say automatically.

He folds the silver paper neatly until it's no bigger than a postage stamp, pulls out a matchbox and stows it inside. He glances up. "You can fuck off now."

"I don't get it. Oh." The penny drops. "You're smoking it."

"Duh." He taps his chin in the teenage sign of idiocy.

"Not good for you, gives you Alzheimer's."

"What are you on about?"

"The silver paper. Coats your lungs with silver liquid; forty years later, Pam!, brain meltdown."

"Fuck off. You don't know what you're talking about," he says suspiciously.

"Well stands to reason doesn't it? Silver foil is made for food preservation, it's not made to be ingested into the lungs." I hitch up my tights. "You don't by any chance have a ciggie, do you?"

The junkie stares at me. "I could stab you, you know," he says wistfully.

"Why bother," I realize I'm now about as drunk as it's possible to be without passing out and am going to have to find my way back to the club in order to call a cab. I turn on my heel which promptly breaks. I hobble down the street in the direction of the party. He bounds after me and taps me on the shoulder. "Hey, you want a cup of coffee?" He cocks his head. "There's an all-night caff down the road, you'll have to pay of course."

"Can't really," I stifle a giggle which turns into a hiccup, "but it was sweet of you to ask."

Close to, a horn sounds loudly. A car screeches to a stop next to us. Rufus bounds out and, before I know what's happening, is standing protectively in front of me glaring at the junkie. "Get in the car, Kit," he says curtly, "I'll deal with this."

"OK," I say amiably.

"Hey," the junkie bunches his fists, "this plonker bothering you?"

"Yes."

"Oh," he says and does nothing.

Rufus waits till the passenger door closes behind me then walks round to the driver's side.

I wind down the window and poke my head out. "Need a lift anywhere?"

"Kit," Rufus explodes.

"Byeee." I wave at my new friend.

By the time we hit the Edgware Road I am overcome with a raging hunger. "Do you think," I ask Rufus's stern profile, "we could possibly stop for some fish and chips?"

"No."

"Please?"

"I'm taking you home."

"Pretty please?"

"Christ, you're more bloody trouble than my dog. No way."

"Fish and chips, chips and fish," I sing, "chips and ham, chips and spam, chips, chips, CHIPS!" I shout through the open window.

"Oh, for goodness sake," he says exasperated. "All right."

Double parked outside Praed Street I discover I haven't got my bag.

"I'm so sorry." I frown with the effort of remembering. "P'raps it was on a separate coat ticket."

"I see." He starts the car again.

"Are we going back to the party?" I ask hopefully, licking the last of the salt and vinegar off my fingers.

"Nope." Rufus is beginning to look world-weary and tight-lipped.

"How do I know you're not going to gang-bang me then throw me out of the moving car?"

"Firstly you can't gang-bang someone on your own and secondly I'm bollocksed if I'm going to spend hours driving across London trying to find a gang just to oblige your drunken fantasy."

"So where are we going then?"

"To Willesden where I can murder you in the privacy of my own home."

"Oh, goody," I say, "how romantic."

Crouching on the edge of a strange bath. Somewhere in Willesden. What now? What if he makes a pass? Would I like it? What if he makes a bypass. I snort at my joke, then hiccup again. Perhaps he's expecting me to come slinking out in a G-string and seduce him. Maybe he thinks I left my bag behind on purpose. Maybe I did? Perhaps in some cunning Freudian way I have engineered this entire bag-leaving episode in order to present myself with a romantic encounter of this nature — or any nature for that matter. I try to garner my thoughts. How long have I been sitting here? Five seconds, five minutes, five hours? Nose is streaming, head is aching. I think I have flu. The joint was definitely a mistake. Ha. No kidding. *Just a chain-smoking writer, toking on the best years of her life*, I hum the Michelle Shocked tune. I haven't been this out of it since how long? One year? Two? A decade? I try to remember then lose my train of thought and before I realize what's happening, pitch forward, only dimly aware of a thud as something, probably me, hits the floor below.

CHAPTER
TWENTY-TWO

There's something warm between my legs. A gentle nudge pressures my thighs, brushing against my skin. Tickling. Lovely. I must be dreaming. I try to open my eyes but they're locked together with the glue of sleep. I wait for the familiar noises of Praed Street opening up for business: none comes. Then I remember where I am and freeze. Rufus has snuck in during the night and crawled into the bed. I make a cursory effort to push him away but the feeling of pleasure compounds the weakness in my limbs. There seems little point resisting. The roughness of his buzz-cut scratches my stomach, I hear a snuffling noise. Oh God, I've given him my cold. I reach my hand down, he nips my fingers. I groan and turn over. His tongue trails a cold line along my body. I stretch out and arch my back. Then, hazily, I become aware of another sound, the creak of the door opening. Alarm bells ring in my head. His daily? His girlfriend? His mother?

"Rufus stop." I shove him away with my foot and turn apprehensively in the direction of the noise. Rufus is standing in the doorway, eyebrows raised, bowl in hand. He whistles softly and with another painful nip on my backside a large bull terrier bounds up through the covers and propels itself off the bed, immersing its head almost fully into the bowl of water, strenuously wagging its tail with a heavy-metal rhythm on to the wooden floorboards.

"Been awake long?" asks Rufus.

"Lovely dog," I croak. "Always had dogs in my bed when small."

"Of course you did," he says soothingly. "Here take these." He hands me Alka Seltzer in a glass of water. I swallow it down then sink back against the pillows and wince as my head fills with a Benjamin Britten cacophony of unrelated chords.

"So," Rufus sits down on the edge of the bed, "I suppose a blow job is out of the question?"

"Very funny," I mutter. "I see you left my clothes on at least."

"Talent, my Bully," he glances fondly at the brute by his feet, "is unusually prudish on first dates. Here," he pulls a T-shirt out of a chest of drawers, "put this on if you like, I'll make you some coffee."

I peel off the ostrich dress. My stomach is a soupy mess of strawberry daiquiri, chips, vinegar and now Alka Seltzer. Another flash and I know I'm going to lose it. I make it to the bathroom just in time, ram my head down the ceramic bowl, open my mouth and out shoots a pink nubbly spray. Designer sick, I think irrationally, if Chanel ever got round to licensing it. When I'm sure there's no more I gulp some water from the tap, steal some toothpaste and do my teeth with my fingers.

Back in bed I rearrange myself into a tragi/vulnerable position. Rufus comes back carrying a steaming mug. He peers at me closely, "What on earth were you on last night? Crack, helium?"

"I should go home."

"You don't look so good."

"It's just a hangover."

"Hm," he says putting his hand on my forehead and looking straight ahead like Doctor Finlay. "I'm not so sure." He disappears into the bathroom. When the thermometer registers 102 I immediately feel much worse and curl up under the blanket with a morbid groan.

"Looks like you're not going anywhere." This is quite possible. I feel very ill. Through closed eyes I graph the rise and swell of my stomach as it surfs on waves of nausea till finally I drift out of consciousness.

When I come to, the room is dark except for a fragile trail of light pushing its way through the curtains. I'm boiling, my heart beating unnaturally fast and fever runs in crooked lines of pain up and down my body. When I was eight I contracted pneumonia. My temperature reached 105. Mum never called the doctor, she hated doctors. Instead she popped me into a cold bath and bought me a bumper pack of Toblerone. I remember being depressed that I was going to die before I got the chance to eat it.

"Trying to get some sleep young lady?" questions a man in the doorway. "Not feeling too well I hear?"

241

"What a massive understatement," I think heaving myself on to the pillows to dispel the waking nightmares.

Hello, Doctor Death.

"Tell me what's been going on then," says the doctor with a charismatic smile. His teeth glisten in the dark. I use them to chart his progress round the blackened room. As he sits down, the bed dips sharply to the right and I find myself annoyed that the symmetry of my sheets has been disturbed. *Square is good, good is tidy, tidy is square.*

"How long have you been feeling like this? What have your signs been?"

Dead end, I feel obliged to confess, *facilities undergoing refurbishment in this area, sorry for any inconvenience, these have been my signs, for weeks and weeks now. Oh, please help me, doctor.*

"Bit queasy," I croak, "a little hot maybe . . ." The doctor nods his way through my list of symptoms with a suitably wooden expression. As he unbuttons a thermometer from its pouch I notice the dark hairs on his hands disappearing under the cuff of his shirt.

"Open your mouth please." The doctor pops the thermometer in. "Try not to swallow," he jokes mechanically. Obviously not a Freud freak then. Positioning the thermometer still with the underside of my tongue I watch him, peculiarly light-headed, as he shuffles equipment round his leather bag. Without looking up, he dexterously plucks the thermometer from between my teeth then switches on a small torch and shines it down my throat.

242

Looking for love, oh Physician of Doom, I sing.

"Aaaaaaaaarrrrgggggh," I sound faintly. The doctor leans in close, balancing the weight of his body on one hand, feeling my throat for swelling with the other. As his fingertips stroke against my tonsils I notice that the black hair also extends to his throat where a good inch is visible crawling upwards to his Adam's apple. Close-carpeted from armpit to armpit.

"Pull up your T-shirt," the doctor orders, fixing a stethoscope into his ears, "and breathe deeply."

Through the stethoscope the beat of my heart sounds deafening. *Terpocket . . . terpocket . . . terpocket.* I am Mrs Walter Mitty. Famous medical phenomenon, about to stun the world with the highest recorded temperature ever. The torch is now shining in my eyes and without warning my vision short circuits to black . . .

Naked now, I sit balanced on the doctor's erection, legs wrapped around his back. Roughly I grip the wiry hair on his chest and pull, only mildly surprised when the whole thing comes away in my hand. A chest toupee, I think through my arousal, how very unusual. Holding my balance I rage on top of him, but on the brink though I am, I can't reach orgasm. God the frustration. Why not? Subconsciously I realize there must a reason. Something is amiss . . .

With an effort I bring myself back to consciousness. Blackness fuses to colour. Rufus and Talent are standing in the doorway silently watching us.

"So what is it then?" asks Rufus. "Just a bug?"

The doctor zips up his bag, Talent patters round to the bed and grabs a mouthful of blanket. "A virus, yes I'm afraid so, and a particularly virulent one. There's been a lot going round. It'll take at least another forty-eight hours or so; your girlfriend has a very high temperature indeed." I hear the quiet murmur of their voices as they descend the stairs.

"Slightly delirious," comes the doctor's faded prognosis. "Plenty of sleep and of course, most importantly: nil by mouth."

Rufus perches on the bed and spoons Tom Yom Gum into his mouth. The room is comfortably messy, Talent eats three chicken satay and most of the peanut butter sauce. It's Monday night and I feel better but when I tried to get up this morning, Rufus became quite bossy, insisting I stay in bed at least for the rest of the day, calling in sick at Film A for me and lecturing in the mode of a Victorian nanny about setbacks and relapses until I genuinely began to feel another week's rest wouldn't be out of order. After he'd left to pick up my bag and go to work, I wondered not unhopefully whether this might turn into a *Story of O* situation, with me prisoner and Rufus forcing me to squat on all fours and pretend to be a table when he returned. This seems unlikely however because during the three days I've been here, Rufus has pointedly kept his distance. He has neither said nor, more significantly, done anything that could be remotely construed as a pass and I'm beginning to wonder why. Is he asexual?

Anti-sexual? Extra Terrestrial? I sneak a look at him as he flicks through the paper.

"Starting in a minute we have the third of Kamikazitsky's fascinating interpretations of post-modernist love among the survivors of an avalanche in Southern Mongolia," he reads. "Kamikazitsky's ability to merge the harrowing with the pathos and utter lack of sentimentality of brutal reality makes the feasibility of this success a foregone conclusion. Three hours, twenty minutes. Subtitles." He looks up at me. "You love a bit of Arthouse. Fancy it?"

"Hm," I say doubtfully. "What do you think?"

He snaps on the television with the remote. "I think I'd rather cut my wrists and slowly let the blood drain from my body."

I laugh — he makes me laugh. There's this undercurrent of humour to everything he says, and not constantly self-deprecating either. My humour is a defence, his is an observation and I find that so attractive. I guess I got Rufus all wrong — what I identified as a hopeless lackadaisical, was more a question of someone at ease with himself, someone who doesn't feel the need to shout out his worth to the whole world. Luke is so different to that. Luke is defined by his success, and I suppose I *aspire* to being defined by my success, but Rufus? Rufus just seems centred enough to quietly get on with the job of taking what he wants from life.

The remote locks on to Sky Movies Gold. "*You're a preppy millionnaire*," complains Ali MacGraw to Ryan O'Neal. "This is more like it," Rufus says, "*Love Story*

— one of the greatest B movies ever. Bet you anything your dad is watching this."

"You know what movie we're in don't you?" I ask him.

"What?"

"I'll give you a clue, I'm Shirley MacLaine and you are . . .?"

"Don? Alistair?"

"Don't be silly, you're Jack Lemmon, the schnooky bachelor insurance clerk, and I'm the elevator girl with a pixie haircut."

"Doesn't ring a bell."

"*The Apartment*." I say amazed, "How can you not know these things? Billy Wilder. Six Oscars. I, Shirley, take an overdose, vomit a lot and you, Jack, save me from myself."

"Do you need saving from yourself?"

"Of course I do. I'm suicidal. I've just been ditched by Fred MacMurray."

"Oh sorry, you meant you Shirley?"

I look at him suspiciously.

"Actually I think this is more *Dying Young*," he says. "I'm Julia Roberts and you're Campbell Scott."

"Gee, bald, terminal, thanks a lot."

"At least the premise is more accurate. I, Julia, selflessly nurse you, while you, Campbell, sweat, throw up, lie around in bed and talk endlessly about your hair." He hops off the bed and starts packing up the debris of the takeaway.

I watch him as he stacks the silver containers on top of each other and chucks napkins, rippled with grease

246

back into the plastic bags. The alarm clock by the side of the bed reads nine fifteen. It's late. I'm cured. There's no real excuse to stay any longer. "I should go," I say.

"Oh, should you?" he says coming over all formal and polite. "Are you sure you wouldn't prefer to see the end of the film?"

I'm about to say, of course I would, I'd prefer to stay all night as it happens, when for some reason I remember a Stephen Leacock story Dad once read to me, "The Awful Fate of Melpomenus Jones". A married couple invite a curate to come for supper, and when he gets up to leave, the couple purely out of politeness insist he must stay a little longer and the curate out of equal politeness feels obliged to do so, and on and on it goes until he ends up living there for ever or being murdered, I forget which.

"No," I say firmly, "I definitely must go, absolutely. Right now."

The car sits in a tailback at the lights. It feels like I'm being driven back to boarding school after a weekend spent listening to my parents explain about their divorce. Out of the window a phalanx of drunks squat on the courtesy benches, warming themselves in the light reflecting from KFC and Quick Kebab, out of whose doors the mingled fumes of batter, spice and all things nice sail high over their heads. *All the lonely people* . . . I realize I haven't seen Dad for a month.

The lights change and the cars surge forward, each driver breathing a guilty sigh of relief as they pass the windscreen cleaners and shoot the crossing; adrenaline flowing as they achieve their narrow escape from the musical chairs of street charity. The traffic lights finally turn red again as we approach. Rufus waves away the skinhead with the dirty cloth who flicks him a V sign.

Personally I like having my windscreen cleaned. I actually look forward to a time when street service is expanded from its current *Evening Standards* and bunches of stunted roses, to people holding up Sainsbury's bags marked, "Weekly shopping for the newly minted spinster!" "Fat-free snacks for obese family of four!" Maybe even waiters from local restaurants could one day be persuaded to run alongside vehicles like FBI men and feed hungry drivers on delicious pieces of dim sum, but I don't muse on this out loud because the vibes in the car are pretty bad.

"Sure you've got your bag this time?" Rufus interrupts the silence.

"Yes, yes, you don't have to worry."

"It's not me that's worried." He picks up on the defensive tone right away. "It was your suggestion to leave."

"Oh, you know." I shrug. "Common politeness sort of demanded it."

"Because," Rufus says vaguely, "I thought we were having a nice time."

"No, no, we were."

"Nice movie, nice food. Even your hair was looking . . . nice."

Pause.

"No, you're right of course. It was all very, very . . ."

"Nice?" he supplies.

"Haven't we already driven round this roundabout, Rufus?"

"So if you, sorry correction we, were having such an unequivocally nice time there was surely no reason really why you couldn't have . . . well you know . . . stayed a bit longer."

Another pause.

"No, I suppose I could have done." I don't dare look at him.

"It's not like it was that late or anything."

"No. No, you're right, it was . . . well . . . before midnight anyway."

"Well bollocks then," Rufus explodes. "We could have finished watching *Love Story* and it wouldn't exactly have compromised your reputation would it."

"Rufus," I say grinning, "how many more times are you going to drive around this stupid roundabout?"

"How many more times are you going to make me, Kit?"

Climbing back out of the car in Willesden and I'm still grinning. One of those inane ones that actually hurt the muscles of your mouth. Rufus grins back, courteously taking hold of my arm to help me up the steps as if I'm too old and infirm to negotiate them without a tragic accident. He then completely ruins the effect by pushing me violently against the door and kissing me. The corner of the number 3 nudges the side of my head. I can't kiss him properly because my mouth is still in the grips of some kind of spasm and all I can think of is that episode of *Friends* when Rachel and Ross are getting it together for the first time and Rachel keeps getting the giggles and Ross gets antsy, then finally shags her under the dinosaur skeleton. Rufus fumbles the lock with one hand, eventually getting the door open and pulls me inside after him. I trip over the welcome mat, he straightens me up, closes the door with his foot and kisses me against the communal side table. A bunch of letters and several copies of *Property Weekly* slide to the floor with a thunk.

Then, momentarily, he loses his nerve. I lean against the wall. He stands in front of me, not quite touching.

"So," I say lightly, "what now?"

"I think the doctor would suggest," he whispers, "that the sooner we get you out of these warm, dry clothes the better. We don't want you in any danger of getting over your cold, do we?"

"Certainly not."

My eyes flutter closed. He presses his mouth against mine.

"But wait a minute," I feel obliged to add, "surely the doctor also said something about nil by mouth."

"God Almighty," Rufus slumps back against the pillows. "How on earth do you do that?"

"Muscle control."

"Amazing."

"Classy huh?"

"Sexy, who taught you?"

"Well, Dad actually."

250

"Your father?" He sounds shocked.

"Oh, he was pretty liberal about these things when I was a teenager."

"I'll say."

"Want me to do it again?"

"Can you so soon?"

"Sure." I blow another perfect smoke ring. "Smoking in bed is such a disgusting habit," I say happily.

"Repulsive," he runs his finger up my arm, "please don't do it in anybody else's bed but mine."

"Luke used to say . . ."

"And please let's not talk about your ex."

"OK."

"Although I heard he's on the verge of getting the part of Cool Boy," he adds slyly.

"How did you know that?" I snatch my arm away.

"Rumour at the Film A party. Would you mind?"

"Of course not," I lie. "Why should I?"

"It's a normal human reaction to wish pain, suffering and failure on all exes."

"Popular myth has it you must be best friends."

"That's just a sinister sort of test to find out whether you were really in love with someone; if you end up friends you definitely weren't. Right. Come back here." He pulls me against him, wrapping both arms around my waist. His chin digs into my back.

"I suppose you've had a long line of tragic, wrist-cutting relationships?" I mumble over my shoulder.

"No real blockbusters, a few straight-to-video affairs maybe. I nearly got married once."

"What happened? You got cold feet?"

"She didn't show up."

"I think that's rather glamorous, shades of *The Graduate*."

"Except she ran off with Dustin Hoffman and I was the Aryan dork left at the altar."

"Oops." I shift my back against his chest. "Sorry."

"I'm not. Hey." He flips me round to face him.

"What?"

"You wouldn't consider lying on top of me again, would you?" He reaches his hand to my face and tries to twist a curl of hair round my ear and while he's doing so he looks at me in a way that I find quite unnerving but that I also like; as though he's trying to discover stuff without me having to tell him, and he manages to do it without looking wishy-washy, and I find myself soppily thinking what an incredible organ the human heart is because only last week it had Luke's name scrawled all over it in indelible ink and now . . .

"Wait." I catch his hand and place his palm against my cheek. "There's something we have to talk about."

"What?"

"I'm sorry to bring it up and, um, I don't want to diminish your enjoyment or anything but I need to know whether it's safe to have sex with you again."

"Didn't we have this conversation about an hour ago?"

"Actually, this isn't the Safe-Sex Issue, this is something else . . ."

"You've lost me." He props himself up on one elbow.

252

"Phone Hysteria Disease. The thing is, I've had bouts of it before and it's really nasty."

"Ah." He looks at me amused. "OK. I think I'm with you."

"So a girl needs to take some precautions you see." I squirm. "Discuss your calling the next day policy."

He looks at me intently for several seconds. "Well, I always do it, absolutely, yes."

"You do?"

"Usually I try to make contact before lunch, or failing that teatime at the very latest."

"So you agree it's really important?"

"Vital, I mean it's more important than the actual shag right? Look," he adds warming to the theme, "I'm even in favour of electronic tagging. All men should agree to have a microchip planted into their brain, hand, maybe even their dick. First-time offenders will not be allowed to move within a hundred yards of the telephone, multiple offenders no more than a foot until such time as they have called the one-night standee to say the following:

"a) Did you get the flowers?
"b) You were great.
"c) You left your watch in my bed. Can you come
    and collect it, preferably naked?"

He pulls my hair. "OK. Satisfied?"

"Oh yes, think so. Absolutely."

"Marvellous, now can we fuck?"

"Of course, um . . . where were we?"

"I was asking whether you wouldn't mind lying on top of me."

"Oh. Yes. Would that be all of me?"

"All of you," he pulls me down. "Unless bits of you were thinking of making an excuse to take a cab home."

CHAPTER
TWENTY-THREE

In the offices of Film A the phone rings: Johnny Too-Fat.

"Linda wants to move to the country."

"Hm?"

"She wants to sell the house and move to Maidenhead."

"Terrific," I say, not that I'm listening. "Let her."

I'm not listening because I'm hysterical. There should be a definition, a technical term for the moment when Post-Shag Euphoria turns to Pre-Phone Hysteria and once there's a name there will have to be an investigation. Then, when the findings are leaked there will be an outcry in the Commons whereupon the thousands of women who have previously suffered in humiliated silence will be forced to come forward, because let's be quite clear about this — what we're talking about is a sexually transmitted disease. Pre-Phone Hysteria is a fatal plague that has eroded and killed the ego of millions of women. It's catching and hereditary, passed from father to son, from male to male. Soon goddamnit the *Daily Mirror* will take up the case, public funds will be raised, benefits given until such point as a cure is discovered and a small tablet manufactured which will have to be ingested within twenty-four hours of infection and would work, I imagine, in much the same way as the morning after pill.

It's too late for me though. It's a lot longer than twenty-four hours after infection and Rufus still hasn't rung. He didn't ring Tuesday before lunch and failing that latest at teatime. Ha, ha. There were no flowers waiting at Praed Street when I got home and definitely no message to say I was great. Of course everyone else in the whole world has rung: Andy Kramer, Michael's new rather foxy girlfriend twice at lunchtime, Caroline from BA Special Services and an LA rights lawyer about some missing script or other and yesterday, can you believe it, even Luke called.

"Sounds like your ex-boyfriend on the phone," Pigtails had come down to tell me, "says he can't get through to your direct line. Apparently you've still got some stuff in his flat he'd like you to take away?" My stomach had contracted with anger. I told Pigtails to keep him on hold as long as possible and then cut him off every time he called back.

"She said it would be better for the children," Johnny says.

"You don't have any children, Johnny," I say wearily. How long am I supposed to give him? One more day, two, a week? Where did I go wrong? If the pilot for the new sitcom, *Kit Falls in Love* had been screened live last Monday night in front of a demographically applicable audience, what would their criticisms have been?

"Hey, that crack about the Phone Hysteria thing," one might say, "personally I think that was really needy."

"Plus, you shouldn't have her smoking in bed," another might chip in, "I mean whichever way you slice it, smoking's a turn-off."

"But if we did?" Too-Fat perseveres.

"Did what?" I ask, deeply irritated.

"Have children?"

"Oh? And what method would Linda be planning here, immaculate ejaculation, martian impregnation?"

"She said she wanted me to commute."

"Johnny, the country's a horrible place. It's crawling with nature and I read an article only the other week which said that city children were far stronger and healthier than country children."

"Linda would say that was only because city children were always breaking into cars or keeping fit by running away from paedophiles."

"Johnny."

"What?"

"Linda would never say something as witty as that."

"I know."

"Leave her, Johnny," I say gently.

"Actually," he says falling into a short silence during which he indulges in some sinusy sniffing, "she's already thrown me out."

Too-Fat brings a suitcase, a toothpaste stained spongebag and, rather inappropriately, his wedding

257

photograph in a silver frame. I scrutinize it as he prowls the house like a psychopath, looking for alcohol to abuse.

"I hate that whole displaying of wedding photographs thing." He unscrews the top off a bottle of whisky. "It's like an affirmation you were once happy, just in case anyone who sees you together afterwards should doubt it." He takes the frame out of my hand and puts it back into his case.

"Divorce might not be so bad, Johnny."

"Divorce is a greater commitment than marriage. At least if you're unhappy in a marriage then things can stay as they are. On top of the nightmare of going through a divorce you then have to somehow be happier, to justify doing it in the first place." He pours half the whisky down his throat. "My dreamboat," he moans, "what will I do without her?"

"Get laid, hopefully." I hold my glass out for a drink.

Later. The sofa. Lying pissed on it I ask him, "How many of the three big lies have you told, Too-Fat?"

"Remind me what they are?" He lolls next to me, nursing the bottle between his thighs.

"1) The cheque's in the post.
"2) I love you.
"3) I'll call you."

"All of them."

"Why do people say 'I'll call you,' then don't?"

"Which people, Kit?" He turns to look at me.

258

"At least if they said '*You* call me,'" I ignore him, "that would put the control in our hands."

"Is it Luke? Because my darling, I hate to say it but what do you expect? You're never going to change the guy. You can't . . . what's that saying," he slurs, "put a square peg in a round hole or plug a hedgehog into an electrical socket . . . however how much fun it is trying," he muses as an afterthought.

"It's not Luke."

"Who then?"

"I can't tell you." (quavery voice)

"Tell me or I'll stab you."

"Rufus." (inaudible)

"Rufus!" He jumps up. "Rufus from the Bush? Honestly, Kit."

"What?"

He stares wildly at me. "Hasn't it ever occurred to you that I . . . that we?"

"What Johnny? What?"

"No," he says sadly, "I don't suppose it has." He starts pacing round the room. After a few minutes of silence he says, "Look, if you want control so much take it. Call him and tell him that you aren't ready for anything serious right now."

"Oh, come on, this is like an episode of *Seinfeld*, the kind of thing Kramer would suggest to Elaine, she'd do it and it would backfire horribly."

"No it's not. It's a no-lose situation. If he wasn't going to call your pride will be intact. If he was going to call you the fact that you're unavailable will make him come running all the faster."

"You've got a point." I consider. "But it would only work if it sounded . . ."

"Spontaneous."

"Friendly."

"Yes, but not cold."

"Exactly."

"You're right," I say struck. "It's an inspired plan." Actually it's not, it's a stupid plan, but alcohol works as a great enhancer of stupid plans so I pick up the phone and begin to dial. Somewhere in the logic compartment of my brain, a muffled alarm sounds. I hang up.

"Go on, Kit," Johnny eggs. "Just do it while you've got the nerve."

My palm is sweaty. This is ridiculous. Only creeps don't phone, and I can handle creeps. Downing another mouthful of whisky I pick up the receiver and without further hesitation make the most expensive local call of the year.

Much much later. Sofa. Lying on it, even more leery than before.

"Let's make a toast," slurs Johnny. "Kit Audrey Butler, you first."

"Right then. Five years down the road, I am going to win my Oscar." "My noscar," I actually say, being plastered.

"Course you are my dreamboat, a lovely li'l Oscar." He slumps back against the cushions and strokes my hair.

"I yam." I swill the warm whisky round in my glass. "I yam, I yam. I yam."

"Five years from now," says Johnny, "I shall win an advertising BAFTA, for most convincing portrayal of a man with an impotence problem."

"Five years from now, Touchstone Pictures will option my screenplay for a record two point nine squillion. Hand me that bottle."

"Certainly, your Dryness." He passes it over. "Five years from now, I shall leep with Kim Basinger."

"I don't care who I have to leep with, but I'm going to win my noscar and keep the Orange open. I'll shagthelotofthem 'cos after all, needs does must when the Devil does drive," I slur.

"You can say that again, my little Erogenous Zonelet," says Johnny. "If you can of course."

The telephone rings. I instantly sober. "Johnny, it's him," I hiss. "It's Rufus."

"I'll get it," he says knocking over his glass. "Tell him to bugger off."

"Are you crazy?" I snatch the receiver out of his hand. "Hello? Hello?"

"Who is this?" a man's voice, not Rufus's demands. "Who's this?"

"Oh, yes, sorry, it's Colin. Is Alice there?"

"No, Colin," I barely skip a beat, "Alice doesn't live here anymore." Then I fall about laughing.

"What?"

"*Alice Doesn't Live Here Anymore*, film quiz, geddit?" I'm doubled up at my own cleverness. "Oh, never mind," I gasp. "Wrong number." I slam the phone down. It rings again immediately.

"My turn." Johnny grabs the receiver. "Do please go away, Colin," he roars, "Kit and I are having sex here."

"Yes," I shriek, throwing my head back and sucking the dregs from the whisky bottle, "with animals and children and everything."

Johnny slams down the phone giggling uncontrollably. "My Whim in a Squillion." He snuggles his sweaty head against my shoulder, then abruptly, terrifyingly, starts to kiss me.

Travels of a script – 8

Chateau Marmont. The Bed

The Independent Producer sits on a specially constructed foam cushion to relieve the pain of his haemorrhoids. He holds a dead phone in his hand. On the other end of the line Film A have reported back that they've drawn a blank. So has the rights lawyer. It's now only a matter of time before Paramount begin to smell a rat.

. . . And smell a rat they do. It's not that the Independent Producer doesn't want to close the deal they realize, he cannot close the deal, he doesn't have the Chain of Title. Now the tables are turned, the Independent Producer starts to ring the Development Executives but they're not getting back to him, they're all far too busy ringing their counterparts at MGM, Universal, etc., to give them the scoop. Word gets round, the fruit baskets go mouldy, a piece appears in *Variety*, the Grade A actress snubs him at a party.

The circle completes, the project dies.

CHAPTER
TWENTY-FOUR

"I'm crazy about your lovely breasts," says Johnny Too-Fat. "Can't you come over to the showroom?"

"I'm busy," I hiss. It's ten-thirty and Michael's buzzing me incessantly from his office.

"Couldn't you just send your breasts over on their own then?"

"You know they're much too small to travel unaccompanied."

"All right my dreamboat, I just didn't want you waiting for *my* phone call."

"Yes, well that was sweet of you," I say uneasily.

"Kit," he says, "everything *is* all right isn't it?"

"Yes, yes, of course. Look, meet me later, six o'clock at the Greek restaurant." I hang up quickly and groan.

Handbook of Relationships — Basic Rules

1) It is foolish to sleep with someone you find deeply unattractive.

2) It's downright insane to sleep with your best friend.

Sleeping with Johnny was always going to be a mistake. Not only a mistake, but such a cliché that at the point when both of us started drinking and snuggling up in what began as an enjoyable orgy of self-pity the entire demographical audience would have been writhing in their seats behind the two-way mirror shouting things like, *Oh Lord, don't let them actually do it. Oh please, dear God, a little common sense!*

"The tickets are here," I put the envelope on Michael's desk, "and I've done your itinerary."

"I hate flying," he groans. "Every night I have the same dream. I'm sitting in the plane. I look out the window. The wing falls off. Pam! Plane crashes."

"That's not going to happen."

"You know what I see when I get off that little bus on to the runway? I don't see a plane, I just see a heap of mangled metal. It's a sign I'm going to die."

"It's a sign that you're flying too much, that's all."

"I hate this business."

"No, you don't," I say mechanically. *How could I have slept with Johnny? How could I be so stupid?*

"I've never had a moment's satisfaction from it. Not a single moment of glory."

"How can you say that? You've won a fistful of awards."

"Always somebody else's moment of glory. Where it counts that means nothing."

"Where does it count then?" I'm really in no fit state to play positive to Michael's negative.

"Oh, you know," he waves out the window, "out there, the Big Guys."

"To most people, you are the Big Guy."

"Kit, one thing you'll learn very fast in this business. However successful you are, there is always someone with more control and power than you. Life is relative, satisfaction is relative. Success is relative." Michael swivels his chair round and stares out of the window. "I'm going to give it all up."

"And do what?" *What am I going to tell Johnny?*

Sorry Johnny, but let's not make such a big deal, it was, after all, just a comfort fuck.

The thing is, Too-Fat, I knew I wasn't going to like it, and guess what? I didn't. But hey! No hard feelings huh?

"I don't know, take up Tai Chi, become a second-hand car salesman."

"Terrible idea." The words just pop out of my mouth. "I just slept with one."

"You did?" Michael's face lights up.

I nod miserably.

"You wouldn't happen to know if he has a 1965 Cobra for sale would you? I've been trying to track one down for months."

"How can you be so insensitive?" I give an operatic snuffle.

"Kit, Kit," he swivels his chair around, "is it that time of the month?"

"No it is not," I say furiously.

"Then what? Come on, tell me the problem, I'm good at other people's problems — makes me feel so much better about my own."

"Fine, all right. In the last week, I have slept with my ex-boyfriend who I hate. Then I slept with someone I really liked but who hasn't called me since. Last night, like an *idiot* I went to bed with my best friend."

"Male or female?" Michael asks, looking interested for the first time.

"MALE," I shout, "and now I never want to see him again."

"You see," Michael shrugs, "this is proof of what I just said. Success is relative. For you, sleeping with three different men is a disaster. For me sleeping with three different girls in the space of one week would give me Paradise Syndrome. And please," he adds handing me a tissue from the box in his drawer, "please tell me the best friend you're never going to see again *isn't* the one with my Cobra."

Rufus is waiting outside Film A. He leans against the wall, arms crossed. He looks awful. A three-day stubble peppers his face and the bandage on his wrist is creased with dirt. My heart flip flops. He is dejected, crushed with love, Hugh Grant when he discovers Andie MacDowell is going to marry someone else. Johnny was right, he's come running and although it's frankly a little sick that all you have to do is reverse to force someone to advance I don't care, I want to jump into his arms. I take a step towards him.

He takes a step back. "Kit." He acknowledges me with a nod and it doesn't take a supashrink to work out something is badly wrong. The look in his eyes is icy. It's not Hugh Grant at all, it's Cary Grant and the expression is the one he gives Ingrid Bergman in *Notorious* when they're sitting on the park bench and she tells him she's agreed to marry uranium-producing

Nazi, Claude Rains, and Cary makes out like she's a whore.

"What's wrong?"

"What the hell were you doing giving me that tragedy sob story about not wanting to wait by the telephone," he says coldly, "that whole Pre-Phone Hysteria I'm so vulnerable bollocks. What kind of game do you think you're playing anyway?"

"I'm not playing any game," I stammer, horrified by his tone. "I just didn't want us to be a . . ."

"To be a what?" he raps.

"To be a . . . to feel like a . . . well, to be a one-night —"

"Oh, right, I see. So you decided to give it what? Twenty-four hours, more? Less? Was there a pre-set deadline? Was I on a timer?" His voice rises angrily. "Is that all it comes down to for you?"

"It's just that you didn't call, and —" I'm so taken aback I can hardly get the words out.

"Firstly, I've been stuck in an editing suite for the last three days solid," he interrupts. "I've been given the chance to show the film and . . . anyway that's not the point. I mean . . . For God's sake, Kit, you think you have exclusive rights to angst, well you don't."

It occurs to me that he's overreacting. This was the last response I'd expected. When I sobered up this morning I reasoned there could be a couple of different responses to my message. Either nothing or a teasing phone call. I certainly didn't reckon on this white-hot anger. "Rufus, look," I say carefully, "I was a bit hammered when I left that message and . . ."

"What message?" he snaps.

"On your machine. Willesden."

"I haven't been to Willesden, Kit. I just told you. I haven't slept or had a bath, let alone been home, I've been here, in Soho, editing for three days."

"So what are you talking about then?" I ask bewildered. "Why are you so upset?"

"I'm talking about you jumping into bed with someone else," he shouts, "two minutes after jumping out of bed with me."

Oh no, I find it hard to swallow. Johnny couldn't, wouldn't have told him?

"I obey your explicit instructions and ring to tell you that you left your watch in my bed but it appears your office is under orders either to cut me off or not put my calls through. So finally I try you at home and some guy picks up quite clearly in the middle of your big moment."

It all finally dawns on me. "But that was . . ."

"Don't deny it, Kit. I heard you in the background. You were screwing someone. You were weren't you? Weren't you? Go on just say it."

I am of course about to deny it, laugh it off even, because what happened with Johnny wasn't sex, it was a mistake. We were just fooling around don't you see? It should never have happened. But the fact is peripheral. It did happen and even were it possible to think up an explanation that didn't sound weary my face has already given it away. I feel choked up, not with guilt really, just with how bloody stupid I've been.

"Forget it." He holds up his hands. "I actually don't want to hear you say it. You're right, I don't know why I'm getting so upset. It's none of my business." He turns away.

"Rufus . . . wait." I can't think of a way to stop him leaving.

He spins round and takes a step towards me. "You know what makes me angry, Kit? That you don't seem to care about anything. The Orange, your father . . . us. Correct me if I'm wrong, but it seems to me that there's nothing you believe in strongly enough to fight for." He looks hard at me like he's willing me to say something, produce some last-minute mitigating circumstances, and I want to tell him he's wrong, that he doesn't understand. There are lots of things I believe in, the problem is I just don't believe in me; but it's all I can do to stop myself crying, so I end up digging my nails into the palm of my hand and saying nothing at all.

"You know something, Kit," he says, unbearably soft. "I knew you were unhappy. I knew that. I suppose I just didn't realize how truly unhappy you were, that's all." Then he gives a nod like he's finished the whole unpleasant business to his satisfaction, turns on his heel again and strides off down Berwick Street.

The window of the Greek restaurant is steamed up from within. I can just make out Johnny at a table in the corner reading a copy of *Hot Tickets* and glancing every now and then towards the door.

Here's my plan: we're going to talk, agree to pretend last night never happened. Then, to cheer Johnny up, maybe we'll go see *Mystery Science Theater 3000: The Movie*. Johnny will sleep on my sofa until he gets himself together and life will return to normal. I certainly believe in *our* friendship enough to fight for it . . . I feel numbed by what Rufus said. Frozen. Like someone could prick my finger and it wouldn't even bleed. I slept with Rufus on the rebound from Luke, Luke, as it happens, on the rebound from Luke, then Johnny on the rebound from Rufus. Johnny, of course slept with me on the rebound from Linda. All that's left is for me to have a lesbian affair with Linda, then the whole lot of us can get together and write a screenplay for Woody Allen. Somewhere in the city, thunder sounds. A storm is coming. As I wrench open the door to the restaurant a bell chimes with tinny Christmas cheer.

"I loathe pantomimes. I loathe Cliff Richard. I loathe poinsettias. I fucking loathe Christmas," Too-Fat says vehemently as I sit down. "And can you believe it, you're supposed to bring your own alcohol here. Next time we come, we might as well bring the food too."

"Johnny."

"And another thing," he says pointing at the sign, **The owner eats here**, "I hate it when they say that. I mean where else is the poor man going to eat? Round the corner at the dentist? Of course the owner eats here for Christ's sake." He refuses to meet my eyes.

"Johnny."

"It would be pointless and uneconomical wouldn't it, eating somewhere else, if you owned a restaurant?"

"JOHNNY!"

Finally he looks at me, then his eyes slide back down to the table.

"I'm sorry." I take his hand.

He slumps back against his chair. "Why didn't it work for you, Kit? Because you know, it worked for me."

"I just don't know. I'm so sorry."

"All those times you told me I was a God, and I said you were gorgeous."

"But Johnny, that's what friends say."

"But the point is, you were lying and I was telling the truth."

"You are a God, Too-Fat," I say sadly. "Just not the right God for me."

"Linda's right, I'm repulsive. It's not your fault. You weren't to know just how repulsive."

"Stop it, Johnny. It wasn't anybody's fault."

"Do you remember what we used to say?" He shreds his napkin methodically. "That if we were both single when we hit sixty we'd get married?"

"Of course."

"Well, who's going to live with me in the old folk's home now we've screwed our friendship?"

"We screwed each other, I think it's only fair to leave our friendship out of this."

"Kit, don't be flippant. I don't think I can stand it."

"Oh, Johnny . . . we were both miserable that's all."

"And drunk."

"That's true." I smile at him. "We were very, very drunk."

Johnny sighs and stares at the wall where a batch of dog-eared celebrity photos are glued. "Oh please, look," he says in disgust, "Michael Douglas with the owner. Michael Douglas, I mean who do they think they're kidding? This is not Hollywood Boulevard. These aren't the streets of stinking San Francisco. Why would Michael Douglas ever eat in Shepherd's Bush in his whole life? Where do these things come from?"

"Probably in packs of ten with the olive oil, like football cards." I pick up the plastic menu and scour it despondently.

"Look, they've even got your dad's favourite."

"Shelley Winters?"

"No, Burt Baby," he chuckles, "that other well-known Hammersmith resident." I look over to where he's pointing; a photograph of Burt Reynolds, grimacing from under a ludicrous hat, arm around the owner.

"Look at the cheese on those smiles," says Johnny in awe. "You could peel it off and melt it on top of a burger . . ."

But something else has caught my eye, a signature and next to it, some figures. "Johnny, look at the date," I say frowning.

"What about it?"

"It's this year."

"So?"

"It's dated September." Something cracks in my head.

274

"So what? Hey, where are you going? Kit, what's so funny?"

I push my chair into the table, still chuckling and put on my coat. My tin man's heart is beating unnaturally fast. In my head there's a clanking of machinery, the one that sets and re-sets the pattern of lost relationships, and suddenly it shifts and moves on to a different track and all I know is that I have to get out of the restaurant before I laugh so hard I actually burst into tears, before Johnny misinterprets it, and before I have to waste time trying to explain what I haven't a hope of understanding myself.

The storm breaks as I press the buzzer on the security gate. Rain slides down my neck as I make my way down the spiral staircase and on to the metal walkway below. Lights switch on in the houseboat marking Dad's passage along its innards.

When I get on to the pontoon I stop. How on earth am I going to explain myself?

Gee, Dad, I saw a picture of Burt in a Greek restaurant and, wouldn't you know, it made me realize just how much I really care about you, you know, deep down?

I realize I've made a mistake, the whole scene is cringe-making, but just as I turn to abort Dad swings the door open, squints at me and holds out his hand. I hesitate then, ignoring his hand, step up on to the boat

275

and down into the wheelhouse shaking my head and showering Dad with drops of rain like a St Bernard.

Another clap of thunder rolls overhead, almost immediately car alarms on the street above us begin to wail.

I gaze out of the porthole. A muddy Tesco's bag attaches itself on the glass before it's sucked off.

"They should invent some kind of global vacuum cleaner," Dad says. "Suck all the garbage into space." He walks in front of me down the steps of the wheelhouse, through to the sitting room and into the kitchenette. The wind sways the boat, swilling some boiling water out of a saucepan where it spits and dances on the hob.

"Here." He hands me a strand of spaghetti. "Taste this."

"You should put it in a bigger saucepan." I bite it gingerly, one end is still hard, the other overcooked.

"In space garbage might be rather beautiful," Dad muses thoughtfully, "like multicoloured confetti spinning around Earth. They could consign it to one of the planets we don't need. Planet Trash they could call it."

"Earth *is* Planet Trash, Dad," I say, throwing myself on to the sofa. "Didn't you know? Somewhere up there is a planet populated by the perfect people, the ones that never get ill or depressed." I feel around for my cigarettes. "Do you think cars ever break down on Planet Perfect? Do you think there are cripples, dwarfs, plagues? Are there oil slicks, broken hearts and suicides? Of course not. We're just the waste bin where God keeps his broken gadgets."

276

Dad turns off the cooker ring and comes slowly out of the kitchen area wiping his hands on a drying up cloth. "Why are you always so angry, Kit?"

"Why did you leave me behind, Dad?" Finally it's out. Painful as a choked up fishbone, God help me, and now what? We glare at each other. I look away first.

"If you're coming to me for answers, Kit, you're going to be disappointed, I don't think I have them. I can tell you what happened if that's what you want to hear but I haven't got the answers."

"You can manage that one though, can't you?"

"Can I?" He sits down at the table opposite, thrusting his hands deep into the pockets of his cardigan.

I wait.

"Because I didn't feel I had anything better to offer you?" he says eventually. "Because your mother needed you more than I did? There are lots more but they're all excuses, not answers."

"You knew what Mum was like, you must have known what might happen."

"How could I?"

"You must have, Dad."

"I don't know if I did or not." He takes off his glasses and folds the sides in carefully. "There were certain things of course, things that made me fall in love with her, things which one day began to scare me."

"Like what?"

"Unimportant things. Her laugh, her dreaminess, individually they meant nothing, but when you slotted them all together, I don't know." He knuckles his eyes tiredly before putting his glasses on again. "Remember that Meg Ryan movie? *When a Man Loves a Woman*, when she's an alcoholic, and at first Andy Garcia likes that she's quite wild and dances in the road at night. He thinks it's charming, but soon he comes to realize that it's not because she's charming, it's because she's drunk and he starts not to like it any more. You see, Kit, the behaviour is the same, but the reason behind it is different. Slowly I came to realize that your ma wasn't just whimsical, she was . . . well you remember how she was don't you?"

Of course I remember. To prove it here's a flashback that's just popped up. And the title? *Mad Mrs Butler and Her Keys. This comic short has a distinct Jacques Tati feel to it folks.*

Usually Mrs Butler puts her keys under the dustbin when we leave for school. Security worries her, naturally it does. Lots of things worry her. One morning, instead of under the dustbin, she throws the keys in the flower bed. It's summer, and the roses are out. Proper English roses and they smell glorious. She spent hours planting them one spring. They fall over each other, a tangled mass of pink, red and white on either side of the path, all the way up to the gate. Today she just tosses in the keys at random. Nobody will find them there, she says. When I get back from school the roses are gone, two straight lines of amputated stems, both sides. She couldn't find the keys, she says, so she cut down the whole hedge. She has a spot of blood on her cheek when she tells me.

"She was mad," I say simply.

278

"She wasn't," Dad protests. "No, no, no, eccentric maybe, but not mad." He shakes his head like he's trying to convince himself. "What she was though, was very, very unhappy. You have to be very unhappy to behave the way she did." He shifts in his chair. "I didn't want Aunt Pauly to tell you, you know?"

"Why not?"

"Because it's pointless that's why. What would it change? I still messed things up for us. Anyway it's easier to accept your father's a shit than your mother's a . . ."

I hold up my hand.

"I went away when she started her second affair. Vietnam. They didn't want to send people with families but I asked for the job. When I came back the affair was over. I could have moved back in I suppose, I was still in love with her you see, but I was angry. I screwed around."

I light a cigarette and look away uncomfortably. The word "screwed" sounds extraordinary coming out of my father's mouth.

"It was for revenge though, not love, not even for sex really. Too many people doing things for the wrong reasons. I didn't see then that she needed help." His face twists. "I took any job abroad I could, the riskier the better . . . the whole thing with your mother . . . I felt I had something to prove."

"But what about me?" I hear my voice saying.

"I got very good at finding excuses not to feel responsible for you." Dad looks away. "By the time I realized what I was doing it was too late; the fighting, the reporting, it had become the means to some kind of goal."

"Which was what?"

"The goal of overcoming the challenge of getting there I suppose. I was going along so fast in a straight line, Kit, I just clean forgot to look at the view and I of all people should have realized that the view is more fun than the destination. That's why road movies are so successful."

"But where were you trying to get to?"

"I never worked it out." He permits himself a wry chuckle. "I suppose I'm a Groucho Marx kind of a person, I never thought of an achievement as an achievement if I personally managed to reach it. The goalposts kept moving."

"Only because you kept moving them."

"Yup, that's your father: good at football but lousy at scoring."

"I think you're just trying to confuse me with a bad analogy."

"You're exactly the same as me, Kit. I see it all the time. We're both impatient."

"I thought I was supposed to be so like Mum."

"You might look like her, but you're not at all like her. Your mother was depressed because she didn't know where she was going. You know exactly where you're going but you just can't get there quick enough — but you'll get there in the end. At least I think you will."

For a moment I nearly lose it. "You're trying to make me cry, Dad, and I'm not going to cry."

280

"Kit," he takes off his glasses again and wipes the lenses carefully on his cardigan, "you cried in *Star Wars*, you cried in *Peter Pan*, you even cried in *Airport 77* for some extraordinary reason."

"It's easy to cry in movies, it's not real life."

"Some psychiatrist," he gets to his feet, "would have a bloody field day with you."

"Like I don't suppose they'd be pointing the finger at you or anything?"

Dad takes a bottle of whisky from the cupboard and pours out two tumblers. "Let me tell you something about guilt," he says quietly, handing one to me. "It treats you like a punchball. It hits you from behind, it hits you from the side, every time you get up off the floor it smacks you in the face and still leaves you reeling. Do you think a single day goes by without me feeling guilty about your mother, about you?"

"You don't have to feel guilty any more, Dad. It was a long time ago."

"I don't need you to absolve me, Kit," he says. "It doesn't work like that."

He walks into the kitchenette where he prods doubtfully at the solidified strands of spaghetti hanging out of the saucepan.

"Are you going to eat that or what?" I say awkwardly.

"*I think that falls into the or what category,*" he quotes brightly.

"Dad," I protest feebly.

"I miss you, Kit." He turns round. "That's all there is to it."

He picks up his glass and swallows down a mouthful. "I made you promise me once, in the days when you were still young and impressionable, of course, that when I was old and senile you would take me to the movies; nights when you hadn't got a boyfriend or a confirmed date. Well," he looks at me, "you don't seem to have much in the way of a boyfriend right now . . ."

". . . And you're virtually senile," I say flippantly, "so I guess we could go anytime."

"Anytime is too vague, how about we go right now?"

"Dad, come on. It's nearly midnight."

"Well? You've got your own bloody cinema haven't you?"

CHAPTER
TWENTY-FIVE

The key turns in the padlock of the Orange's back entrance. Dad stands behind me, hunched into his overcoat. The rain has stopped, leaving only the wind blowing a cold corridor between us. I re-lock the padlock on the chain, unbolt the inner doors and glance up and down the alleyway where the street lamps shine a pea-soup colour on to the wet pavement. The place is deserted.

I feel like I should have called Julie or Callum, but it's not as if we're doing anything illegal and technically I am still the manageress. All the same I feel like I'm breaking into a stranger's house and the quietness gives me an uneasy knot somewhere in my stomach.

"Get on with it will you, it's freezing out here." Behind me Dad's breathing is slightly bronchial. I turn round, his eyes are watering and close-up, bloodshot, but he's smiling, and when I turn back to push open the door he lets out a tiny giggle, a high-pitched schoolboy giggle. It's such a surprising noise from him that I laugh as well.

"We're going to get ourselves arrested, Dad."

"Oh, I do hope so," he says, helping me push the heavy doors shut.

On the ground floor I snap on the lights to the box office and theatre. Dad stands shivering in his overcoat and gazes around him. Cream paint bubbles off the walls like a facial peel and the floor is coming up in the corners. The Orange's general air of neglect looks worse than ever. Maybe it's the cold. I switch on the heaters. Dad runs his hand over the plaque nailed to the door of the storeroom. "EALING IRON WORKS," he reads out loud.

"Those doors came off a battleship."

"Really? That's lovely. You have my dream job you know that? Running a cinema."

"Really?"

"Absolutely. It would satisfy every requirement of my life; I could sit around all day with my feet up watching films and eating popcorn. Running a cinema is a very romantic thing to do."

"You're the romantic, Dad, not the job."

"Maybe," he concedes. He blows on his hands. "So, what do we do now?"

"You decide where to sit. I'll go sort out a film." I start up the steps. "What do you want to see? It'll have to be a video, I can't work the projector properly."

"You choose then."

"No you."

He looks at me warily. "We like different things."

"No," I turn round. "Not really."

I allow myself a bit of a private smile when I see Dad hunched in the front row over a bucket of cold popcorn and nursing a bag of sweets. Not exactly playing cool about being eager is it?

284

"Can I interest you in a jelly tentacle?" he asks when I sit down.

"Don't mind if I do." I feel around in the striped bag. It's intensely odd to be this close to my father. Arm's length, suddenly reduced to finger's width, then to hair's breadth. Any minute now I'm in danger of sitting on his lap and sucking my thumb. Dad is aware of it too. I feel I ought to say something, something philosophical and profound, but I can't think of anything appropriate. I chew on the jelly tentacle instead.

"Well this is all very civilized, Kit."

"Clever of you to get the best seats."

"Aah . . . well there are some circles in which I still have clout."

"Which circles would those be? Corn? Knitting?"

"Stop being so cheeky and eat your pick'n'mix." He plops the bag in my lap. I snout around for a Sherbet Alien then plop it back in his. Dad turns to look at me quizzically, but he can see that I'm smiling and enjoying all of this, and I am, and what's more I know why: for the first time in a very long while we're having a conversation which doesn't include sniping or humouring. I'm not having to manoeuvre my words past the lump of bile in my throat because the bile's just not there at the moment and it feels good, it feels right. I feel like a proper person and so far it's been quite easy. It wasn't as if Dad had to go prove himself, dress up in a fake moustache and flasher's raincoat like Clint Eastwood, he didn't have to trash lots of expensive cars like Sean, in fact he didn't have to do anything at all and obviously it would be facile to think that's the end of it, but it's certainly a beginning and so, yes, it feels good, in fact it doesn't feel good, it feels bloody great.

"Pay attention," says Dad, squeezing my arm. "It's starting."

There's a reasonably enjoyable B movie called *Backdraft* which boasts a fantastical performance by Donald Sutherland as a giggly loony who can't resist a bit of arson on the side. *Backdraft* casts the fire itself as the bad guy, the unpredictable serial killer, hiding in corners, bursting out when you least expect it, particularly in old dark buildings like this one. Frankly it's a lousy movie but it managed to lodge a vague unease in my mind that fire has an intelligence and speed I hadn't previously been aware of. Therefore when forty minutes or so into *King Kong* Dad sniffs the air once, then again, turns his head to look at the deserted entrance behind us, sniffs for a third time, digs me in the ribs and finally says, "Do you smell something?" I immediately conjure up a cunning streak of smoke flitting in and out of corners of the Orange, hovering in passageways, trying to remain undetected long enough to take control of the place. I feel a corkscrew twist in my guts, because I do smell something. I smell fire. Not a pleasant winter bonfire smell of burning leaves or roast chestnuts but an acrid, frightening smell.

My seat pings behind me as I head quickly up the aisle towards the exit sign. At the back the smell is stronger. Dad is calling my name. I turn round. He's

286

standing up, a small figure silhouetted black in front of a giant hairy ape. I turn back and break into a run.

Down the steps and speeding up. Round the corner, past the disused dressing rooms, towards the basement and already I'm watching rushes of this scene which are running in front of reality by about three seconds. I see myself racing towards the heavy doors knowing the fire is behind waiting to engulf me. My head fills with the charred smell of tar as flames envelop my clothes. By the time I actually arrive at the doors I'm so carried away it's far too late to counsel caution. I yank on the bar with the full expectation of being carried backwards by the impact and close my eyes in expectation. Then, when nothing happens, I open them again. Instead of a blast and choking flames, a man stands in the middle of the cavernous room, his back to me. He's holding a burning cloth to a pile of damp-looking rubbish and bits of scorched wire on the ground. As the door grinds he spins around and takes a step forward, face illuminated by the smouldering rag in his hand.

It's odd isn't it, how you think you'll react to an act of violence against yourself, you wonder whether you'll lie there and take it, whether you'll scream like Fay Ray, or be outraged and indignant like those ninety-year-old women who, when mugged at knifepoint, utter such classics as, "How dare you, whippersnapper, these pearls belonged to Great Aunt Edwina?" Personally, I'm just mad with anger. Without stopping to think, I run at him and grab the sleeve of his shirt, finding myself in possession of a fistful of purple nylon.

Mr Rashid Hassop of the council is as surprised as I am. His arm pulls back but whether in self-defence or act of aggression it's impossible to tell because at that moment I'm shoved out of the way. Something flies by me at great speed, making an odd growling noise. It's Dad, hands raised in comic Master of the Universe style and in spite of the situation I nearly burst out laughing.

"Be careful," I implore. But I needn't have bothered because Dad is already in the throes of an incredible kung-fu-style punch which somehow involves his arms and at least one of his legs but all with such deadly speed it's hard to gauge the exact choreography. It catches Hassop on the bony part of his jaw and the force of it rattles him from skull to sternum. He drops to the floor and lands on his back, face-up, lips making an odd pursing shape like a stunned fish gasping for oxygen. Almost immediately after that he passes out.

Dad stands astride his body, rubbing his hands with a look of pure joy as though he'd just KO'd Amir Khan in the opening rounds of the World Featherweight Championships. A trickle of blood crawls down Hassop's nose.

"Dad," I say in awe, "that was magnificent."

"Impressive, eh, for an old kipper like me."

"I'll say." I start to laugh then stop abruptly. "God, he's not dead is he?"

"Of course he's not bloody dead. If you want to kill them, you have to apply a similar force directly to the base of the spine. Or the bridge of the nose like this."

He makes a chopping motion through the air with the side of his hand.

"Oh, I see," I stammer. "Poor Mr Hassop, background in electrics, I don't suppose he's that clued-up on martial arts."

"Hang on, Kit. You know this man?" Dad looks astonished.

"Well yes. He works for the council."

"What on earth is going on here then?"

I tell him about Ron Chambers, about Neville's will, about the dead cat, the rats, the endless health inspections, the attempted bribe, the temporary licence. "Maybe he couldn't afford to wait for the appeal. I mean he's obviously paid Hassop."

"Why did you never talk to me about all of this?"

"Why? What could you have done?"

"What do you think I spent all those years in Afghanistan doing?" Dad looks affronted. "Knitting yashmaks? Believe me, Kit, I would have thought of something."

"I'll go and call the police." I make for the door.

"Wait, not yet." Dad puts a hand on my arm. "Let's hold off till he comes round, much more fun."

"What do you have in mind?" I ask suspiciously.

"I don't know. Tie him up, torture him, taunt him, tickle him. There's got to be something more interesting than handing him over to the authorities. Once the police are involved we'll lose our edge."

Dad sits down on a crate of Coca-Cola. I perch next to him.

"Let me get this straight, Dad. We're going to keep him hostage?"

"I don't see why not, send his turban through the post to your grieving landlord, demand an extortionate ransom, feed him on shards of mango chutney and withhold all yogurt drinks until the money is forthcoming."

"This is not a joke you know."

"Alternatively we could break his legs like in *Misery* or try to make him fall in love with you like in that John Fowles book." Dad is refusing to take this seriously. I give up.

"*The Magus?*"

"No"

"*The Ebony Tower?*"

"I could think of it if only you'd stop interrupting."

"*The Collector?*" I interrupt.

"That's it, butterfly loony Terence Stamp keeps girl prisoner in cellar."

"An intellectual prequel to *Silence of the Lambs.*"

"Except that Terence Stamp is imbued with far too much middle-class angst to do anything to Samantha Eggar and anyway she's far cleverer than he is. He just wants her to fall in love with him."

"With my record I couldn't even get a loser like Rashid to fall in love with me."

"What happened to that new boyfriend then, have you seen him off already?"

"Mm."

"Was that a good idea?"

"I s'pose."

"Come on, Kit, you can't pull the wool over my eyes. Baaa." He makes an idiotic sheep noise.

"That's a pathetic joke, Dad. Where did that come from?"

"Oh, spur of the moment thing like many of my witticisms. You liked him though didn't you?" he adds craftily.

"I suppose."

"Is it retrievable?"

"I don't think he's interested any more."

"Well, he was certainly interested back then."

"Dad, I really don't want to talk about it." The truth is I'm not sure I can handle my father's metamorphosis from estranged parent to agony aunt in the space of a single evening.

"You're not good at relationships," he says bluntly. "You've inherited that from me I'm afraid."

"Yes, well thanks."

"Hark." Dad puts his hand on my arm. Rashid lets out another groan. "He's coming to."

"Now what?"

"Beats me," says Dad cheerfully.

Rashid Hassop opens both his eyes at once. His pupils seem to have slipped their moorings and travel wildly around his sockets searching for the correct fixture to enable 20/20 vision. With his turban askew and swivelling eyeballs he looks like a toon from *Roger Rabbit*, a humanoid imbued with cartoon-like characteristics, and so much so that it would be tempting to fire him from a cannon or drop a ten-ton safe on his head had either prop been remotely handy. Instead I tap him roughly on the shoulder. Dad prises a can of Coke from the crate underneath him. "*The Indian Patient*," says Dad holding it to Hassop's lips. He winks at me.

Hassop's eyes complete their circuit and click into focus, he sips the Coke staring dazedly at the pair of us. As the river of E courses through his veins he begins to look a little better. Colour returns to his cheeks. He shifts himself into a sitting position and leans against the meshed cage behind him. Inside, the mechanism for opening the old safety curtain has rusted to a blackish red.

"Meri tabiyat thik nahi ha . . ." he says.

"What's that?" Dad asks.

"I really am feeling most unwell."

I squat down and put my mouth close to his ear. "Serves you right."

Hassop pushes himself up further upright against the cage and fixes me with an aggrieved look. "Since I am coming to this country I have driven a mini-cab, I have been a cleaner in a bank, even made egg McMuffins. When my friends came here Thatcher was in power. Clever people made money. I am not a criminal. I have a degree, I have a wife and twin daughters."

"Ron *bunged* you, didn't he?" I say scornfully.

"I am not familiar with the word 'bung'," he says vaguely. The trickle of blood from his nose has not quite reached his mouth, but coagulates in a blob on the topside of his lip. Hassop becomes aware of it, dabbing it with his finger then examining the red smear on the tip. "Mr Chambers has a very substantial offer from Quick Kebab." He sighs. "A percentage of this offer is worth a lot of money and the deal is expiring this end of December."

"Do you know how many independent cinemas there are left in London?" I ask him.

"No."

"Why don't you persuade your new boss to invest some money into the place, try to make it more profitable?" says Dad.

"And how much money to invest," Hassop protests, "to make this profit?"

"Well, besides the repairs, we'd need some extra seating capacity," says Dad matter of factly as though having a meeting with his friendly bank manager. "Re-open the Gods, some of the balconies. A bar would be good," he thinks for a second or two. "Let's say a hundred, maybe a hundred and fifty thousand."

"And where is this coming from?" Hassop reaches into his pocket and for an insane moment I think he's going to present us with a bank draft, but his hand emerges holding a small tin with a picture of an Indian girl on the front. "Where is even one thousand coming from? There are easier choices." He flicks the tin open and takes out a thin cheroot. "I am not without morals but life is a question of survival."

"Just not ours," says Dad wryly.

"I wasn't to be knowing anyone was here," Hassop says apologetically.

"How did you get in anyway?" I ask. He nods at the wooden ladder bolted against the wall. Dad's eyes follow it up forty, fifty feet to the dome.

"There's a broken pane of glass at the top," Hassop says.

"That's a vertiginous piece of climbing by any standards," Dad says impressed. "You know, Kit, this is one hell of a space back here, surely you could do something with it?"

"Like what?" I look helplessly round the cavernous room; the damp walls are lit by naked bulbs, random pieces of industrialia lie upended on the wooden floor.

"I don't know, I don't know," he says slowly, "but leave it to your old man. I'll come up with something."

Hassop eases himself up. Dad gives him his arm. "You are very kind," says Hassop politely.

"I'm making a report of this," Dad says in a quiet voice that sends a little shiver down the back of my neck. "I will not be sending it to the police right now. But you interfere with my daughter, her job, her safety, or her cinema and I will. I promise you I will."

"You are what in Hindi is called a *dada*, a *mastaan*."

"I'm not even going to ask what that means," says Dad.

"Don't be worrying. It is a compliment, it means tough guy. Of course it is slang. If I had used the word *kameenay*, which means a third-rate fellow, that would be an insult."

"Charmed though I am by this lesson in colloquial Indian, I think it would be more appropriate if you left." Dad puts his hand under Hassop's elbow and together we escort him shakily towards the exit. I pull back the bolts top and bottom and Hassop, giving his nose one last wipe steps out into the night. As we're about to re-lock the door behind him, he pops his turban back in.

"Can I be asking what you are doing here?" As if it's only just occurred to him.

Dad says nothing for a second. Finally he looks at me then at Hassop. "Where else do you go when you're in love or when you're single," he says, "when you're happy or when your head's about to explode with black thoughts? Where else can you take someone when you have nothing left to say or have not yet managed to say anything . . . we're here to see a movie of course."

I stare at my father. Hassop stares at him too. I have a sudden and mawkish urge to cry but am saved by Dad pinching my arm. Hassop gives us a grim smile and rubs the fading red mark on his jaw. "Well," he says eventually, "don't be forgetting to switch off all the lights." Then he disappears without another word into the inky darkness outside.

CHAPTER
TWENTY-SIX

"Say you'd shot a movie but you weren't sure of the ending?"

"Yup," Michael says bored.

"Look, I need some advice."

"Oh, all right, give me the premise then."

"Small-time girl —"

"Pretty?" he interrupts.

"She has her moments."

"She'll be pretty by the time we finish with her," Michael says matter of factly.

"Whatever. Small-time girl is a writer. She has three scripts in the back of her filing cabinet."

"Kit," he groans, "how many times do I have to tell you. Come the next flood, Noah would save William Goldman and Nora Ephron, hope they were sexually compatible and leave the rest to drown. Most of the writers I meet can't even put down a coherent shopping list, let alone a memorable piece of dialogue. Scriptwriting is for mugs, and we don't need a heroine who's a mug."

"Yes, but that's the story."

"Fine. I hate it so far, but carry on."

"OK, this girl is a mug on all kinds of personal levels as well. Mother dead, doesn't get on with father, loses boyfriend she thought she might eventually marry."

"Yes, yes, yes, does she at least have a drug problem?"

"Not yet."

"But unemployed, garret-style existence writing her fingers to the bone."

"She runs a cinema, an old dilapidated cinema."

"Hm," he considers, "I quite like that, shades of *Cinema Paradiso* and *My Beautiful Launderette*. Could she be a lesbian?"

"I don't think so," I say doubtfully.

"Pity. So where's the Unique Selling Point? The big idea?"

"There's a bad guy, he wants to close the cinema, she has to raise money to keep it open."

"She becomes a prostitute," Michael says hopefully, "a hooker with a heart, we'll call her Hazel, or Heather maybe."

"No. She's fed up with her life, she takes a job she doesn't really want, abandoning the cinema. She doesn't care about it any more, then one day, she sort of makes up with her father and realizes she wants to save the cinema all at the same time. How does she do it? How does she get the money?"

"Firstly that's not really a plot, secondly it's trite."

"I know. That's the problem."

"Can't you introduce some element of sexual deviancy? Could the father have been imprisoned for a crime he didn't commit?"

"Well, he's kind of a serial adulterer, if that's any help?"

"No good. Old people having sex, *Cocoon*, it's been done already, is there any other love interest?"

"No."

"OK," he considers, "here's my advice. How about — girl stops sleeping with second-hand car salesmen and has affair with depressed boss of job she is clearly about to resign from who then, in role of mentor, helps her raise money?"

"That's what you're suggesting?" I ask incredulously.

"Actually I was joking. Why?" He perks up. "Would you do it?"

"Have an *affair* with you?"

"Sure, what's wrong with me? I'm rich, successful. I've got a nice car. You're the one always telling me I'm a great package."

"You are a great package, but I think I'll pass if you don't mind."

"But this is a chintzy way of resigning, right?" Michael doesn't seem that upset.

"I can't come back after Christmas."

"Couch casting," he sighs, "just ain't what it's cracked up to be."

CHAPTER
TWENTY-SEVEN

VOICE OVER (*unseen*) It's fucking ridiculous, Ben Moor is God's sacred land, and they want to charge a pound for climbing it. What happened to the effing Right to Roam?

CALLUM Well I suppose there is all that litter, and what about how much it costs to rescue all those people year after year?

JULIE (*shouting*) Leave them there, if people are stupid enough to climb a mountain and get themselves stuck they don't deserve to get rescued.

CALLUM What about road accidents then? If people are hit by a car when they're crossing the road, they should be left there too, on the grounds, I suppose, that people have no business crossing the road in the first place.

JULIE That's completely different and would cause inconvenient traffic congestion but if you left all the dead morons on Ben Moor they wouldn't get in anybody's way, better still, the next generation could do that thing of walking up the mountain and finding their father trapped, perfectly preserved under the ice. Take the kids to see Grandpa. A nice day's outing and beats a bloody trip to the cemetery any day.

CALLUM A sort of Generational Theme Park. That's neat.

JULIE (*sulky*) At least it would be worth charging a fucking pound for.

I tilt my chair against the wall and smile. My cinema, Mine. *My Beautiful Laundrette, My Beautiful Cinema.* It's fantastic to be back.

Christmas has passed, New Year has passed, neither as bad as they threatened to be. It was never going to be the kind of holiday spent frolicking in the fountain in Trafalgar Square, then again, neither did I spend them munching on Tesco's turkey for one and watching Lunn Poly adverts for spring away-breaks.

In the end Dad, Aunt Pauly and I had a perfectly delicious roast lunch on Christmas Day itself. Then on Boxing Day, Dad and I embarked on a marathon film crawl. We started with *When We Were Kings* (Dad's surprisingly arty choice) at Screen on the Green, during which I decided George Plimpton was a God, and we ended with *Flirting with Disaster* (my choice on video) which featured a bisexual FBI agent licking Patricia Arquette's armpit.

300

On New Year's Eve Dad appeared to suffer from some kind of aberration and announced he had bought tickets to the theatre. He hauled both me and Aunt Pauly off to some Iranian director's revamping of *Twelfth Night* at the Barbican. Aunt Pauly appeared to enjoy herself hugely, but personally I hate the theatre. I don't know what he can have been thinking.

January.

Sleep has returned to me like an ex-boyfriend in search of sloppy seconds. It woos, cajoles and tantalizes with its promise of luxurious nights to follow. By the time it came back however, I was over it. Bit by bit, I've fallen for the wakeful state. It might not be ideal, but it's there when I need it, a relationship conducted in companionable silence, and anyway, I know it's only a matter of time before sleep regresses back to its old selfish ways. The difference is that during the night now, I've begun to write. The block has lifted, the filter gone. I write until the darkness outside begins its fade to light, until the silence is broken by the twittering of the irritating birds, and I don't stop until the twittering is drowned by the early morning traffic. Then I crash.

Dad works my mornings for me at the Orange. He doesn't get paid. It's not a formal arrangement as such, just a hobby that's beginning to slide into permanence. Naturally it's been couched as a favour to me, but it's clear he's having the time of his life. He's hardly sat around twiddling his thumbs either. It's taken him about three and a half minutes to change the Orange from Arthouse to Kitsch House.

He's produced a book called *Bad Movies We Love* written by a couple of reporters from *Movieline* magazine in LA. It's his new Bible — not, you understand, that he consults it for inspiration, it's more that he believes it to be a justification of his taste, his opinions, his entire reason for living.

"Listen," he says gleefully, "to what they say about the *Poseidon Adventure*."

Overacting in a grey wig that makes her resemble Miss Piggy's grandmother, Shelley Winters performs the most crazed of the film's many madcap surprises. When Hackman is trapped underwater, Winters waddles in and does an underwater ballet unparalleled in Bad Movie madness.

He's even copied their spiel off the back cover of the book and stencilled it up on a poster outside the Orange. It reads:

GASP AT SCENERY-CHEWING PERFORMANCES!
MARVEL AT GLORIOUSLY ABSURD PLOT LINES!
QUIET GOOD TASTE? NEVER HEARD OF IT!

To be fair he's been thoroughly sensitive and reassuring about the change of direction. "Don't think we're not going to be choosy, Kit. The Orange won't be showing just any old turkeys, it won't show megabudget

302

debacles, we will be showing pure B movies and only very bad ones at that."

At his instigation, we've struck a deal with the distributors. We don't give them a percentage of bums on seats any more, just a flat fee. We're allowed to run the film for as long as we want, rather than the usual two weeks. Any film we can't get permission to show, we screen free and ask people for a donation. Most people hand over at least their ticket's worth, occasionally some smart alec refuses, but just as often a film Samaritan puts in a twenty proving a touching nostalgia from the locals.

And of course we're a cult hit. We've even had a write-up in the *Guardian*. In the evenings the Orange teems with new faces. Earnest looking movie buffs with goatees hang around after hours, drinking coffee and with great dedication discuss the finer moments of *Mandingo*. Recently some attractive local women have even found the time to indulge in heated arguments with Dad about whether he should have double-billed *Mommie Dearest* with *Towering Inferno*.

Naturally I try to maintain the air of being slightly miffed but it's hard not to be carried by Dad's sheer exuberance. One day when the projector breaks down, he and Julie even perform the final scene of *Gone with the Wind* to rapturous applause. "Face it, Kit," Dad said, when *Valley of the Dolls* outsold the takings for last year's *Crash* by ten to one, "you're about to revert to a dedicated low-brower just like me."

Dad's and my relationship has fallen into a sort of *Bringing Up Baby* pattern where Katharine Hepburn gets her way the whole time by distracting Cary Grant with non-sequiturs and irrelevancies and is generally so annoying you want to stab her. Secretly though, you come round to her in the end because she's irrepressible and of course she's an *enthusiast* isn't she? Well that's Dad and me, Cary Grant and Katharine Hepburn: the only incongruity in this scenario being that it's Dad, not myself, her namesake, who gets to play the part of Katharine.

Occasionally we talk about Mum, but not often. There isn't that much to say. Sometimes I tell Dad stories, the funny ones, and we both do the decent equivalent of laughing at them. Sometimes Dad talks about her. I listen to him but I don't say much. If Luke was around he'd probably say this was the moment for opening all those doors, but I believe there are some doors that should not only remain shut but locked with a state of the art security system fitted to them. So even though Dad talks to me about his guilt I can't talk to him about mine. I don't think I'll ever be able to talk about it, not to him, not a supashrink, not to anyone: the fact that the strongest emotion I felt after she died was not grief, not loss, not love even — I felt all those things of course, but they were overshadowed by a dull sense of relief. That's my guilt and I have to live with it, but at least I've stopped blaming Dad for it: I figure he has enough on his plate already.

From Ron Chambers and Hassop, there's been barely a squeak, although they did turn up one morning before I came in. Dad dealt with them. Presumably the Quick Kebab deal has now fallen through so Dad seems sanguine about the whole thing. I'm less sure. I mistrust loose ends. Every time I watched the *Wizard of Oz* as a child one thing always bothered me. What happened to Miss Gulch? The film ties itself up neatly in every other sense except this one. I used to lie in bed at night worrying about it, because if Dorothy wakes up and finds Oz all a dream, then it would be fair to assume that Miss Gulch is still in posession of her legal order — which means that one day, sooner or later she will bicycle around with it, take Toto away in her wicker basket and have him put down . . .

In the meantime we're raising cash. I've applied for all kinds of different grants, filled in a million forms, begun to hassle yet again for Free Money. People are buying seats. They pay £200 to put their names on them, dry-cleaned or not. We've started a collection box — people drop money in it. Michael Ryan, heroically, is holding a charity screening at the Orange and donating the proceeds. Callum wanted to make a chart, you know, one of those corny ones with a giant thermometer they use when raising money for hospitals, but we've settled on Xeroxing black and white movie negatives blowing them up life-size at Pronto Print then colouring them red, frame by frame as the money comes in; and it's coming in, it is, it's actually, unbelievably, slowly but steadily starting to happen.

These days Johnny and I frequent a new restaurant which has opened up two streets away from the Bush. It has things like shaved parmesan and pumpkin risotto on the menu. We don't go to the Bush any more, not that it would matter anyway, because I hear that Rufus is hardly ever there. The Mexican has taken over the management role, if that's the word for it. Ray Charles is out, Elvis is always in. Occasionally when I pass by on the way to the bank or the doughnut shop I wonder what would happen if Rufus was there: if he looked up, out through the window and made eye contact, what then?

"Linda has a new boyfriend," Too-Fat says. "Too stupid to walk in a straight line, too stupid to know he's in England for goodness sake. What can she see in him? Do you think he's enormously well hung? Maybe he hires himself out to fill swimming pools, or demolish warehouses. I bet you anything *it's* bigger than our three-bedroom flat. If Linda asks him to move in with her, he'll be the first man in England who's had to apply for planning permission for a penis extension . . ."

Plus there's definitely something going on with Julie and Callum. The other day when I walked into the Orange I could have sworn they were holding hands. I'm having quite a problem getting my head round this one. These two people are simply not compatible — either physically or mentally. When you look at them together, it's not like you're thinking: Bonny and Clyde, Rhett and Scarlett, you're thinking more along the lines of Little and Large, or even something deeply politically incorrect out of *Viz* Magazine.

Luke, aka Dr Hybrid, aka (you won't be surprised to hear) Cool Boy, is also reported to be having an affair with some cool girl. And me? Sex, the Final Frontier? Ha! I went out with a journalist from the *Guardian*. He was actually quite cute but when he confessed he'd walked out of *Strictly Ballroom* twenty minutes after it had begun, I realized we had no future together.

At the end of February, Rufus screened his short in Soho Square. It seemed quite a serious sort of an affair. Three or four times to choose from and proper invitations. The Orange got sent four tickets. None of the tickets had individual names on but I assumed one was for me. Johnny, Julie and Callum all went. It wasn't a bile issue, or even a God of Cringe issue. I just didn't want to go.

Johnny said the film was nothing special, which meant the reverse. Julie, who went at an earlier time, said it was full of agents and snappy-looking TV executives. The Mexican told Callum that right now, the sun was shining golden on Rufus and that film companies all over the place were sending him scripts by the busload.

So I guess the nub of it is that someone else has had the luck and eye to recognize the divinely talented young director, with his asymmetric features and barely any money. I have heard that he will be showing his revolutionary short in selected cinemas for three weeks exactly, playing before Ang Lee's new release in the early summer. During this time, if it hasn't happened already, he will no doubt be discovered and internationally revered as the new Orson Welles and although I got my one shag on the floor of the box office, I suppose my personality was simply not haunting enough to keep him from departing for Hollywood, neither my script nor me in his arms, just an empty shopping bag waiting to be filled with his own hopes and dreams. So I probably won't find myself included in *Halliwell's Guide* as most influential person of the Post-Tarantino era, but that's OK, and the reason that's OK is that I've snapped out of my depression. My inner psyche has let up juggling with feelings of anger and low self-worth; both good and bad things have happened in the last six months. And it's not like I'm back to being a twenty-something know-it-all, or worse a thirty-something self-awareness freak, but it has occurred to me that out of the seven kinds of movie plots, my life recently has been a combination of all of them and that the final result, with a touch of artistic licence, might almost qualify as Rites of Passage: a phrase I've never fully understood before but which I now take as meaning becoming a proper person or at least the next best thing to it.

Michael Ryan was right. Everything is relative, a question of perspective. The width of failure or success depends on how philosophically you take it. A few months ago for instance, when I looked at Luke and I looked at the scripts in the back of my cupboard I thought: that's three years down the tubes, up the spout, or wherever these things go when your confidence feels like disappearing on you. But nothing is ever wasted — everything is just stored up to be churned out later. So I've become an optimist again, and although I often catch myself thinking about Rufus, I also have faith that one day love will fall like a bolt from the sky. I will find myself in a traffic jam on the Uxbridge Road, bumper to bumper with a million other bodies sandwiched in their mobile sardine cans, when a complete stranger will roll down his window, hand me a card and say:

"Hey, lady, will you marry me?"

I'll smile and laugh, be flattered. I'll take the card and it will say:

DON DIAMOND
PLUMBING CONSULTANT

And I'll think: hey! . . . wait a minute,
Me and Don.
Why not?

CHAPTER
TWENTY-EIGHT

The first thing I'm aware of is the noise going on inside my head. What is it? My brain floats effortlessly towards an explanation and my brain is nothing if not a pragmatic organ over which I normally pride myself on having full control. Maybe the buzzing isn't internal at all, it goes on to amend, surely no one's head makes that kind of noise until it has the misfortune to meet with the edge of a pathologist's saw.

At the word pathologist my brain does some lateral gymnastics and suddenly a giant TV screen opens up; a man in a white coat is beamed into my eyeballs. *Quincy!* Jack Klugman. The Corpse's Sleuth. I can even remember the theme tune if I try hard enough, and to prove it, the noise in my head obligingly hums it what soon becomes an irritating number of times until finally, loudly, it registers itself as the telephone.

"Is that Katharine Butler?"

My eyes snap open at the voice of authority. Dad, I think, something has happened to Dad.

"Is that the hospital?" I fumble for the light switch.

"Are you the keyholder of the Orange Cinema, Shepherd's Bush?"

"Yes, yes," I say impatiently. "What's going on?"

"This is the police madam, Acton Way. I'm afraid there's been a fire."

It takes forever to get there. Despite the empty streets my car throttles along at its usual strangulated pace and anger grows with every yard. The image of the cinema reduced to embers is unbearable. I stare through the windscreen hoping to see sinners Ron and Hassop, transported by flames up to heaven's door, denied entrance by God's angels, bouncers of the most exclusive nightclub of all, then dropped unceremoniously down to hell. But Ron and Hassop in hell, prison, or anywhere else won't make a damned difference. The Orange will still be gone.

By the time I swing the car into the inside lane of the roundabout *The Tragedy of Orange* has taken on mythic proportions. The scene to come stamped in my head: helicopters circling, weary but heroic firemen, faces scorched and smeared with grease, bringing out body after body. The chief of police, careworn yet strangely attractive will knuckle his eyes in frustration; Shepherd's Bush and indeed most of London already written off as a disaster area.

Remembering the water tanks on the roof I'll shimmy up the hot metal of the fire escape, dynamite in teeth and blow up the place, tragically sacrificing myself in the process. I will be canonized after all. Martin Scorsese will weep. A small but beautifully bound book of my film and video criticisms will be released and become an international bestseller, profits going to a special screenwriting award bearing my name.

Real and actual smoke only makes itself visible when I turn off the Uxbridge Road. Clouds of it hover under the surly tinges of the street lamps, then rise up and over the bricked skyline. I turn off into Blondine Road. Two police cars are criss-crossed at the other end, blocking the entrance to Queen Street. I wrench the car up on to the pavement, cut the engine and run.

I feel the heat before I see the flames. Ash floats past my face, and there's a distinct smell of burnt toast, not unpleasant but all the more ominous for its Marmite connotations. Round the corner now, duck under a police barrier, still running. The keys to the Orange cut into my palm. Firemen in shiny suits dart around with their rubber anaconda, struggling to control the jaws of the hose as it spits great gushes of water. The smoke is overwhelming; thick and black as molasses it pours over the houses on either side of the street. My lungs ache, I stop and take a gulp of air, at the same time realizing that I'm already halfway along the street, way past the corner and that the clumps of people standing around in semicircles are not pointing at the Orange at all — because it isn't the Orange on fire.

The cinema stands veiled by smoke but untouched. No ladders against its brickwork, no men in gas masks, housewives in gingham dresses tossing expensive silk stockings out of windows. No, the fire is further along, in the laundromat and the building next door to that. It's the Bush on fire, the Bush Restaurant, and for a moment I feel so insanely relieved that I can only stand, rooted to the spot as the heat grows stronger against my face. When it starts to burn I take a couple of steps backwards and bump into someone behind me. I turn round and my heart dips.

"There's never a superhero around when you need one, huh?" Rufus says lightly.

Out of breath. Unprepared.

"I've always thought there should be a superhero Yellow Pages." He clears his throat. "You know, Starsky and Hutch, filed under lovable Protestant'n'Hebrew police team. Spiderman, Batman, Superman could be advertised in a special section for airborne." He trails off. Talent sinks his nose as far up my crotch as possible and inhales reverently. Rufus shortens the lead over his wrist. "Kit," he says, but I suppose shock or relief, something anyway has stamped itself on my face because he grips my shoulders and gives them a shake.

"It's not the Orange, Kit. They're just damping it down as a precaution." He points to where the firemen have broken through the side exit of the building. "They couldn't wait for the keys." He turns me round to face him. "Are you OK?"

Tears have welled up and started to run down my face without me even feeling them. I nod turning back to what was the restaurant. The fire has reached the roof and flames are skidding across the top, shooting up fifteen feet through the billowing smoke. The effect is mesmerizing. We stand watching it, side by side. I'm intensely aware of how close Rufus is, his elbow brushing mine. Tension flies alongside sparks and ash but thankfully the heat in the air disguises the heat starting to build around my neck. I know I should do one of two things here: find some decent words to tell him how I feel or walk away, but I don't seem to be up to either.

"Just kids," he says after a minute or two. "At least that's what they said."

"Oh."

"Kit." He turns to face me. "Kit, I've been wanting to call you," he says quietly.

I feign a sudden and profound interest in my feet.

"Those three days in the editing suite." He rubs the top of his head violently. "They were hell. I couldn't concentrate. All I could see was you and that took me by surprise. It scared me and it wasn't as easy as I thought to just pick up the phone. I didn't know what to say or how I was going to say it. When I finally got hold of you," he stops, "well the reality was so far from the fantasy I guess I just freaked."

He's looking at me searchingly and I can see he's still, after three months, waiting for some kind of explanation, but my tongue is tying itself into ever more complicated knots. If only I could pull down a screen in front of his eyes, roll out the special effects, fade in a red beating heart . . .

"Three years, Kit, that's how long it took for you to agree to go out with me. Three whole years. Then you break my wrist, you vomit all over my bathroom, have sex with my dog, then with me, then with some other sucker, probably his dog too for all I know, after that you tell me you never want to see me again. Fuck it, I mean this is not a conventional way to start a relationship. What was I supposed to do? Come swinging through your bedroom window with a bunch of flowers and a box of Milk Tray?"

"Yes." I finally free up my tongue. "Don't you see? That's exactly what you were supposed to do. How could you not know that?"

"How *could* I know that?" he asks amazed.

"I thought it must be pretty obvious."

"What was it that was so obvious?"

"That I —" I know what he's waiting for me to say, but I'm wound up too tightly inside.

"What was that? I didn't catch it."

"Nothing, nothing." I back-pedal.

He steps closer. "Please, Kit, please say something," he says gently. "I need you to say something . . . anything, really, it is your turn . . . come on, look at me at least?"

And finally I do. I look at him and words travel up through my throat. They reach my lips and very nearly make it to the open air when I spot them — out of the corner of my eye — Hassop, standing a hundred yards away, staring blankly at the fire and a few feet from him Ron. Then there's a suspended moment of belief because by Ron's side, chatting as if they were the oldest buddies in the world, stands Dad.

It takes about two seconds for the reality to sink in. Shock tugs at my stomach, and it's so strong I feel like my vital signs must be about to crash. For a minute, I can only stare at the three of them, then Hassop turns and looks our way. He alerts Dad who beckons me over with a wave.

"No," I say before I can stop myself. "Dear God, no."

"What?" Rufus says. "What is it?"

I try to shake him off but he's holding my arms in an iron grip as though panicked I'm about to commit some kamikaze act of heroism, rush into the collapsing restaurant and rescue the Mexican's Elvis collection or his favourite potato peeler or something.

"Let me go." I pull away, desperate for Rufus not to see them, but then there's a shout and it's too late.

"Kit," Dad shouts again. He starts waving and despite the din of the fire engine, enough of the shout filters through and Rufus looks over in his direction.

"Hey, isn't that your father over there?" He breaks off then adds surprised, "With Ron Chambers?" Something changes in his voice even as he says it. His tone takes on a suspicious, incredulous tinge as he makes the connection and starts to think: surely not even strange unhappy Kit and her lonely damaged father could possibly be responsible for this?

"Kit?" he says, looking at me disbelievingly. He lets me break away then, no problem, and I push through the clumps of people feeling his eyes drilling into my back.

The three stooges stand in a semicircle.

"Bleeding shame," says Ron, shaking his head dolefully. "Kids. They break in, have a fag, dog it out on a piece of cardboard and before you know it . . . bingo!" He balls his fists deeper into his overcoat. "Tragic really," he adds.

316

"Very sad indeed," agrees Dad, also shaking his head like a nodding dog.

"But every negative has a positive, every cloud a silver lining," says Hassop.

"Which is?" I ask, purely because it's there to be asked and it might as well be asked to dispel any small hope that my father is not responsible for this, but already I can hear his insanity plea being read out loud in court: *It was all the wars that broke him Your Honour, that and his wife leaving for the Land of the Nymphos of course, it was only a question of time before his mind went completely.*

"Which is that the money on selling these two sites will allow us to invest in other ailing businesses," says Ron gravely, sounding like a politician discussing the saving of the NHS.

"I think what Ron is trying to say is that he sees himself not so much as a businessman these days but more as a patron," says Dad kindly. "Don't you, Ron?"

"A patron, that's right mate," he claps Dad on the back. "And which patron did you say I was like?"

"A Charles Saatchi," says Dad helpfully.

"Yes, that's it, darling. I see myself as a Charles Saatchi of the Cinema."

I walk away.

Standing alone in the street, the air around me is flecked with specks of red. The rusty backdrop of night is slowly rolled up as the beginnings of dawn unravel over the city. Someone touches my elbow.

"How could you, Dad?"

"Simple business arrangement."

"You could go to jail."

"Have a little faith."

"You might have killed someone."

"No, Kit," he says gently. "That simply wasn't a possibility." I turn to look at him. My anger has died down with the fire. Instead, some other emotion is taking over. The sense that this is Dad finally running his red light for me is overwhelming and I suppose I am in some ways to blame. I should have had the guts to tell him months ago that the red light itself was always enough. It never had to be more than a simple token. I stare at him and he no longer looks like a very familiar stranger to me, he looks like the reverse, a very strange bit of my family and that's all there is to it. It hits me forcibly that sooner rather than later I'm going to have to make the decision whether to accept it or not.

"Kit, all I did was divert them, waylay, flatter. I made Ron do what he was going to do anyway a little differently, but that little difference will give us everything we want."

"You sound like a third-rate villain arguing the ends justifies the means."

"Don't be so bloody pompous. Don't tell me you wouldn't rather have an old folk's and orphans' home burnt down before your cinema. Ron will have his venue to sell to Quick Kebab and in return we'll buy the Orange's lease cheap and . . ."

"We?" I say.

"You, me. We."

318

"I see, and with what exactly will *we* be buying the lease?"

"I've sold the houseboat."

I open and shut my mouth. "Oh, Dad . . . where will you live?"

"Here," he waves carelessly in the direction of the cinema, "under the dome. Basement with café and ancillary flat. *A proposal to restore, regenerate and retain this historic building as a working cinema open to the public.* Hassop, I think you'll find, will be recommending the application to the planning division. You'll be able to think of me if you like, as a sort of Phantom of the Orange."

My jaw is beyond dropping again. It remains glued shut.

"Kit, I'm sick of kowtowing to fate. I'm sick of hinting at what I want and hoping someone up there sees fit to give it to me. I'm running out of time to have such good manners and I'm too old to flirt with chance." He puts his hands on either side of my face and presses his forehead against mine.

"Movies were our therapy, Kit. They may not have been a very successful therapy but they were the only way I had of working it all out. I thought you knew that. When we stopped going, I lost you. That was twenty years ago and even then it was you that came to me. Well now your old man's getting proactive. I'm taking what I want and I'm taking it now. I want you, I want the Orange and I want some kind of life together."

"Dad," I whisper, "for pity's sake." His hands are still on either side of my head and I see what this must look

319

like to the onlooker, the bystander. A man with grey hair, only his forehead pressing against the girl's. She, arms by her side, not around him because of course she hasn't put her arms round him for the whole of those twenty years and it would be too strange and difficult to start now — but then my arms are around him and as I hold him tightly I wonder whether I should attempt to maintain my role as moralistic daughter of a lunatic father, but the situation is too profoundly ludicrous. Besides, when I finally swallow the lump in my throat I'm aware there's a strong tickling sensation there instead. At first I think it's smoke inhalation, then I realize I'm about to get appalling giggles.

"Dad." I break away. "You're telling me you actually sat down with Ron and struck this deal with him."

"In a manner of speaking, yes. We had a charming bolognese lunch together."

I shake my head. "There's not a big chance of you not interfering for ever in my life is there?"

He sees something of a smile on my face and pounces on it. "Absolutely none at all," he agrees. Then adds slyly, "So how about a kiss for your old father then?"

"God Almighty, Dad," I say gruffly, "don't push it."

The fire is out. It's six-thirty a.m. Most of the spectators have drifted off but the roads are still blocked by the police. I make my way back to the car and unlock the door. I've got the lights on and the ignition fired up before I realize there's something on the windscreen. At first I think it's a parking ticket and outraged, open the window and try to sweep it towards me with the wiper. It's not a parking ticket, just a flyer, and sod's law it's stuck. I open the door and rip the paper from beneath the blades. I'm about to screw it up when I realize it's not a flyer at all, it's a note. Foolscap, folded down the middle. I unfold it. There are two pages of scribbled writing, I scan the first few lines.

The restaurant is deserted. Ray Charles scratches on the record player. The manager polishes a glass dreamily, watching a girl in conversation at a table in the corner. From the goofy expression on his face it is clear he is smitten . . .

I speed-read the rest. From the fish shop through to the party, the weekend in his flat, the fire. It's all in there, right up to me standing reading the note by my car. Everything that happened, everything he feels. I turn the second page over but it's blank. For a moment I think the final piece must have blown away but then I hear the familiar rasp of canine snot and realize I've been ambushed.

"See, the studio," Rufus says, "they just weren't that happy with the ending — you know how difficult these executives can be. General comment was it lacked romance, feel-good factor. Audience might complain they weren't getting their money's worth. They reckon it needed a bit more schmaltz, they reckoned the ending might even need rewriting, God forbid." He looks steadily at me.

Unbelievably long pause.

"So what now?"

"Well." He takes a step closer. "Rumour has it you're not entirely without talent in that department."

I can't look at him, only the general area he's occupying in front of me. "So, I was thinking, it's up to you." He takes a biro out of his pocket and hands it to me. "Here's the deal, Kit. I'm commissioning another draft of our affair, a better ending — if you're interested in taking the job that is. But if you are interested, then I thought maybe when you've mulled it over a bit, you could bike it round or I don't know, better still, deliver it in person, perhaps later this morning so we could . . . er . . . discuss it at some length." He takes a curl from in front of my eyes and hooks it behind my ear. "I have to tell you that I'm pretty much happy to work on anything you might have in mind." He flashes a quick smile, turns and walks away towards the Uxbridge Road, Talent pattering along behind him.

I watch him, grinning broadly until the noise of a car door slamming snaps me to. The two police cars at the entrance to Queen Street finally reverse and move slowly off. It's practically light, the air less opaque. Four Canada geese fly by. At the other end of the street, Rufus and Talent have reached the corner and are turning left towards the tube station. A light wind rustles the blank paper in my hand.

Falling in love with someone whose wrist you've broken, whose bathroom you've passed out in, whose dog you've seduced and now, on top of everything, whose restaurant you've burnt down probably *isn't* the most conventional way of starting a relationship. But then again, what is?

322

Vince and Joy

Lisa Jewell

The love story of a lifetime

The cream of pop fiction   **Glamour**

Vince and Joy have always been looking for something:

In their teens, in family holidays and bathroom mirrors. In their twenties, in messy London flats and messy London relationships. In their early thirties, in marriages that appear stable — but feel anything but.

And in the near future, Vince and Joy are going to have to ask themselves the same troubling question: could it be that they'd actually found what they've both been looking for when they first met back in the mid-eighties, in a holiday park by the sea?

ISBN 0-7531-7559-2 (hb)
ISBN 0-7531-7560-6 (pb)

The Laments

George Hagen

A fine novel, about family, migration, identity and the struggle to find and hold onto it **Roddy Doyle**

When Howard and Julia Lament secretly adopt Will, a baby switched at birth in a bizarre hospital debacle, it marks the beginning of a journey that takes them from Rhodesia to the Middle East, Britain to the New Jersey suburbs — for no matter where the Laments set up home, the grass always seems greener on the other side of the ocean. As the Laments discover that living somewhere doesn't necessarily mean belonging there, Will grows up struggling with his sense of identity in the shadow of his anarchic twin brothers, Julius and Marcus. Yet when disillusion and mishap threaten to tear his family apart, it is Will who fights to hold them together.

ISBN 0-7531-7507-X (hb)
ISBN 0-7531-7508-8 (pb)

My Sister's Keeper

Jodi Picoult

A beautiful, heartbreaking, controversial and honest book **Booklist**

Anna is not sick, but she might as well be. By age thirteen, she has undergone countless surgeries, transfusions, and shots so that her sister, Kate, can somehow fight the leukemia that has plagued her since she was a child. Anna was born for this purpose, her parents tell her, which is why they love her even more. But now that she has reached an age of physical awareness, she can't help but long for control over her own body and respite from the constant flow of her own blood seeping into her sister's veins.

And so she makes a decision that for most would be too difficult to bear, at any time and at any age. She decides to sue her parents for the rights to her own body.

ISBN 0-7531-7443-X (hb)
ISBN 0-7531-7444-8 (pb)

Mr Starlight

Laurie Graham

The Boff brothers live at home with their Mam. They have a lav down the yard and a tin bath in front of the fire on club nights, but they are also rising stars at the Birmingham Welsh and the Rover Sports and Social. Cled tinkles the ivories while Sel slips on his gold lamé jacket and serenades the ladies. When Sel tries his chances in America, Cled tags along, into a world of sequinned suits and mirrored ceilings, heart-shaped tubs and stretch limousines. And so, eventually, do the rest of the family.

But it's tough at the top and times change. The kids want rock 'n' roll. And then there's family. You just never know what skeletons they're going to start dragging out of your walk-in closets.

ISBN 0-7531-7327-1 (hb)
ISBN 0-7531-7328-X (pb)

Hunting Unicorns

Bella Pollen

Maggie Monroe is a fearless New York journalist — the more cutting edge the story, the happier she is. So when her next assignment turns out to be a documentary on the decline of England's ruling classes, she's furious at being sent to cover a bloody tea party.

Her difficulties multiply when she meets the family that will provide the material for the documentary. The Earl and Countess of Bevan are eccentric and maddening. Their eldest son Daniel is attractive but also a hopeless alcoholic, and the responsible younger brother Rory seems to be perpetually angry. But soon Maggie finds herself torn between her journalist ideals and the dawning comprehension of the loyalties in play within this strange family.

ISBN 0-7531-7225-9 (hb)
ISBN 0-7531-7226-7 (pb)

ISIS publish a wide range of books in large print, from fiction to biography. Any suggestions for books you would like to see in large print or audio are always welco   ᴅ   ιent at:

A full list   ᴅm:

   Ulver   **:d**

(UK)
The Green
Bradgate Roa
Leicester LE7
Tel: (0116) 2   22

(USA)
P.O. Box 1230
West Seneca
N.Y. 14224-12
Tel: (716) 674 4270   Tel: (905) 637 8734

(New Zealand)
P.O. Box 456
Feilding
Tel: (06) 323 6828

Details of **ISIS** complete and unabridged audio books are also available from these offices. Alternatively, contact your local library for details of their collection of **ISIS** large print and unabridged audio books.